better

than

this

better

than

this

Cathy Zane

SHE WRITES PRESS

Published: 2018
Printed in the United States of America
ISBN: 978-1-63152-403-5 paperback
 978-1-63152-404-2 ebook
Library of Congress Control Number: 2018932741

For information, address:
She Writes Press
1563 Solano Ave #546
Berkeley, CA 94707

She Writes Press is a division of SparkPoint Studio, LLC.

for Ruth

Chapter 1

S arah's gaze traveled to the darkening sky just outside her class-room windows. It was one of those days when the grayness felt suffocating. After nearly ten years in Seattle, she longed for the abundant sunshine of her Southern California hometown. She never imagined she would settle here when she came for college, or that she'd end up teaching high school English, but here she was. Life never turns out as you expect. There are always unexpected turns and detours along the way.

She sighed and glanced at the industrial clock on the wall. Ten seconds until the final bell. *Leave it to you, yet again, to be the buzz-kill,* the voice in her head admonished. She couldn't help feeling a bit like the Wicked Witch when it came to assigning homework, especially on the weekend. She looked out at her students as they crammed books and notebooks into their already overflowing backpacks. A few were already done and positioned to bolt out the door. She inhaled deeply before broadcasting her voice over the noisy activity.

"Remember that your essays are due next Friday. If you don't have a rough draft completed, be sure to finish it before Monday."

There it is, she thought as several students grimaced and moaned. *The audible groan.* Never mind that they were supposed to have the draft finished this week! She wasn't going to be the bad guy in this scenario. Besides, it was supposed to rain all weekend. They'd have plenty of time indoors to work on it.

Sarah's internal dialogue continued as the bell rang, drowning out the frenetic chatter of her students as they bumped and jostled their way out of class. She hoped the rain would hold off until the morning. Slogging around in a downpour never worked when you needed to look good, and she definitely needed to look good tonight. Things hadn't been going well with Robert lately. He was distant and irritable and nothing she did seemed to please him. He was always traveling for work and they never had fun together anymore. She had tried to convince herself that maybe it was to be expected after five years of marriage, especially with a kid and busy jobs. But other people managed to do it. Why couldn't they? *You should try harder. You need to do something to rekindle the romance. To make him happy. To get things back to the way they were.*

Her thoughts wandered back to the moment she and Robert met. It was the beginning of her senior year of college and she'd been going through a tough time: her boyfriend of two years had graduated the previous semester, and when he did he'd decided they should break up. She was devastated. The school library felt claustrophobic, so she spent her study time at a nearby Starbucks. The constant bustle made her feel less alone and, ironically, helped her concentrate. It kept her mental demons at bay.

The last thing on her mind had been meeting someone new. She smiled now as she remembered picking up her coffee and crashing into Robert as she turned away from the counter. He was incredibly handsome, and old enough to be her father. And he was clearly not happy about the coffee now decorating his crisp white button-down shirt.

Sarah's immediate reaction had been one of fear, like a child waiting to be smacked. She blabbered an apology and, on the verge of tears, waited for him to yell. But he didn't. His anger just melted away and he smiled that charming smile of his. He was so charismatic and playful. He made her feel comfortable and at ease. And he made her laugh.

She missed that. She couldn't remember the last time they'd laughed together. And she was at a loss about what to do to make things better. *There must be something you can do. You need to put forth more of an effort. Stop being lazy about it.*

She jumped slightly when Maggie bounced through the door, dressed, as always, in an odd assortment of what Sarah considered mismatched clothes. Maggie called it her own unique style. Sarah thought of it as a mix of old hippie and Earth Mother. As a loyal Nordstrom shopper, she thought the "style" part of Maggie's dress was debatable. But unique? That she couldn't argue with.

Maggie dramatically threw herself backward across Sarah's desk. "Thank God! Another week over."

"Ah, ever the dedicated teacher!" Sarah pushed her back up off the desk.

"Hell yeah! Dedicated to getting out of here." Maggie motioned toward the door. "Let's get going. I want to buy you a birthday drink."

Sarah glanced up at the clock and shook her head. "No time. I need to get Lizzy from day care and pick up my dress for tonight from the cleaners." Her mind was already spinning with all the things she needed to do before Robert got home.

Maggie frowned. "Your dress? For Luigi's?" She motioned toward Sarah's tailored slacks and cashmere sweater. "You'd be fine like that."

Sarah turned away and busied herself with straightening her desk and packing up her bag. "Change of plans. We're going to Maxwell's," she said without looking up.

"Maxwell's? Seriously? You hate that stuffy old place."

"I know," Sarah said, trying to sound upbeat and nonchalant. "Normally it wouldn't be my first choice. But Robert made a big deal about wanting to go to a nice restaurant for my birthday. And I think he's right. I want it to be a nice night."

Maggie frowned, then shrugged and slumped down into a chair. "If you say so." Her disappointment filled the room like a dark cloud. Sarah was always amazed at how quickly her friend's mood could change. And she couldn't deal with it today. She was stressed enough on her own. She needed to fix this.

"How about I take a rain check for next week? You can buy me a beer then."

Maggie didn't respond and Sarah knew what her silence meant: she was planning her next argument. She'd never give up without a fight. She was one of the most persistent people Sarah had ever met. And she always managed to get her way. So, when she brightened and sat up in her chair, Sarah braced herself. *Be strong, Sarah. You know you shouldn't go today.*

Maggie motioned toward the clock. "You know, we still have time. One quick drink and then I promise to have you on your way by four fifteen. That'll give you plenty of time to get to the cleaners."

"I'm sorry, Mags, but I really can't. I need to get some food for the sitter and—"

"You can do that after the cleaners," Maggie said, jumping up from her chair.

"I don't know . . ." The voice in Sarah's head was shouting. *This is a terrible idea. Don't encourage her. You can't be late or the cleaners will close. You have to have that dress. You know Robert wants you to wear it. You can't start the night off with him in a bad mood.*

Maggie dropped to her knees, hands folded prayer-like, in front of Sarah. "Please. Please. Don't make me drink alone. I need you!

Please don't abandon me. I would never abandon you. Just one drink. That's all I ask."

Sarah rolled her eyes. "You're seriously pathetic. Get up . . ."

Maggie jumped up, bouncing and pumping her arms like a cheerleader. "Say you'll go! Say you'll go! Say you'll go!"

Sarah looked nervously at the door. *Someone is going to hear her. This is really embarrassing. You need to get her to stop. She's doing this on purpose. She totally knows how to mess with you.* "You're crazy, you know that? Now stop!" she said in barely more than a whisper as she glanced toward the door again.

Maggie stopped, slumped down onto the top of a desk, and feigned a pout. "What? You don't like my cheerleader routine?"

"Cheer-bully, more like."

Maggie shrugged. "Whatever works. So, you'll go?"

"Okay, but only one quick drink." Sarah had a nagging feeling she was going to regret this, but she pushed it away. Maggie was right. She was her best friend; she shouldn't let her down. "I mean, I can't miss celebrating with my BFF!"

"Damn straight!" Maggie grinned and linked her arm through Sarah's. "Rusty Hub, here we come!"

A cold wind and light rain hit Sarah's face when they stepped out the front door of the school. She frowned when she looked up at the dark sky and unhooked her arm from Maggie's so she could get her umbrella out of her bag.

"This is not good," she said more to herself than to Maggie. She prayed that it wouldn't rain any harder—that the real storm would at least hold off until after she and Robert got home from dinner.

"Oh, come on! It's just a little rain. Chill out and enjoy," Maggie said and then burst into a booming, "I'm singin' in the rain, just singin' in the rain," twirling around a street sign, a mailbox, and a fire hydrant as she sang.

Sarah looked around nervously to see if anyone was watching. She hated it when Maggie acted like this. It always made her question how they'd ever become friends in the first place. A classic case of opposites attract, she decided.

"Please stop. You're embarrassing me."

Maggie laughed, linking her arm back through Sarah's. "I know. That's what makes it so much fun. You really need to lighten up a little. And I'm the one to help you do it. That's my gift to you, my dear Sarah. Happy birthday!"

Sarah raised her eyebrows. "I thought you were buying me a beer for my birthday."

Maggie reached out to open the door of the Rusty Hub. "That too!"

Sarah closed her umbrella and stepped inside as Maggie held the door. It was a little busier than usual. There were only a few seats left at the long mahogany bar, and most of the booths were full. Probably the weather. It was a good place to escape the cold and rain.

Maggie pushed past Sarah, who had stopped to put her umbrella in the bin by the door. "I'm going to grab those stools," she said, nodding toward the only two adjacent seats still left at the bar.

Sarah looked around as she followed Maggie across the room. She always felt nervous that she might see someone who knew Robert, but in all the time they'd been coming here, it had never happened. This really wasn't the kind of place Robert's acquaintances would frequent. She told herself to relax and scooted up onto the barstool next to Maggie.

"Hey there, stranger," Maggie said to Alex, the bartender, who was stacking some clean beer glasses behind the bar. He looked up and smiled.

"Well if it isn't the Dynamic Duo! What can I get you today? The usual?"

Sarah nodded as Maggie interjected, "And the wings platter. In honor of the birthday girl!"

"No—" Sarah started to object but then stopped herself. Why bother? The strongest linebacker in the NFL couldn't stop Maggie once she'd made up her mind about something. Might as well just go with it.

"Well, happy birthday!" Alex said.

Sarah smiled. "Thanks."

Alex called out the order for the wings as he pulled the tap to fill two glasses. He tossed a couple of coasters onto the bar and sat their beers down in front of them. "Enjoy!"

Maggie raised her glass to Sarah as Alex moved to greet an attractive man who had just taken a single seat at the other end of the bar. Sarah noticed her checking him out. She grinned. "Like what you see, huh?"

Maggie sighed deeply. "A girl can dream."

"Whatever happened with your date from last weekend?" Sarah asked—and then immediately scolded herself. *You idiot. You should have asked her on Monday. How could you have forgotten that!? You really are a lousy friend sometimes.*

"Total bust." Maggie sipped her beer. "I need to take a break from the online stuff. It's just too weird to me. It's like shopping for shoes. Lots look good until you try them on."

Sarah followed Maggie's gaze back to the dream guy, who was now talking to the equally attractive woman sitting next to him.

"Do you think he knows her?" Maggie asked. "Or did they just meet? Do people ever really meet someone decent in a bar? I certainly never have."

Sarah didn't answer. She knew the questions were rhetorical.

Maggie turned back to Sarah. "I'm officially on a break. Time to focus on me for a while. I was thinking of trying that yoga class you told me about."

"That would be great," Sarah said, and then stopped to consider what to say next. She needed to be careful. Talking to Maggie about her luck with guys was dangerous territory. The flypaper of her fun, crazy persona tended to catch the equally fun but non-committing types. And she inevitably got swallowed up by a black hole when she talked about it. Sarah couldn't go there today. She needed this to be a quick drink. Better to shift gears to safer territory. Something that would provide a distraction.

"Could you believe Jessica in the staff meeting this morning?" she said, shaking her head.

Maggie loved to dissect colleagues, especially when they acted in ways she found offensive or suspect. Sarah watched her guilt creep in. She felt like a terrible person when she gossiped, but her anxiety about her evening with Robert was eating away at her and she was feeling desperate. This was an emergency, she rationalized. She couldn't deal with Maggie in a puddle today.

"Oh, my God!" Maggie said, taking the bait. "She is such a lame suck-up. She totally said the complete opposite thing to me last week. She's just trying to impress McCarthy. I know she has her eye on the department chair position. It's total bullshit. I have half a mind to . . ."

And we're off, Sarah thought as her mind raced forward into the evening ahead. She had to get Lizzy, pick up her dress, and then make a quick stop for some food. Something the babysitter could heat up easily. Then she'd get Lizzy into the bath so she could change and put her hair up. Oh, and she couldn't forget to check the house to make sure everything was tidy the way Robert liked it . . .

Chapter 2

It had taken longer than Sarah anticipated to pick Lizzy up and now she was running late for the cleaners. If she didn't get that dress, Robert would be disappointed and the evening would be ruined. *Serves you right. You are so stupid. You knew the Rusty Hub was a bad idea. Why do you let Maggie talk you into things so easily? You'll never learn.*

She slammed on her brakes, nearly rear-ending the car in front of her, when the driver hesitated at the four-way stop. The traffic was ridiculous. *Why do drivers turn into morons when it rains?* She glanced down at the clock and pounded on the steering wheel. "Oh, come on!" She winced and rubbed her chest before plunging her hand into her purse on the seat beside her, searching for her TUMS. *You seriously need to clean out your purse. It's a mess. No wonder you can never find anything.*

"What's the matter, Mommy?" Lizzy asked from the backseat. Sarah glanced in the rearview mirror at her daughter, who'd been narrating a gossip session between two Barbie dolls about which girls liked which boys at school. *What five-year-old thinks like that?* Sarah certainly hadn't when she was five.

"Nothing. Just lots of traffic."

Lizzy became more animated. "We made bird feeders at school today!"

"That's nice," Sarah said, fighting the urge to scream. Sometimes Lizzy's precociousness was more than she could handle.

"Mrs. Johnson said they have to dry, but we can bring them home next week."

"Great," Sarah said as she finally made it through the intersection. She glanced back in the rearview mirror and noticed Lizzy looking around, confused.

"Mommy, this is the wrong way."

Sarah pressed on the gas pedal and navigated a quick left turn in front of traffic into the strip mall. "I have to stop at the cleaners."

"What for?"

"A dress."

"What for?"

"I need it for dinner tonight with Daddy. Now, stop with the questions," she said, barely containing her urge to yell and cry all at the same time. She glanced at the clock as she pulled into a parking spot in front of the cleaners. 5:02. She grabbed her purse and turned back to Lizzy.

"Let's go."

"I don't want to."

"Lizzy, please. I'm in a hurry."

Lizzy crossed her arms. "No. You can't make me."

Sarah felt her body tense. She was not in the mood for this today. "We have to go! Right now!" She got out of the car, slammed her door, and pulled Lizzy's door open forcefully. Lizzy was getting too big to carry, but if she was going to be a total brat then Sarah had no other choice. She unbuckled Lizzy and pulled her out of the car.

Lizzy started kicking and screaming. "No. I don't want to go. I don't want to get my dress wet."

Sarah looked around. *People are going to think you're a terrible mother. And it's true. You can't even get your own kid to behave.*

She held Lizzy tight to her body as she pushed the car door closed with her back and ran up under the awning. She reached the door of the cleaners just as a young man was turning the OPEN sign to CLOSED. She put Lizzy down and motioned to him to open the door. He pointed to the sign and turned away. Sarah shook her head and pounded on the door. "Please, open the door!" She had to get that dress. She couldn't take no for an answer.

The store clerk turned around, noticeably frustrated, and opened the door slightly. "Lady, we're closed."

"I just have to get one dress," she said, holding up her receipt. "I need it for tonight."

He shook his head. "I can't. I've already closed out the register."

"I can pay cash and you can reconcile it tomorrow."

He shook his head again. "Sorry."

He's not going to give it to you. Robert will not be happy. And it's your fault. You never should have gone out with Maggie. How are you going to explain that to him? You know how he feels about your friendship with Maggie. He'll be furious. You are such a fuckup!

She burst into tears and frantically pushed on the door. "You don't understand. I have to have it. Please!"

Lizzy looked up at Sarah and grabbed for her hand. "Mommy, what's wrong?"

Sarah pulled away from Lizzy, holding up the receipt as she pleaded with the employee. "Please! I really have to have this dress."

He looked down at Lizzy and then back to Sarah. "What a day

for the boss to leave early," he said, shaking his head. He opened the door. "Okay. But we need to make it quick."

Sarah rushed in. "Thank you. Thank you so much. This really means a lot to me. You're a lifesaver!" *Stop gushing. You sound like an idiot. What is wrong with you?*

The clerk turned away. "Yeah, whatever." He disappeared into the back to retrieve her dress.

He thinks you're a total nutcase. He's probably right. Something is seriously wrong with you. Sarah felt shaky. She took a deep breath and tried unsuccessfully to choke back her tears. She felt like a dam had burst open; she couldn't stop crying.

Lizzy reached for Sarah's hand. "It's okay, Mommy. He's getting your dress. Everything's okay, right Mommy?"

Sarah looked down at her daughter and nodded, smiling weakly but unable to speak. She took a deep breath and told herself that everything was okay. It was going to work out. She just needed to let this be a lesson and not ever do it again. She took another deep breath and started to feel more composed. She wiped her face just as the clerk returned with her dress.

"It'll be $9.50," he said as he hung the dress on the rack next to the cash register. Sarah opened her wallet and gave him a $10.00 bill.

"I don't have change," he said, taking the bill. "Remember, I told you I already closed out the register."

She waved her hand, avoiding eye contact. "Don't worry about it." She grabbed the dress from the rack and pushed Lizzy toward the door. "Thanks again for your help. I really appreciate it." She rushed out of the store without looking back.

The rain had slowed to a drizzle by the time they reached home. Sarah turned into the driveway and pushed the remote for the garage door, ticking through a mental list of all the things she needed to do before Robert got home. She pulled forward into the garage and turned off the car.

Lizzy jumped out of the car, Barbies in hand, and pushed open the door to the kitchen. "Daddy, Daddy, we're home!"

Sarah grabbed her purse, dry cleaning, book bag, and grocery bag and leaned her back into the car door to close it, struggling to not drop everything. "I don't think Daddy's home yet sweetie, but he will be soon." She still felt a little shaky after her breakdown at the cleaners, and she was determined to be more composed. *You need to get back in control. Stop being such a baby. You can't let Robert see you like this. He hates it when you're needy. You need to be strong. And you need to get Lizzy settled. You know he'll be upset if she's cranky when he gets home.*

She maneuvered through the door into the kitchen and lifted her bags onto the counter. "Let me put all this away and then we'll get you into the bathtub."

Lizzy frowned. "I don't want to take a bath yet. I want Daddy to see my new dress."

Sarah took a deep breath and blew it back out forcefully. She couldn't deal with Lizzy's obstinacy today. Why couldn't she just behave? She quickly glanced into the dining room. *Good, nothing to clean up in there.* She glanced at the clock and felt a sense of dread. She'd never be ready in time. Why had she agreed to go out with Maggie? *Stupid, Sarah. Really stupid. You'll never learn, will you?*

She turned her attention back to Lizzy. "He can see it later. You need to take your bath before Amy gets here. And you know better than to drop your Barbies on the floor. Now pick them up and let's get going."

Lizzy clenched her fists and stomped her feet on the hardwood floor. "No! I don't wanna wait 'til later. I want Daddy to see my dress now!" She turned and ran out of the room, heading for the den.

Sarah took a deep breath, trying to calm the urge to scream. She knew from past experience that yelling would only make Lizzy dig her heels in more. She forced herself to take a couple more breaths before picking up the dolls and following her into the den.

Lizzy had crawled up onto the sofa and was sitting with her arms crossed defiantly, an extremely exaggerated pout on her face. If Sarah hadn't been so angry, it probably would have made her laugh.

"Lizzy, I have a lot to do before Daddy gets home and I need you to be good." She handed the dolls to her daughter. "So, take these to your room and get ready for your bath."

Lizzy took the dolls but glared at Sarah. "No!"

Sarah felt the anger building in her body. Why couldn't she just cooperate? She silently repeated the mantra she'd learned at a parenting class. *Focus. Stay calm. Don't yell. Be firm.*

"Lizzy, I need you to do as I say. Now go to your room right now and get undressed."

"No! I'm staying right here until Daddy comes home."

Something snapped inside Sarah. "The hell you are. You're going to your room right now and getting undressed or I'll do it for you!" *Get a grip. What is with the swearing and yelling? You are such a terrible mother.*

Lizzy started to cry. "No!" she screamed, her volume increasing. "You can't make me! Daddy would want to see my dress." She threw the Barbies at Sarah as she jumped up off the couch and ran out of the room.

"Fine! Be that way!" Sarah loudly stomped back to the kitchen. *What is wrong with you? You're as bad as she is.* Sarah tried to breathe some more, remembering the parenting experts' advice. *Take a time out. Calm yourself before going back to Lizzy. Give her some space to calm down.*

"Fuck the experts," Sarah said aloud. "They don't know Lizzy. They talk about the 'terrible twos,' but what about the terrible threes, fours, and fives? She throws a fit any time she doesn't get her way. I'm so tired of it." She stopped for a moment, leaning with both hands on the counter. She was on the verge of tears again.

She straightened up and put the food for Lizzy and the sitter in the refrigerator before carrying the rest of her things to her room. She put her book bag neatly beside her desk and hung her dress up in the large walk-in closet before steeling herself to go to Lizzy's room. She could do this. Lizzy was a child and she was the adult. She needed to start acting like one. *Just keep breathing and stay calm.*

Lizzy was face-down on her bed, crying, when Sarah opened her door. Sarah sat down on the bed and tried to gently put her hand on her back, but she jerked away.

"I hate you," she said, her voice muffled by the blanket underneath it. "You just don't want Daddy to see my new dress."

"That's not true," Sarah said, struggling to manage the irritation in her voice. "There just isn't enough time. Amy will be here soon and Daddy and I need to leave for dinner."

Lizzy curled up on her side and scooted even farther away from Sarah. The time-out clearly hadn't done the trick. Robert would be home soon and she needed Lizzy to be calm. And she still had to get dressed. She knew the tough approach never worked. It was time to play nice. She hated giving in to Lizzy—she knew it only made things worse in the long run and it made her feel like a terrible mother—but she was at the end of her rope. She couldn't do it anymore. She needed a break. And she needed to get Lizzy out of her dress and ready for the sitter.

"Hey, I have a great idea," she said, hoping Lizzy would buy it. "You can put your dress back on tomorrow morning and surprise Daddy. You know how stressed he can be when he gets home from work. In the morning he's always happier, right?"

Lizzy continued to lie silently on the bed. Sarah reached out slowly and gently touched Lizzy's back. Lizzy didn't pull away this time. Sarah took that as a good sign. She was making progress.

"But we should hang it up now so it doesn't get wrinkled. And if you take your bath quickly, you can have a special treat. How about a Tootsie Pop and a video until Daddy gets home?"

Sarah pushed away the voice that started to criticize her for bribing Lizzy. She had to stay focused on not upsetting Robert. That was the most important thing right now. And that meant getting Lizzy in a good mood.

Lizzy sat up slowly, still pouting. "Okay."

Sarah breathed a sigh of relief. Her body relaxed slightly and she put her arm around Lizzy.

"Good girl. Now you get undressed and I'll go start the bath."

With Lizzy bathed and settled in to watch a video, Sarah began straightening the den and cleaning up the kitchen. Tidiness wasn't her strong suit. She was comfortable with clutter. It made a house feel lived in to her. But not so with Robert. He liked everything in its place, and Sarah had learned that nothing triggered Robert more quickly than having the house out of order. Although he never offered to help. He'd wanted to hire a live-in maid and nanny when Lizzy was born, but Sarah had been uncomfortable with the idea, so he had reluctantly compromised on a weekly cleaning service. But he had been clear that any additional cleaning needs—and childcare needs, for that matter—were her responsibility.

She heard the front door open and quickly tossed the plastic take-out bag in the trash just as Robert walked in. Her body immediately tensed. She'd perfected the skill of sensing his moods within a few seconds, and she could tell that today was not a good day.

He dumped his briefcase and keys on the counter and began to take off his overcoat. "I need a drink." He tossed his coat over the back of a chair.

Sarah caught her breath. She knew she needed to tread lightly. Be good. Be supportive. Not say anything to upset him more.

"Rough day?" she asked, trying to calm the quiver in her voice as he walked around the center island and opened a cupboard.

"Something like that," he said as he grabbed a glass. He continued to fix his drink, getting ice from the refrigerator and vodka from the liquor cabinet, without looking at Sarah.

"Want to talk about it?"

"Nope." Robert poured the vodka over the ice.

Sarah searched for something to say. Being supportive wasn't working. Maybe a distraction would help. "Lizzy's been asking for you. She wanted to see you when you got home."

"I need some downtime and a shower." He picked up his drink and kissed Sarah quickly on the forehead as he passed. "Be a dear and put a video on for her. I'll see her in the morning." He strode out of the room, drink in hand.

Sarah slumped back against the counter and slid to the floor, cradling her head in her hands and fighting back the tears. She felt so alone. Again. She knew it was probably stupid to keep expecting something to change, but she was really tired of feeling like a single parent. She tried to do everything she could think of to make him happy, but it never seemed to work. He was so distracted and irritated all the time. Where was the fun, charismatic man she had married? She wanted to try to talk to him, but that always seemed to backfire. It always turned into her fault somehow. How was it possible to be married and feel so lonely?

The doorbell startled her and she jumped up from the floor and headed for the door. Amy was early. Maybe that was a good thing. Lizzy wouldn't be so focused on seeing Robert before they left. She opened the door, welcomed Amy, and distractedly went through the motions of showing her the food in the refrigerator and letting her know where they were going and how late they would be. As she started up the stairs she heard Lizzy's squeal of excitement. She was glad Lizzy liked Amy. That hadn't always been the case with Lizzy and babysitters. The fact that she really clicked with Amy made everything so much easier.

Robert was still in the shower when Sarah walked into their large master suite. She quickly went into the walk-in closet. She wanted to put her dress on to surprise Robert when he came out of the shower; maybe it would help shift his mood. She took the plastic off the dress and slipped it over her head, tugging slightly to get it over her body. It was tighter than she remembered. Could it have shrunk? Had she gained weight? *You haven't been good about weighing yourself every day. You should be more careful.* She tugged the zipper up and heard the fabric rip just as the shower stopped running.

"Shit!" she said under her breath as she quickly pulled the dress off and stuffed it and the plastic cover into a drawer. *You idiot! How could you be so careless? Robert's already stressed out. You don't need this tonight.* She quickly grabbed another dress and pulled it over her head just as Robert came out of the bathroom with a towel wrapped around his waist. He was using a second towel to dry his full head of hair. He was still toned and fit despite the beginning of some recent greying at his temples. Sarah tentatively came out of the closet and turned to have him zip up her dress.

Robert frowned. "I told you I wanted you to wear your black dress."

"I know. I rushed to get to the cleaners after I picked Lizzy up, but the traffic was awful because of the rain." A white lie. Really not that bad, she told herself, if it kept the peace.

"Too bad. I love that dress on you." Robert moved into the closet to begin dressing. "I closed another deal today." His voice was distant and distracted, as if he was talking to no one in particular. "I need to go back to LA on Sunday. I'll be there for a few weeks to oversee the installation."

"But you just got home." Sarah heard the whine come out of her mouth before she could stop it. She plopped down onto the bed, pouting. "Sometimes I think we should just move to LA."

Robert frowned as he came out of the closet. "Don't be ridiculous. This is our home. Your job and your friends are here. My family is here. And right now, I'm here too." He walked over to Sarah, reached out, and gently pulled her up from the bed to look into her eyes. "And you look beautiful and it's your special day. So, let's forget it for now and take you out for a wonderful dinner, okay?"

Sarah nodded and smiled meekly, her body relaxing.

"Good girl," he said. He kissed her forehead and went back into the closet to finish dressing.

Sarah sat down to freshen her makeup and put up her hair, glad that Robert seemed to be in a better mood. She shouldn't be mad when he was being so sweet. Maybe it would be a good night after all. *As long as you can keep your stupid mouth shut.*

Chapter 3

Sarah was quiet on the drive to the restaurant. She was aware of some lingering frustration and disappointment and knew she needed to keep herself in check. She didn't want to do anything that might upset Robert. He was lost in his own thoughts, as he often was, and that was where she wanted him to stay. Silence was always better than the alternative. She'd been worried when he came home that it might be one of their bad nights, so she was grateful that his mood had improved. Maybe all the work she'd done tidying and making sure Lizzy was distracted when he got home had helped.

The vodka likely had something to do with it too.

But he was still going back to LA and she was upset about that. Being alone with Lizzy all the time was wearing her thin. She needed him home more. She wished there was some way to make him understand. But trying to find the right thing to say and the right time to say it was always tricky with him.

Robert pulled up in front of the restaurant and handed the keys to the valet before walking around the car to open Sarah's door. Sarah stifled a snicker. He never opened her car door. Except when they came here. Such a performance!

Stop it, she quickly cautioned herself. Thoughts like that might make her say something she'd regret. She needed to be positive. He was being nice right now. She should enjoy it. She tugged at the hem of her mini-dress, attempting to adjust it inconspicuously as she stepped out of the car. Robert took her arm and led her into the restaurant.

Sarah knew the routine and the part she was expected to play. She smiled sweetly as they were greeted immediately by the maître d'.

"Good evening Mr. Jenkins. Mrs. Jenkins. You both look wonderful, as always."

"Thank you, Joseph." Robert smiled warmly and turned toward Sarah. "We are celebrating Mrs. Jenkins's birthday today."

The maître d' nodded politely. "Happy birthday, Mrs. Jenkins."

Sarah smiled demurely. "Thank you." She felt self-conscious and uncomfortable whenever they came here. It represented Robert's world of old money and prestige. A world she knew she didn't belong in. And Robert's mother, she reminded herself, would be the first to agree. She hadn't approved of Sarah from the start, and she still related to her more as hired help than family.

The maître d' turned back to Robert. "I have your regular table reserved as you requested, Mr. Jenkins." He motioned for them to follow and seated them at a private booth. Robert discreetly slipped him a tip as they sat down. The maître d' nodded and handed them their menus and the wine list as a waiter approached.

As the waiter placed their napkins in their laps and poured water in their glasses, Robert handed the wine list back to the maître d'. "We'll just have our usual cabernet."

The maître d' nodded. "We had the pleasure of having your parents in last night," he said to Robert.

Robert smiled and nodded knowingly. "For their standing Thursday night date."

"Yes, sir," the maître d' said, bowing slightly. As he and the waiter turned to leave, his eyes met Sarah's, and she caught a slight smirk on his face. She smiled slightly. They had their own little inside joke—their shared opinion that you could say a lot of things about Robert's parents, but "a pleasure" wasn't one of them. Entitled, snobbish, arrogant? Yes. But a pleasure, definitely not.

Sarah watched Robert quietly read his menu, wondering what was going through his mind and chastising herself for what was running through hers. *You're being a bitch again. What is wrong with you tonight? Do you want to blow it yet again? This is your night. You're in an exclusive restaurant with your handsome, charming husband. Get a grip. You need a major attitude adjustment. Now!*

She tried to focus and read the menu, but her stomach was churning. Nothing looked appetizing to her. The waiter returned with the wine and poured a small amount in Robert's glass. Robert swirled, smelled, and tasted the wine before nodding to the waiter, who returned the nod and poured them each a glass.

Sarah didn't really like red wine; she would have preferred a beer. But she would never say that to Robert. She remembered back to their first dinner out together. He had actually said that no woman of his would ever drink beer. So she had learned to tolerate wine. And she saved her beer drinking for Maggie at the Rusty Hub on Fridays after school. It was one of those secrets married couples have. It seemed innocuous enough to her.

"I'll be back in a few minutes to go over our specials for this evening," the waiter said when he'd finished pouring the wine.

As he left the table, Robert raised his wine glass. "Happy birthday to my beautiful wife," he said with a warm, relaxed smile on his face. He tapped the rim of Sarah's glass and returned to perusing his menu as he sipped the wine.

Sarah studied him, trying to see him as others might in his obviously tailored and expensive suit, exuding power and having dinner with his much younger wife. He was definitely charismatic. She'd give him that. And handsome and sexy. She knew she was the envy of many women. She was sure there were women in the restaurant tonight, and probably men as well, who had noticed them. She lifted her wine glass and took a large chug, checking to be sure Robert wasn't watching. She knew he wouldn't approve. Wine was to be sipped and savored. But she still felt shaky from this afternoon and she was angry at Robert about Lizzy.

She thought the alcohol would take the edge off her anger and help her keep her mouth shut, but instead it seemed to weaken her resolve. The words rose up in her throat like a dormant volcano finally being released. She couldn't hold them back.

"Lizzy really wanted to talk to you tonight."

"I'm sorry. I was beat," Robert said without looking up from his menu.

"It's hard for her having you gone so much." Sarah knew she was pressing it.

"Sarah, please," he said, still focused on his menu. "Not tonight."

He's warning you, Sarah. Loud and clear. Stop now. Don't do this. You know you will just piss him off. And that always gets ugly. Just keep your mouth shut. But she couldn't stop the flood of emotion coursing through her. She pushed the voice in her head aside. "But she really misses you."

Robert looked up from his menu, scowling, his voice low and stern. "How many times do we have to have this conversation? You knew my priorities when you decided to keep the pregnancy. I didn't want kids. I agreed because you wanted it so badly."

"It? That's our daughter you're talking about!" Sarah was aware that her voice had risen slightly.

Robert shot her a harsh look and then glanced around to see if anyone was looking their way. "Stop it." He leaned in toward her, his voice low and terse. "You will not embarrass me here. You know I adore Lizzy, but I could never be a regular dad. I keep you both very comfortable and I don't feel like you appreciate that very much. I'm tired of you being so selfish and childish."

Sarah's stomach roiled and her chest tightened; she felt nauseous and it was hard to breathe. Her mind raced desperately as she struggled to think clearly. She felt spacey and scared. Something was wrong. Maybe it was the wine. *Why did you chug that on an empty stomach? You're messing this up. You're making Robert mad. Focus. Concentrate. Say something. You need to fix this.*

"You're right," she managed to say over the lump in her throat. "It is selfish of me, but I just miss you and I get really lonely sometimes." Tears welled up in her eyes and one spilled down her cheek.

"I know." Robert reached across the table and took her hand. "All the more reason not to waste the time we do have together fighting."

Sarah nodded and dried her eyes with her napkin.

Robert pulled his hand back and returned to his menu. "So, let's find you something wonderful to eat. I know you like the salmon here."

Sarah tried to take a breath, but her chest still wasn't cooperating. She just nodded again, unable to speak and knowing that she wouldn't tell Robert that she didn't really want the salmon tonight anyway.

Sarah was diligent the rest of the meal about keeping the focus on Robert. She asked about work, and got him to talk about his family.

She'd learned that when Robert closed a conversation, she needed to let it go unless she wanted things to go south. His temper had gotten worse with each year of their marriage. Much of the time she was fairly successful at managing his moods; she'd learned how to act and what to say to keep him happy. She looked at him across the table as he studied the bill and remembered once hearing a woman call it her "wifely duty" to please and appease her husband. Sarah wasn't sure she was cut out for the wife thing. She certainly didn't feel very good at it.

Robert paid the bill with cash and looked up at her, smiling. "Ready?"

Sarah nodded, folded her napkin, and laid it on the table as Robert slid out of the booth and came around to help her up. She still felt a little woozy from the wine so she stood up slowly, trying to steady herself. Robert didn't seem to notice; he was busy smiling and waving to an acquaintance across the room. He motioned to Sarah to walk ahead of him and she gingerly made her way through the crowded tables, trying to avoid bumping into one of the other customers. As she passed a table of two casually but nicely dressed young men, one of them met her eyes.

"Sarah?"

Sarah hesitated briefly before recognizing him. Her face lit up. "Matt! I can't believe it. How are you?"

"I'm well," he said, smiling broadly. "How amazing to run into you!"

"I know. It's been so long . . ."

"It has. You look wonderful . . ."

Robert stepped up and authoritatively reached out his hand to Matt. "I'm Sarah's husband, Robert."

"Oh! I'm so sorry, how rude of me." Sarah felt her face flush. "Robert, this is Matt. Matt Herringer."

Matt shook Robert's hand. "Good to meet you, Robert."

"My pleasure," Robert said, his voice curt.

Matt motioned to his dinner partner who was still seated. "This is my friend, Nate Stevenson."

Nate stood up and nodded. "Nice to meet you both."

Sarah and Robert both replied simultaneously, "You too."

Sarah turned back to Matt, smiling. "Are you back in Seattle?"

Matt shook his head. "No, I'm just in for a couple of days from Boston. I did my residency there and never left. How about you? Are you busy writing?"

"Not really . . ." Sarah hesitated, wondering how to explain having given up something that was so important to her when she and Matt were together. He had been her biggest champion, encouraging her to write even when she doubted herself and her abilities.

"No?" Matt said. "I thought you would have finished a couple of books by now! Those short stories you published in college were wonderful."

Robert pressed closer to Sarah and she felt her body tense. *You know he's not happy about this. You're pressing your luck. You better cut this off now.*

Nate's eyes opened wide. "Published? You're a writer?"

"She's a great writer," Matt said before Sarah could respond. "She won the top award in the English department at U-Dub."

Sarah blushed and glanced nervously at Robert. "It was no big deal—"

"Sure it was," Matt said. "I remember how excited you were."

"It was a long time ago," Sarah said.

Robert stepped closer and put his arm around her. "She teaches now."

"Really?" Matt asked. "High school?"

Sarah nodded "Yes. Literature and composition."

"That's great. So, you must enjoy it," he said, more a statement than a question.

"I do. It's really rewarding—"

"We should get going," Robert said.

"Oh, I hate to rush off. I'd love to catch up more," Sarah said impulsively—and immediately regretted it. *Why did you say that? He's going to be pissed. You really need to learn to keep your mouth shut.*

Nate motioned to the table. "Why don't you join us for a drink or some coffee?"

Sarah smiled and glanced apprehensively at Robert, who shook his head. "No, we have to go. We really shouldn't keep the babysitter waiting."

"Wow!" Matt said. "You have a—"

"It was a pleasure meeting you both," Robert said as he nodded to Matt and Nate and firmly steered Sarah away from the table.

"Likewise," Matt said.

"Good meeting you!" Nate called after them.

Sarah looked back over her shoulder and waved slightly. "It was great to see you, Matt!"

Matt smiled and waved back. "You, too!"

"What was that all about?" Robert said when they stepped outside. He was furious. He didn't need her carrying on like that with an old boyfriend. And he hadn't liked the way the conversation was going. The last thing he needed was someone encouraging Sarah's fantasies about writing again. He thought he'd finally put that one to rest. He grabbed her wrist and pulled her down the sidewalk toward the valet.

"Ouch!" Sarah winced. "That hurts."

"Don't start with me. You know everyone in that restaurant knows me and my parents. How do you think it looks for me to stand around while you flirt with an old boyfriend?"

Sarah tried to pull away, but Robert held firm. "Oh, for God's sake! I wasn't flirting."

"Keep your voice down," he said as they neared the valet stand. He handed over the ticket.

Sarah was quiet until the valet was out of earshot. "I was just catching up. It was good to see him. I haven't talked to him in six, almost seven years."

"And you won't start now. You were embarrassing in there." She was so immature sometimes. And she definitely lacked certain social graces. His mother was right about that.

The valet pulled to the curb in his new BMW sedan. He squeezed Sarah's wrist again and said under his breath, "Just get in the car and shut up." Then he let go of Sarah's arm and moved around to the other side of the car. He smiled pleasantly as he tipped the valet.

The valet nodded. "Thank you, sir."

Robert returned the nod and stepped into the car. He was as frustrated with himself as he was with Sarah. Why was it so hard to control his anger with her? He knew it wasn't right but he couldn't help himself. She was so aggravating. He'd need to do something to smooth things over. And then just get the hell out of Dodge again.

Sarah felt her stomach lurch as her anger dissolved into fear. She knew that tone of voice and where it could lead. *Idiot! You've done it again. Why can't you control your mouth? You'd better do something to*

try to calm him down. Her hand shook as she pulled her door closed. Robert silently put on his seatbelt and accelerated quickly into the street. Neither of them spoke for several miles.

Sarah quietly and tentatively broke the silence, "Babe, I really wasn't trying to flirt—"

"Sarah, stop. I don't want to hear your voice right now."

She wanted to kick herself. Her timing was off. She'd approached him too quickly. She coached herself to breathe, calm down, be quiet and patient. She stared out the passenger window, barely aware of the passing scenery. She sensed the tension in Robert's body beginning to ease and her body relaxed ever so slightly.

As they approached home, Robert broke the silence. "Sorry," he said, his voice quiet.

"It's okay." She was ambivalent as to whether to reach out to him or hold back for now. She was aware of the part of her that was angry and wanted to fight back but quickly pushed that away, thinking instead about all she'd done to trigger the fight. *You shouldn't have had so much wine. You know it makes it harder to keep your comments in check. And you shouldn't have been so friendly with Matt. You should have cut him off when he started talking about the writing. You know Robert hates that. You should have talked more about Robert. That would have helped. Why didn't you think of that? Why do you always fuck things like this up?* She sat very still and continued to stare out the window.

Robert spoke again as they pulled into the driveway. "Do I need to drive Amy home?"

"I can take her if you want," Sarah said, reaching for the car door.

"No, it's fine. I'll just wait here. You can send her out."

"Okay." She got out of the car and walked quickly to the front door, not wanting to make Robert wait any longer than necessary.

Amy was curled up on the sofa with her feet tucked under her, reading a book. She shoved her book into her backpack and stood up to greet Sarah. Sarah felt a bit numb as they exchanged the appropriate pleasantries. She wanted to appear the good, concerned mother, but also wanted to get Amy out of the house and into the car as quickly as possible. When Amy walked outside, she closed the door behind her and watched as Robert backed the car out of the drive before collapsing on the sofa, feeling drained and depleted. She hated the way these arguments left her feeling. Each time they happened she felt a little worse, a little more like a failure. Why couldn't she figure out how to do things differently? How did she always manage to screw things up? She'd been with Robert over six years now, but it only seemed to be getting worse.

She closed her eyes and felt the tears well up. *No, you can't cry. You know that just makes things worse. And he'll be back in a few minutes.* She took a deep breath and tried to muster the energy to pull herself up. She straightened the pillows on the sofa, scanned the room, and went to check the kitchen. She cleaned up the leftover dishes and was just finishing wiping down the counters when she heard the front door open. She walked out to greet Robert, who took her arm to guide her upstairs without speaking. She knew he might be quiet like this for a while—days, even—so she quietly ascended the stairs and went into the closet to change. She stripped down to her panties and grabbed her nightshirt.

When she came out of the closet she began to pull the nightshirt over her head. Robert had taken off his shirt and unbuttoned his slacks and was sitting on a chair to untie his shoes.

"Leave it off," he said.

Sarah looked up at him and saw the look on his face. She knew that look. *So, this is how it's going to go.*

He motioned her over. "Come here so I can see you."

Sarah walked around the bed to stand in front of him.

"I want to look at you." He slipped her panties down and kissed her belly. His eyes and hands moved up to her breasts and he fondled them.

Sarah still felt unsettled from their fight. She thought they should at least try to talk about what had happened. "Robert, I . . ."

He put his fingers to her lips. "No talking." He stood up and roughly kissed her mouth as he rubbed her back and buttocks. Sarah knew better than to resist so she returned his kiss and began sliding his pants off. They continued kissing as Robert kicked off his pants and pulled off his boxers. He moved behind Sarah, caressing one breast while he moved his other hand down between her thighs and started rubbing. He guided her onto the bed and entered her from behind. Sarah winced and bit her lip at the pain. She knew it wouldn't be long and she moaned a little for effect. Robert responded by thrusting harder. He quickly reached orgasm, and as soon as he did he rolled over, pushing her aside in the process, and lay on his back with his eyes closed.

"That felt great," he said when he caught his breath. Sarah rolled toward him and reached a hand out over his torso. He leaned over and kissed her head. "Happy birthday, sweetheart." He turned away from her and onto his side.

Sarah touched his back. "I love you."

"Hmm . . . love you too."

Sarah knew he would be asleep within seconds. She lay still for a minute and then turned onto her back and stared at the ceiling. She reviewed the events of the evening, and suddenly she felt sad and confused. She thought about how mad Robert had been about her conversation with Matt. She rubbed her wrist. It still hurt, and she suspected she'd have a nice bruise the next day.

She continued to stare at the ceiling as she tried to dissect the argument. He'd said she'd embarrassed him by flirting. Had she really been flirting? She didn't think so. But she had been excited and happy to see Matt. And mad and frustrated with Robert. Maybe this was her fault.

You were probably trying to make him jealous. You did it to get back at him. To take back control. You always do this. You always do something to piss him off. And this time you ruined your own birthday. Serves you right. Maybe this time you'll finally learn something.

Chapter 4

Sarah struggled to make sense of her dream. She'd almost made it to the top of a hill, tired and out of breath, when she felt something jabbing her repeatedly in the shoulder. It took her a few fitful turns before she opened her eyes and realized that it was morning and Lizzy was standing next to her bed.

"Mommy," she whispered as she continued to poke Sarah's shoulder. "Remember? I need to put on my new dress for Daddy this morning."

Sarah groaned inwardly. Why today? She just wanted to sleep in. She wanted Lizzy to go away and leave her alone. Maybe she could bribe her somehow? She was turning the idea over in her mind when another voice quickly charged in. *You're a terrible mother. What is your problem? Get your lazy ass out of bed and take care of your daughter.*

The voice was right. She needed to get up. She nodded at Lizzy and gingerly slipped out of bed, holding a finger up to her lips with one hand and motioning to her with other hand to leave the room. Lizzy tiptoed out as Sarah quietly grabbed her yoga pants, a sports bra, and a long sleeve T-shirt from the closet. She followed Lizzy into the hall, closing the bedroom door behind her and leaving Robert to sleep.

Sarah used Lizzy's bathroom to get dressed. She splashed some water on her face and pulled her hair back in a ponytail. Her wrist ached, and it was starting to show some discoloration. She stretched her shirtsleeves so they would fall down over her hands and went to help Lizzy get dressed.

Lizzy had already pulled on some tights and was buckling her shoes when Sarah walked into her room. Sarah got the dress out of the closet and held it open for Lizzy to slip her arms and head in. She pulled it down over her body and zipped up the back. This accomplished, Lizzy spun around to face Sarah, her face lit up with excitement.

"Can you put my blue and white ribbon in my hair for me?"

Sarah smiled. "Sure. I saw it hanging in your bathroom. I'll go get it."

Sarah settled Lizzy in at the kitchen table to color while they waited for Robert to wake up. Her mind was a jumble of thoughts while she started to cook breakfast. She needed to find a way to talk to him about the previous night without becoming bitchy. She should own her part. Apologize. Explain to him that she hadn't meant to flirt, she'd just been excited. And acknowledge that what she did had been upsetting to him. Tell him she was sorry she'd embarrassed him and that she would try to be better.

She smelled the toast burning and jumped to pop the lever. She was aware of some tightness in her stomach. She was anxious for Robert to get up; she wanted to go to yoga soon and needed to talk to him before she left. They needed to get back to a good place before he went back to LA. She threw the toast in the trash and put two more slices in the toaster.

When Robert finally came downstairs, Lizzy had finished her breakfast and resumed coloring at the table. Sarah was washing the pan she'd used to scramble Lizzy's eggs. She looked up when he walked in, trying to get a read on his mood.

"Good morning, my beautiful girls," he said as he came into the kitchen. "I'm making a Starbucks run. Can I get you anything?"

Sarah pointed toward the coffee pot. "I made coffee here," she said, trying to be upbeat. "And I need to leave for yoga in about a half hour."

"I'd rather have a latte. I'll go quickly and be right back."

Sarah felt a switch flip inside her. She was trying to be good. She had let him sleep in and made him coffee. She had taken care of Lizzy once again. And yet he didn't appreciate any of that. He was just going to do whatever he wanted to do, without any consideration for her. As always.

"There's not enough time. And besides, I really need to talk to you about last night." Sarah heard the sternness in her voice and glanced at Lizzy.

Lizzy looked up at Sarah and then jumped up from the table and ran to Robert. "Daddy, see my new dress!?"

Robert turned to Lizzy and swept her up into his arms. "Yes, I do! And you look absolutely gorgeous! You get more beautiful every day! How about going out with your dad for some hot chocolate with extra whipped cream?"

Lizzy's face lit up. "Yeah!"

"Run and get your jacket," he said as he let her slide down to the floor. Lizzy excitedly ran out of the room as Robert picked up his wallet and car keys from the counter.

Sarah felt the tightness in her chest and shoulders. "Why did you do that? I told you I need to talk to you about last night."

Robert walked around the counter to Sarah and put his arms around her from behind, kissing her cheek and speaking softly into her ear. "What I remember about last night is that you were incredibly sexy."

Sarah twisted away. "Robert, stop, I'm being serious. Look!" She pulled her sleeve up to show him her bruised wrist, but quickly pulled it down as Lizzy ran back in.

"Here Daddy," Lizzy said, reaching up to Robert with her jacket in her hand. Robert took the jacket and helped her put it on.

"Hot chocolate, here we come!" he said as he shuffled Lizzy toward the door. He glanced back at Sarah as they left the room. "See you later. Have fun at yoga!"

Sarah glared at him, but he didn't seem to notice. The flicker of anger she'd been feeling was snuffed out and she slumped back against the counter, dejected. Tears threatened, but she fought back. *No*, she told herself, suppressing her discouragement. She wasn't going to let him get to her today. She stood up and started to clean the kitchen—then stopped herself.

"Fuck it!" she said out loud. "If you want a clean kitchen, you can clean it yourself." She grabbed her purse and keys and headed out the door.

Sarah was still fighting waves of emotions when she got to the dance studio. Anger, sadness, loneliness, and discouragement rose up into her awareness, but she pushed them away. She didn't want to feel any of them. She was tired of feeling bad all the time. Tired of letting Robert get under her skin. Tired of feeling like a failure.

She pushed open the door to the studio and headed down the

hall. There was a jazz class in progress and she hesitated briefly as she passed, a glimmer of interest and longing on her face. She had danced when she was younger, and missed the mindless joy she'd felt when she was moving in an effortless flow with the music. The instructor motioned for her to join, but Sarah shook her head and held up her yoga mat before continuing on to her class.

She stepped quietly into the open, naturally lit room. Some students were already stretching on their mats and others were quietly finding a spot. She glanced around and saw Kate on the far side of the room.

Sarah had met Kate two years earlier, when their daughters started in the same preschool class. Sarah had always felt theirs was an unlikely friendship. Kate was twelve years older than her, although you wouldn't know it—she was a fit, attractive stay-at-home mom who wrote a food blog and spent a lot of time exercising. Sarah envied her at times, but also knew she would go crazy staying home full time.

Sarah gingerly stepped around the other class participants and quietly unrolled her mat next to Kate. In doing so, her sleeve pulled up to reveal the bruising on her wrist. She quickly pulled it down, tucking the cuff under her thumb.

"Hi Kate," she whispered.

Kate looked up and smiled broadly. "You made it!"

"Yeah. Barely." Sarah felt some of her anger at Robert return.

"Something wrong?"

"No. Just a lot on my mind." *If she only knew.*

"Want to talk about it?"

Sarah shook her head no. She wished she could talk to Kate, but she was too scared and ashamed. Kate was so together. *You can't let her see what a mess you've made of things. She wouldn't want to be friends with you anymore. She'd see you for who you really are: a complete fuckup.* "I just need a little time to relax."

"Well, you've come to the right place!"

Sarah sat down on her mat and started stretching. She felt a little better already. Spending time with Kate always left her feeling lighter. Kate was such a positive person, always calm and friendly. Nothing seemed to faze her.

"Are you still okay to take Emma tomorrow?" Kate asked as she shifted her body to stretch in the other direction.

"Of course. It's all Lizzy can talk about—a sleepover on a school night! You'd think I'd told her she could have ice cream three meals a day."

Kate smiled. "I know. Emma's pretty excited too."

"So, what are you and Will planning? Or is it a surprise?"

Kate laughed. "I think we've been married too long for anything to be a surprise anymore. We're taking a ferry over to Bainbridge Island. I found a great little bed-and-breakfast. And no television or Wi-Fi. We're taking our hiking shoes and we both have books. I think that's about all we'll need!"

"Sounds wonderful," Sarah said, trying not to sound wistful. "I love that you do these date-night getaways."

"A little trick we learned from our marriage counselor."

"Really? But you have such a great marriage. Why would you need a marriage counselor?" *Stupid! Why did you say that? You shouldn't ask a question like that. That's too personal.*

As usual, Kate wasn't rattled. "Well, we work at it. After sixteen years and four kids, you need a little tune-up now and then."

Sarah forced a smile. She wasn't sure a tune-up would be enough. Her marriage needed a total overhaul. There was no way she'd ever be able to convince Robert to go to a counselor. He would just laugh in her face. But maybe a weekend away together would help. Just the two of them, with time to reconnect. He might go for that. Maybe she could go down to LA with him sometime when school was on break. He knew she missed Southern California. She could drive down to San Diego while he was working and see friends. Sarah felt excited at the thought. She would talk to him about it when she got home.

She stretched her legs out in front of her and brought her head to her knees, just resting in the stretch. Her thoughts continued to drift until the yoga teacher stood and calmly addressed the class.

"Good morning, everyone . . ."

Sarah was still thinking about the idea of a trip with Robert when she walked in the front door and saw him sitting in a chair by the window, sipping coffee from a Starbucks cup and reading the paper. Her hopefulness about reconnecting with him faded as her anger crept back in. This was his idea of father–daughter time? Had he come home and parked Lizzy in front of a video?

"Where's Lizzy?" she asked, trying to keep the edge out of her voice.

"We ran into Elena," Robert said without looking up from his paper. "She was on her way to the park with Sonia, so Lizzy went with them."

Sarah's anger erupted. She threw her purse and mat onto a chair. "Seriously!?" she screamed. "You can't even spend two hours with your daughter? You have to pass her off on a friend so you can drink coffee and read the paper? You're leaving again tomorrow and you'll have all kinds of alone time. Don't you care at all about your daughter? She might as well be fatherless."

Robert looked up a Sarah. "For God's sake Sarah, not again. Stop trying to make me the All-American Dad."

"As if that would ever be remotely possible," Sarah said, crossing her arms in front of her body.

"Jesus, get off my back." Robert threw the paper down and got up out of his chair. "All I wanted was a little downtime to read the paper. Besides, Lizzy wanted to go with Elena and Sonia." He turned abruptly and started walking out of the room.

"No way, Robert! Don't you dare leave. We need to talk about last night. You really hurt me. Again!" She rushed over to Robert and held her wrist up to his face to reveal the bruising.

He sighed. "Why are you making such a big deal out of this? I said I was sorry. I certainly didn't intend to hurt you. I can't help it if you bruise like a peach. I'm really tired of your overreacting. It's over and done with, so let's just drop it, can we?"

Sarah shook her head and rolled her eyes. "Fine. Whatever."

"Thank you. Now if you don't mind, I have some work to do." Robert turned to leave.

Sarah wasn't ready to let it go. "What about Lizzy? Do you plan to find some time for her?"

Robert stopped, dropped his head, and turned slowly back to Sarah. When he spoke, his voice was even and conciliatory. "Fine. Why don't we all go out to dinner tonight? We can go to Luigi's like you wanted."

Sarah smiled weakly and nodded her head, appreciating the small victory. Going out to dinner as a family would be good for them. "I think Lizzy would like that."

"Good. Let's make it early so we can beat the crowds. I'm on the first flight out tomorrow, so I want some time to pack before the game starts." He started out of the room, then stopped and looked at Sarah. "Oh, and clean up that mess in the kitchen. It's disgusting in there. You know how I feel about that." He turned again to leave.

"Fuck you," Sarah said under her breath.

Robert turned back. "What?"

Don't go there, Sarah. Stop while you're ahead. He's agreed to dinner. Lizzy loves Luigi's. Just keep your stupid mouth shut for once. Do what he says.

"Sorry about the kitchen. I was running late for yoga, so I was going to clean it up as soon as I got back."

Robert smiled. "Good girl."

Sarah watched as Robert walked down the hall. She slowly picked up her yoga mat and purse before going to clean the kitchen.

Chapter 5

Sarah was glad to be back to school on Monday. The fight with Robert the day before had left her feeling drained. He'd kept his promise of taking them to Luigi's, and had been attentive to Lizzy that evening, but for the most part he'd ignored Sarah. When they got home he had retreated to the den to watch the basketball game, leaving Sarah to entertain Lizzy until bedtime. Sarah had fallen asleep before he came to bed, and when she woke up he'd been gone, leaving her feeling abandoned again.

Being at work and having all her students around helped lift her spirits, but she was still aware of feeling tired and a bit numb. She was grateful to have two composition classes before lunch. She'd put them to work doing some peer editing of their essays so she could ease into her day.

The noon bell rang and her students excitedly filed out of her classroom, on a quest for the coveted off-campus lunch. It was just occurring to her that she hadn't seen Maggie yet that day when she synchronistically appeared in Sarah's doorway.

"Ugh! Monday!" Maggie said as she came into the room and slumped into a chair in front of Sarah's desk.

Sarah smiled. "Hello to you too!"

"I know. I'm a complete drag." Maggie sat up in her chair and leaned forward on the desktop toward Sarah. "How about some lunch?"

"Sure." Sarah stood up and reached out to grab her purse, forgetting about her wrist. Before she could pull her hand back, Maggie spotted the dark purple bruising.

"Yikes! What did you do to your arm?" She stood up from her chair to look more closely at Sarah's wrist. "That looks nasty."

Sarah pulled her arm back; her body tensed. She should've had a story ready. She reached for something to say. "Oh, you know me. Ever the idiot. Trying to carry three canvas bags of groceries and Lizzy at the same time." *What a lame response. She's never gonna buy that. She'll see right through it.*

"Jeez, taking Supermom to new levels. Let the kid walk next time," Maggie said. Her gaze swiveled to the vase of two-dozen roses sitting on the table under the window. "Whoa! Somebody scored!" Maggie took the card from the flowers and read aloud, "Beauty for my beauty. Love, Robert." She held the card up toward Sarah. "Seriously!?"

Sarah just shrugged. The flowers and the card represented something very different to Maggie than they did to her. And she was sure Maggie would feel differently if she knew the whole story.

"I should be so lucky." Maggie threw the card down on the desk. "What's wrong with me that I only seem to attract losers? I can't remember any of my previous boyfriends ever getting me flowers, let alone writing a romantic card." She sagged a little. "I guess we all get what we deserve." She headed for the door without waiting for a response from Sarah.

"Yeah. I guess we do . . ." Sarah said under her breath and followed her friend out of the room.

As they walked the three blocks to the deli, Sarah listened as Maggie talked about her preparation for the spring drama presentation. She did two shows a year and her energy always went into overdrive during those times. Sarah knew Maggie loved teaching history, but the school plays were what she lived for. And they were always great. Sarah was consistently amazed by the professionalism of the production and the talent of the students.

As they approached the deli, Sarah saw the line extending out the front door and beginning to snake down the sidewalk.

"Wow! Busy day today," she said. "Do you want to go somewhere else?"

Maggie answered by joining the end of the line. "Nah," she said, "it usually goes pretty quickly. And if there aren't any tables, we can eat outside. I was thinking that would be nice anyway. We should take advantage of this little bit of sunshine."

"Sounds good to me," Sarah said. She had been enjoying the warm glow that intermittently stole through the clouds as they were walking. She loved the way it melted the tension in her body. She closed her eyes and lifted her face, soaking up the relaxing heat.

Maggie had fallen silent. Sarah glanced at her, wondering what was going on. She had been so talkative on the way there, but now seemed preoccupied. Had she said or done something to upset her, or was it just one of her moods? She waited a few minutes before breaking the silence. "Hey, Mags. You okay?"

"Huh?"

"You seemed gone somewhere."

"I was thinking about how much I hate being alone."

"Well being together isn't always so great either!" Sarah regretted the words as soon as they were out of her mouth. *Idiot! Why did you say that? You know how Maggie is. How many fights have you had because she felt you didn't understand? Why don't you ever think before you open your big mouth? You really can be so insensitive!*

"Give me a break, Sarah. Expensive romantic dinners, roses, sentiments of undying love . . ."

"I'm just saying—"

"Cut the crap, I don't want to hear it." Maggie turned her back on Sarah and pushed ahead of her in line. Sarah knew to stay back, keep her mouth shut, and give her moody friend some space. If she tried to talk now it would just make things worse.

They got their sandwiches and found a bench outside the deli, where they sat and ate in silence. Sarah was nearly done eating when Maggie turned to her.

"Sorry," she said.

"It's okay. I know it's hard for you being alone. But I know you're going to find a great guy."

Maggie shrugged. "Let's change the subject. Any hot gossip?"

Sarah thought for a moment. Should she tell Maggie about running into Matt? She'd never really talked to anyone about him. She felt nervous and uncertain. What if she asked about Robert's reaction? She couldn't tell her about that. She'd seen her wrist. She might put two and two together. Although knowing Maggie, she'd be more interested in finding out everything about Matt. Robert's reaction probably wouldn't even occur to her. She didn't know about Robert's temper.

She decided to go ahead and risk it. She knew it would put Maggie in a better mood.

"How about running into my college boyfriend?"

Maggie's eyes popped open. "Really!? You never talked about a college boyfriend."

Sarah shrugged. "Not much to tell."

It was working. Maggie was definitely hooked.

"Bullshit! There's always something to tell when it comes to old boyfriends. His name, how you met, how long you dated, what he was like in bed. Spill! I want to hear it all!" Maggie scooted closer to Sarah on the bench.

"His name was Matt. We met through a friend. Dated for a year. And in bed, well, he was my first. End of story."

"The hell you say! You cannot follow 'he was my first' with 'end of story.'"

"Sure I can. And I just did!" Sarah got up to throw away the paper wrapping of her sandwich. "We need to go. We're going to be late for class."

Maggie jumped up to follow Sarah. "No way. You are not leaving me hanging. I want all the gory details."

Sarah sighed. She knew Maggie would never let this go. She'd wanted her to be in a better mood and it had worked. So now it was time to pay the piper.

"Fine. But not now. We really need to get back. How about dinner at my house, tonight? Robert's gone so we can have a girl's night. We'll make tacos. They're one of Lizzy's favorite dinners."

"Sounds perfect," Maggie said happily. She linked arms with Sarah as they walked toward the school. "It's a date! And I'll bring the beer . . ."

Maggie lived in a one-room loft on the third floor of a small building in the heart of the urban bustle. She loved being in the middle of everything and always felt a little out of her element when she visited Sarah. The suburbs were too quiet for her liking, and Sarah's house looked like something out of House Beautiful. It was tastefully decorated; everything in it was high-end. And the living room furniture was white! Who did that? It made her nervous. She was always afraid she was going to spill or break something.

Sarah had just gone to put Lizzy to bed. She'd told Maggie to settle into the living room while she was gone. She would have been happier to stay in the kitchen! She carefully placed her beer mug on a coaster on the glass coffee table and curled up in a chair to read a magazine.

She'd nearly finished both the beer and the magazine by the time Sarah finally came back.

"Sorry," Sarah said as she came into the room.

Maggie looked up from her magazine. "I just figured you were avoiding me."

Sarah plopped down on the sofa. "She had a hard time settling down. Too much excitement about making tacos and having Aunt Maggie over."

Maggie tossed her magazine onto the table. "So she's finally asleep?"

"Almost. She's listening to a bedtime tape. I think she'll be asleep soon."

Maggie grinned. "Good. So now the real girls' night can begin! Let's get back to this mysterious old beau. Why haven't you told me about him before?"

Sarah hesitated briefly. "I think I wanted to block him from my memory."

"Sounds like it was a bad first time. Let me guess: a smelly dorm room and his roommate walked in on you."

"No! I was just really angry."

Maggie frowned. "About the sex?"

"No. It had nothing to do with sex. He'd finished medical school and wanted to volunteer for a year in Africa before starting a residency."

"Quite an accomplishment. And that made you furious . . . why?"

Maggie was having a hard time following Sarah's story. She really wanted her to hurry up and get to the good stuff.

Sarah glared at her. "Would you let me tell the story already!?"

Maggie gestured for her to continue. "By all means."

"I wasn't angry he was going. He was very up-front about his plans when we first met, which is why he never really got that attached."

"But you did."

"Exactly. He was easy to be with and we had a great time together—"

"And the sex was great?" Maggie motioned with her hand to speed Sarah up.

Sarah picked up a pillow and threw it at her. "Jeez, could you be more impatient!"

Maggie moved the hand holding her beer out of the way and caught the pillow with her other hand. "Careful. Beer on this nice white sofa would not be pretty!" She threw the pillow back to Sarah. "Just get to the good stuff."

"As I was saying . . ." Sarah said.

"I'm all ears," Maggie said, coaching herself to be more patient.

"It took me a while to get up the nerve to tell him I was a virgin. I think he was relieved. My resistance made more sense. And he was very sweet about the whole thing after that. He planned a romantic night in at his place: dinner with candlelight, music, champagne, and then the bed all covered with rose petals!"

Maggie nearly choked on the beer she had just swigged. "You're shitting me!" she said once she was able to swallow.

"Like I could make this up?"

Maggie lifted her beer mug slightly. "Touché." She leaned forward, put her drink on the table, and shook her head. "Hell. My first time was in the backseat of my drunk, pimply faced boyfriend's junker car my junior year of high school. I seriously considered becoming a nun after that."

Sarah laughed. "That good, huh?"

"Nothing like your guy, that's for sure." Maggie sighed and sank back into her chair. This story was another reminder of what a charmed life Sarah seemed to live, especially compared to her.

"Yeah, I guess it was nice of him," Sarah said.

"Nice? Hell, he deserves the Nobel Prize of First Times. What turned this hero into a villain?"

"He thought we should date other people."

Again, Maggie was a little lost. Sarah was holding something back and she was having a hard time reading between the lines. "And you didn't want that?"

"No. I wanted to do the long-distance thing. But he thought I needed more experience. I hadn't really dated anyone before him and I think that made him a little nervous. So, we split up."

"Why do I feel like there's something you're not telling me?" Maggie said, furrowing her brow and scrutinizing Sarah.

"No." Sarah shook her head. "It's nothing, really."

"Let me be the judge of that," Maggie said. "Come on. Out with it."

"I don't know. I feel a little ashamed of my behavior back then."

"Oh no, what did you do?" Maggie was really curious now. As far as she knew, Sarah had never done anything bad in her life. She was the quintessential good girl. It would be fun to finally have some dirt!

Sarah shook her head. "It sounds so stupid now, but I went pretty psycho bitch at the time and wrote a really nasty letter."

"Oh." Maggie felt a little disappointed. She'd been hoping for something more scandalous. She should have known. For Sarah, a nasty letter probably felt reprehensible. "It doesn't sound that stupid. Worse things have been done during breakups. Did you send him the letter?"

Sarah cringed. "Yeah. Bad move, huh?"

Maggie shrugged and smiled. "Maybe not the best. So, I'm guessing you never heard from him."

"No. He wrote me back."

"And?"

Sarah stood up abruptly and grabbed Maggie's empty beer mug off the table. "I don't know," she said as she headed toward the kitchen. "I never opened it."

Maggie jumped up and chased Sarah into the kitchen. "Never opened it? You're kidding? You just pitched it?" She couldn't believe it. What on earth could have made her never open it?

"No, I didn't pitch it. I stuck it in a box with the rest of my college stuff."

"So, you still have it?" Maggie was giddy with excitement. "Where is it? We should get it and read it!"

Sarah frowned and shook her head. "Forget it. I'm married now, remember?"

Maggie threw her hands up. "So what? We're not talking about having an affair. Come on. Don't you want to know what he said?"

"I don't know . . ."

The phone rang and Sarah froze. Maggie watched as she glanced at the caller ID, took a breath, and then tentatively answered the phone. She was puzzled by the distinct change in Sarah's demeanor. She was suddenly more formal—sort of detached. The playfulness was gone. She almost seemed to shrink in size, which Maggie knew was totally absurd, but that was how it seemed. She wondered who was on the other end of the phone call.

"Okay," Sarah said. "I'll wait to have dinner with you when you get home."

Ah, Robert. Maggie had only met him a couple of times. Her impression of him was that he was very proper and sophisticated. And a bit of a snob. A stuffed shirt, actually. But maybe that was to be expected. After all, his family was one of the wealthiest in Seattle. In all of Washington, for that matter. That was probably why Sarah didn't ever invite her over when he was around. She knew she was the farthest thing from sophisticated. And she was proud of it. She was glad that Robert traveled a lot; otherwise, she'd probably never see her best friend!

Sarah hung up the phone. "That was Robert. He's coming home later than planned. Not until Friday night." She slumped a bit, then seemed to remember herself and smiled at Maggie. "He'll be exhausted. I'll have to think of something nice to cook for dinner."

Sarah still seemed far away. Maggie wanted to pull her back. "So, what about that mystery letter?"

"Huh?"

"The letter? From Matt?"

Sarah swiped her hand dismissively. "Oh, I can't think about that now."

Maggie wondered what was going on. Sarah seemed lost in her thoughts. She wasn't used to seeing her like this. "You okay?" she asked, studying her face.

Sarah met her gaze. "Yeah. Of course. Just getting a little tired. I should probably call it a night."

"Yeah. Okay," Maggie said, disappointed. She got up to leave, still puzzled by Sarah's behavior. Had Robert told her something upsetting? She opened her mouth to ask—then shut it. It wasn't any of her business. If Sarah wanted to talk to her about it, she would.

Chapter 6

Sarah checked the food in the oven and glanced at the clock. Robert's plane had been delayed, but he'd called from the town car to say he was on his way. She'd been disappointed about the delay. He was only home for the weekend and she had been counting on having a nice dinner together. But she'd kept it warm and Lizzy was already asleep, so the evening wasn't completely ruined.

She went to look out the front window just in time to see headlights illuminate the rain as the car pulled into the driveway. Sarah watched as the driver got the bags from the trunk and handed them to Robert, who nodded a thank-you and ran for the front door.

Sarah turned on the porch light and opened the door.

Robert gave her a quick peck on the cheek before putting his bags down and taking off his coat. "Damn Seattle rain," he said as he reached back outside to shake off his coat. "It was sunny and gorgeous in LA."

Sarah smelled a strong odor of alcohol and her body tensed. "Had a few drinks?"

"With a three-hour delay, what do you think?"

Sarah felt a twinge of fear but pushed it away. "Well, it's dry in here! Come to the kitchen. I kept dinner warm for you."

"I'm not hungry," Robert said. He handed her his coat and headed for the stairs. "I just want a hot shower and a comfortable bed."

Sarah felt a wave of disappointment but pushed it away, reminding herself that he'd had a rough day. She went to the kitchen to put away the food.

When she got upstairs the shower was running, so she undressed, put on her nightshirt, and crawled into bed. She resigned herself to wait to talk to Robert until tomorrow. She knew he'd pass out as soon as he hit the bed, so she turned off her bedside lamp and settled in to sleep.

Robert came out of the bathroom naked and crawled into bed, groping clumsily for Sarah.

Sarah took hold of his hand. "I thought you were tired."

"Not too tired for some of your sweet thing," Robert said, his speech slightly slurred.

"Robert, you're drunk. And I'm really wiped. It's been a long day."

"I know how to wake you up." Robert spooned Sarah from behind and slid his hand up under her nightshirt to fondle her breasts. Sarah felt his erection against her upper thigh. She scooted forward and gently tried to push his hand away.

"Robert, I'm really not in the mood tonight." The last thing she wanted was more drunken sex. It seemed like that was all they ever had anymore. She wondered if he was even still attracted to her.

"Sure you are, baby," he said as he rolled her toward him and straddled her, using his knee to spread her legs and holding her arms down above her head. "I know you've missed me. You just gotta loosen up." He put his mouth on hers as he forcefully entered her and began thrusting slowly.

Sarah winced and pulled her mouth away, trying to lift her arms to push him off. "Robert, no . . ."

Robert was thrusting more quickly. "Oh, come on. It feels good."

"No, it's hurting."

Robert was breathing harder now. He continued thrusting. "That's because you're too tense. Just relax."

"But—"

"Hang on. I'm almost there," he said breathlessly.

Sarah winced as the pain worsened. "Robert, please!"

"I'm not done yet." He grunted and began thrusting harder.

Sarah felt herself go numb. She lay still until Robert climaxed and rolled off of her and onto his back.

"Ah, great fuck baby," he said, sighing deeply.

Sarah lay very still for a few minutes, fighting back the tears, until she heard Robert's breathing become deep and regular. Then she gingerly slipped out of bed, went into the bathroom, and quietly closed the door before turning on the shower. She stood briefly and stared at herself in the mirror. Tears sprang into her eyes and she turned away. She opened the shower door, tested the water with her hand, and stepped in. She let the water run over her head and face for a minute before she slumped against the wall of the shower and cried.

Robert woke before Sarah with a vague memory of having had sex with her the night before. He knew he'd been pretty drunk and he remembered feeling turned on by his seatmate on the plane. He wondered if Sarah thought he'd been too rough with her. It was something she'd complained about before. Maybe a preemptive strike was a good idea. He quietly slipped out of bed, pulled on a pair of jeans and a sweater, and went down the hall to Lizzy's room.

He found Lizzy already awake and playing quietly. She squealed and jumped up to run to him when he came into her room. He scooped her up in his arms to quiet her.

"I missed you," she said, wrapping her arms tightly around his neck.

"I missed you too, pumpkin. And I was thinking we could do something fun this morning. How would you like to help me make Mommy a nice breakfast?"

Lizzy's eyes brightened. "Waffles?"

Robert opened his eyes widely to mirror Lizzy's. "With blueberries and whipped cream?"

"Yes!"

"I know that's what you want. But what do you think Mommy would like?"

Lizzy frowned slightly. "Waffles!"

Robert smiled. He liked her spunk; she wasn't at all like Sarah in that way. That was her Jenkins blood. It made him proud. "Don't worry, I'll make you some waffles. But I know Mommy likes scrambled eggs and toast better than waffles."

"I want to help. I can make the toast."

"That sound perfect," Robert said as he let her slide down to the ground. "Now you get dressed and come down when you're ready. I'll go get started on your waffles."

"Okay."

He watched her run to her closet, then headed down to the kitchen to begin cooking. It wasn't his favorite thing to do—he preferred to be served and generally ate out when he was away from home—but he could handle the occasional breakfast.

Domesticity was hard for him. He adored Lizzy, but he knew he couldn't be a full-time dad or husband and was grateful that his work was primarily in LA. He loved his life there; it made him feel alive and energized. His Seattle life satisfied his parents and, to some extent, Sarah, although he'd be lying if he said he wasn't aware of her occasional discontent. There was a time when he'd made more of an effort to please or at least appease her, but he was finding it increasingly difficult all the time. He wouldn't go so far as to say he felt trapped—*although*, he mused, *maybe that's exactly what I feel.* He resented Sarah, and at times Lizzy, and trying to pretend otherwise was wearing on him.

Lizzy skipped into the room just as he was pulling her frozen waffles out of the toaster. He smothered them in blueberries and topped them with a generous squirt of whipped cream.

"Yummy!" Lizzy said in approval as she climbed up onto a bar stool at the counter.

Robert readied a breakfast tray as Lizzy devoured her waffles: a single rose in a bud vase, a glass of juice, a cup of coffee, a small pourer of cream, a plate, a napkin, and silverware. He added a small bowl of strawberries and then began cracking the eggs.

"Mommy's gonna be really surprised, isn't she?" Lizzy asked through a mouthful of waffle, her lips stained blue from the berries.

"She sure is." Robert poured the eggs into the pan and gave Lizzy a jar of jam and a plate with a slice of toast. She pushed her waffle plate to the side and got up on her knees on the barstool to take on her task.

Robert finished cooking the eggs, carried the pan from the stove, and scooped them onto the plate. He glanced over at Lizzy. "How's that toast coming?"

Lizzy proudly lifted a piece of toast overflowing with jam up in both her hands for her father to see. "Good!"

"Great job! You're my own special *sous-chef!*"

Lizzy beamed proudly as Robert took the toast from her and

placed it on the plate. He picked up the tray as Lizzy hopped down from the barstool.

"You can run ahead and open the door for me. But don't tell Mommy until I get there. We want it to be a surprise, right?"

Lizzy nodded. "Right!"

"Good. Okay, let's do this!"

"Yeah!" Lizzy said as she ran up the stairs ahead of Robert.

When Lizzy opened the door, Sarah was awake but lost in thought. She didn't even realize her husband and daughter were in the room until they both yelled, "Surprise!"

Sarah startled slightly, then smiled weakly and pushed herself up to a sitting position in bed.

"What's all this?" she asked, trying to muster some playfulness for Lizzy.

Lizzy beamed. "We made you a special breakfast!"

"Because you are such a special mommy!" Robert added as he put the tray down in front of Sarah.

Lizzy excitedly crawled up in bed next to Sarah. "I made the toast all by myself!"

Sarah put an arm around Lizzy and gave her a hug and kiss. "It looks wonderful, sweetie. Thank you."

"You're welcome!"

Sarah noticed Lizzy's blue lips and smiled. "So, did you have your breakfast?"

"Yeah, Daddy made me blueberry waffles."

Sarah gently touched Lizzy's lips. "I thought that might be the case! Sounds like Daddy's been cookin' up a storm this morning."

"Sure have," Robert said. He looked at Lizzy. "And we, my little *sous-chef*, have a lot of cleaning up to do, so we better get on it and let Mommy enjoy her breakfast." He lifted Lizzy off the bed and carried her out of the room.

After they left, Sarah absentmindedly picked at her food. She'd been rehearsing how to best tell Robert how angry and hurt she felt about last night before he and Lizzy had come in with breakfast. And now she felt guilty. How many husbands served their wives breakfast in bed? And he was taking care of Lizzy and giving her a break. *You should appreciate it instead of being an ungrateful bitch.*

Sarah tried to push the anger away by rationalizing Robert's behavior the night before. He'd been drinking. He hadn't realized what he was doing. He probably didn't even remember what had happened. She resolved to focus on the positives: he'd made her breakfast and was taking care of Lizzy, giving her a chance to eat at a leisurely pace and relax on a weekend morning. She smiled and grabbed her book from the bedside table, determined to savor the moment.

Robert had loaded the dishwasher with the breakfast dishes and was sitting at the table reading the paper and sipping a cup of coffee when Sarah walked in with her breakfast tray. He looked up and smiled when she came in. She was still in her nightshirt and thick, fluffy socks.

"You look comfy," he said.

"Yeah, although I was just thinking I felt a little chilled," she said, wrapping her arms around her body. "It was so warm and cozy in bed. It was nice to just curl up and read for a while."

"Good," Robert said and went back to reading his newspaper.

"Where's Lizzy?"

"In the den, watching a video," he replied without looking up.

"Thanks for the breakfast."

"Sure." Robert laid down the paper and looked at Sarah, who had just started clearing off her breakfast tray. He recognized from the tone of her voice that she was in what he called her "spacey place." He wasn't ever sure what triggered it or what it was about, but she often became distant and checked out. He generally ignored it; he really didn't want to know more or talk about it. He had more important things on his mind most of the time. But he was feeling somewhat relaxed this morning and thought that checking in with her might assuage any bad feelings she had about last night.

"You okay?" he asked as he got up from the table to help her.

"Yeah," she said. "Just a little sore from last night."

Robert thought this was a good opening; an opportunity to make her feel good and steer the conversation away from anything negative. He didn't want to get into one of those discussions today.

"That's what you get for being so damn sexy," he said as he reached down to lift Sarah's nightshirt. "Should I kiss it and make it better?"

"Robert!" Sarah pushed his hand away and motioned down the hall toward the den, where Lizzy was watching her video.

Robert let go of Sarah's nightshirt. "I know. Besides, if I go kissing down there I'll just want you all over again." He reached out for Sarah's hand and held it to his crotch. "See, I'm getting hard just thinking about it."

Sarah scowled and pushed his hand away. "Stop it!"

"Fine," Robert said, holding his hands up. "I'll take a rain check." His strategy clearly wasn't working. Yet again, how quickly her mood had changed. Describing her as mercurial was an understatement. He internally shook his head. Much of the time his understanding of her was limited at best, but in this moment, he knew it was better to just leave her alone for a while. He kissed her cheek and grabbed a beer from the refrigerator. "I'll be in the den. It's almost time for the Sonics game."

Sarah's anger reared up again as she watched Robert walk down the hall. She listened to the competing voices in her head as if they were dialogue from a movie.

What is wrong with you? Why didn't you say something?

Don't do anything stupid. Keep your mouth shut. You don't want to make things worse.

You are such a wimp. You can't let him keep treating you like this.

He's being nice. He made you breakfast. He thinks you're sexy. Don't fuck things up. You can't start something today. Lizzy is here. Be a good parent. Be good so you all can have a nice day today.

The voice that told her to lay low, to appease, to not rock the boat, generally won out. But lately, her angry voice had been getting stronger and harder to contain. And Robert's responses were getting more intense. He often blamed her. She wondered if he was right—that she pushed him too hard, that she needed to be more mature and rational, less reactionary. Quit being such a drama queen. Sure, he'd been drunk and gotten a little rough last night. Why make it into a big deal? It was a few minutes; it had felt good to him. It had been her turn to give a little. *Couples make sacrifices for each other*, she reminded herself. *That's how relationships work.*

She took a deep breath and looked around the kitchen. Robert had made an effort to get a few things in the dishwasher, but there was still more cleaning up to do. As usual, he'd left most of it for her.

She reached for the sponge with one hand and picked up a plastic waffle wrapper with the other as she stomped down on the pedal on the trash can.

Don't go there, she cautioned herself as she took her foot off the pedal and began wiping the counter with the sponge. *Focus on the positive.* He seemed relaxed and happy today. Maybe this would be a good time to talk to him about the seminar. She'd been thinking about it for weeks, but no time ever felt like the right time. And now she was up against the deadline for the registration, and he was heading back to LA in the morning. She really needed to talk to him today.

If she waited until the game started, he'd be distracted. She finished wiping the counter and rinsed out the sponge. *Well, no time like the present.* She wiped her hands on a dishtowel and headed to her room to get dressed first. Robert would take her more seriously if she wasn't in fuzzy socks.

Lizzy was sprawled on her stomach on their bed, chin in hands and still in her pajamas, watching cartoons on the television. Sarah went into the closet. "Emma and Kate will be here soon," she called out as she pulled on a pair of yoga pants and an oversized sweater. "You should get dressed."

Lizzy didn't respond so Sarah came out of the closet and tried again. "Lizzy?"

"Yeah," Lizzy said, her eyes still glued to the TV.

"Look at me!"

Lizzy dragged her gaze away from her cartoon and looked up at Sarah.

"Emma and Kate will be here soon to pick you up, so you need to get dressed."

"Okay," Lizzy said returning her attention to the TV. "This is almost over."

Famous last words, Sarah thought, but didn't force the issue. She left the room to go talk to Robert.

Robert was standing with his beer in one hand and the remote in the other when Sarah came into the den. He glanced at her, sat down on the sofa, and put his feet up on the coffee table as he found the right channel.

"Game's about to start," he said.

"Can I talk to you about something?"

"Sure. What's up?" He stayed focused on the TV.

Sarah held out a brochure. Robert glanced at it but didn't take it.

The words tumbled out in a rush: "I was thinking about going to a writing seminar in San Francisco over spring break. The timing's perfect and Jenny Sampson, my friend from U-Dub, is going. We could room together to keep the cost down."

Robert continued to stare at the TV. "What about Lizzy? You know I need to work."

"I know. I thought of that . . . so I asked your mom and she said she could watch Lizzy while I was gone."

Robert turned abruptly toward Sarah, his face stern. "You talked to my mother about this before talking to me?"

Sarah felt suddenly afraid and small. It hadn't occurred to her that arranging this with his mother would make him mad. She'd been trying to take initiative, something he constantly said she didn't do. *You should have asked him first. Why didn't you think of that? Really stupid of you, Sarah.*

She scrambled to explain. "Just to be sure she could watch Lizzy. I knew you'd be too busy. I didn't want to bother you."

Robert took the brochure and scanned it briefly. "Why on earth would you want to go to a writing seminar?"

"I really want to start writing again. I've been thinking about working on some short stories, or maybe even a book."

"A book? You can't be serious. Stop dreaming and be practical. You'd never get a book published. It'd be a complete waste of time and money."

"But it's not . . ."

Robert shook his head. "I agreed to let you teach even though I thought you should stay home with Lizzy." He tossed the brochure down on the coffee table and returned his focus to the TV. "A good mother would spend spring break with her daughter, not run off to San Francisco with some old college friend."

The doorbell rang before Sarah could think of anything to say in reply. She felt defeated. She knew the discussion was over. She wouldn't be going to the seminar.

"That's Kate," she said, getting up from the sofa and heading for the door. "She's going to take Lizzy and Emma to the park for a while."

Robert turned up the volume as Sarah headed for the door. "Great," he said. "Tell her I said hello. And then bring me another beer, would you?"

Sarah pushed away a twinge of anger as she hurried to answer the door. She reminded herself not to go there. She wanted to have a nice day with Robert today.

She greeted Kate with a hug and held on to her for slightly too long. When she let go, Kate stepped back, looked at her, and tilted her head. "You okay?" she asked.

Sarah shrugged. "I just showed Robert the stuff about that writing seminar I told you about and he doesn't want me to go."

"Well, the hell with him. I think it would be great for you to get away. You could use a break. You're practically a single mother most of the time."

"Yeah, well, don't let him hear you say that."

Kate frowned. "What do you—"

"Hang on," Sarah said, her face reddening. "I'll get Lizzy." She spun away before Kate could ask any more questions. *You shouldn't have said that. Why didn't you stand up for Robert? Kate will have a bad impression. She'll think he's a bad husband. You need to take it back. Say something good about him to her.*

She reached her bedroom door to see Lizzy spread out on the bed where she'd left her, still in her pajamas.

"Lizzy! Kate and Emma are waiting for you downstairs. You need to get a move on!"

"Yay!" Lizzy jumped out of the bed and ran down the hall to her room.

Sarah followed, considering what to say to Kate. She could tell her about Robert fixing her breakfast in bed this morning. And watching Lizzy so she could read and relax. That would show she wasn't a single parent. *That will work*, she thought confidently as she followed Lizzy into her room.

Sarah went into the kitchen to make some tea after saying good-bye to Kate. She felt relieved that Kate hadn't seemed to dwell on what she'd blurted out about Robert. In true Kate style, she'd said it was romantic and good of Robert to have taken care of Sarah that morning, adding that we all needed that from time to time. She'd described how wonderful it always felt for her when Will took the kids out for breakfast. Sleeping in was such a luxury!

But Sarah knew she needed to be more careful. She'd let a few things slip with Kate recently. She reasoned that this time it was because she was feeling so off today. She felt irritable and spacey and confused. She wanted to let go of last night. She really did. So why was she having such a hard time shaking it? She filled the teapot with water and turned on the burner. She was sitting on a barstool at the kitchen counter, her head in her hands, when Robert came in.

"Whatever happened to my beer?" he said, irritation evident in his voice.

"Sorry," she said, lifting her head up. "I forgot."

He pulled open the refrigerator door. "Obviously. What's up with you today anyway?"

"Nothing."

"Nothing my ass. You've been a total space cadet. You're not paying very good attention."

"What do you mean, not paying attention?" Sarah felt the anger rush back and her heart pounded forcefully inside her chest. She told herself to take a deep breath. To not say anything stupid.

"Well, my beer for one." He popped off the cap and held it up as if to toast.

"I cleaned up the kitchen and got Lizzy ready to go out," Sarah said, losing the battle to contain her anger. "I've been busy with other things. Forgive me, your highness, for forgetting to serve you your beer."

"Jesus, Sarah. I just asked you to bring me a beer. Don't make a federal case out of it." He turned to leave. "Something is definitely up with you."

"You!" Sarah shouted as she moved toward Robert, her blood boiling. "You are what's up with me. First you rape me and then you tell me I can't go—"

Robert whipped around, his face distorted with anger. "Don't ever let me hear you say something like that again," he said, his face close to hers.

Sarah cringed and started to whimper.

"Damn it, Sarah," Robert said, backing away. "Why do you always make me get like this? I'm really tired of your bullshit. That was a terrible thing to say. Why would you say something like that?"

Sarah began to cry more strongly.

"Oh, for God's sake," he said as she dropped her head to the counter, sobbing. "Here," he said, shoving a Kleenex box toward her. "You are such a fucking drama queen."

He turned and stormed out, beer in hand.

When he was gone, Sarah sat up and took a Kleenex to blow her nose and wipe her face. She couldn't believe he'd just walked out. It seemed so cold. And to call her a drama queen when she was clearly in pain? That was just mean and unfair. Maybe it seemed like no big deal to him, but he'd really hurt her last night, and he needed to understand how it felt to her. The anger flooded back. She jumped up from the stool to follow Robert—and hit her hand on the corner of the cupboard. Pain shot like a lightning bolt from her hand up her arm and she slumped back onto the countertop, clutching her hand and sobbing deeply. *Serves you right. You're being so ridiculous. You shouldn't have said he raped you. That was really stupid. Sure, he was drunk and rough, but you're his wife. He has every right to be mad.*

When she felt calmer, Sarah noticed the reddish-blue bump that had formed on her hand. She opened the freezer and grabbed a bag of peas. *He's right. You are a drama queen. You need to get a grip. And go make up.*

She could hear Robert yelling at the TV as she approached the den. She paused and took a deep breath before going in. Robert was on the sofa, beer in hand. He glanced up at her as she came in.

"What happened?" he asked when he saw her holding the frozen peas to her hand.

Sarah rolled her eyes. "Being klutzy. I hit it on the corner of the cabinet."

Robert smiled, reached his arm out, and motioned for her to come closer. "Come here. You can curl up with me and watch the rest of the game."

Sarah nodded and sat next to him on the sofa. "I'm sorry I got so crazy."

"Me too." He pulled her in close and kissed the top of her head. "Love you," he said, keeping his eyes on the TV.

"Love you too," Sarah said softly as her body relaxed and she snuggled in next to him.

Chapter 7

Sarah pulled into the parking lot at school on Monday morning and realized she'd been on autopilot for the past twenty minutes. She remembered dropping Lizzy off at school and then suddenly she was at work. It always scared her a little when that happened. How could she just lose time like that?

She steered her car into a parking space and opened the door to get out when she heard singing. She smiled and looked back to see Maggie dancing toward her.

"Oh, what a beautiful morning, oh what a beautiful day . . ."

"You're in a chipper mood this morning," Sarah said, giving her friend a hug.

"I am," Maggie said with a quick nod of her head.

"And you're absolutely beaming. Something good must have happened."

"Right again! I had a great date Saturday night. Nice guy. Not bad looking. My love life may not be a complete disaster after all."

"I didn't know you had a date this weekend," Sarah said, genuinely surprised but pleased.

"I didn't either. It was a last-minute blind date. An old friend's brother who just moved to Seattle, fresh out of law school with a job at a downtown firm."

"Sounds promising."

"No shit!" Maggie said.

Sarah reached into her car for her book bag.

"Jeez," Maggie said. "More battle scars?"

Sarah glanced at her hand. She had almost forgotten about it. She thought about the nice day she'd had Saturday—first cuddling with Robert on the sofa and then going out for pizza with Lizzy in the evening. She was happy they'd made up before he went back to LA. The fight, and her hand, had receded into the background.

"Yeah, just call me super klutz," she said, shaking her head. "I hit it on the corner of a cabinet." She was glad she didn't need to make up a story this time.

Maggie winced. "Well, it's not pretty."

"It's fine. No big deal," Sarah said, wanting to change the subject. "So, tell me more about this date. It sounds like you liked him."

"Yeah. I really did. I don't want to get my hopes up, but we seemed to have a good time together. We had dinner at that new Thai place down the street from me. We sat there talking for a long time after we finished eating. I think they were about ready to kick us out!"

"Well, that's always a good sign. What-all did you talk about?"

"Oh, you know. The usual first date stuff. Background, family, education, work, friends. Stuff like that."

"So, you talked about little ole me?" Sarah grinned.

"Oh yeah! He knows all about my uptight, straight-laced, goody-two-shoes teacher friend who I'm constantly trying to corrupt! He can't wait to meet you in person. He couldn't believe you were for real!"

"That's not fair! You make me sound horrible. Did you really say that?"

"No, of course not. I told him you were very nice, conscientious, and proper. Nothing like me!"

"That's for sure, you crazy, wild woman!"

"Hey, who's being unfair now?" Maggie looked hurt.

"I'm teasing," Sarah said. "Boy, you sure can dish it out, but you don't take it very well."

Maggie shook her head. "I'm teasing you back, you doofus."

"Right. I knew that," Sarah lied. "So, back to your awesome date. Did he kiss you good night?" Sarah knew that how a guy ended a date was always a test for Maggie.

Maggie smiled but didn't respond.

"Oh, come on. No holding back!"

"I'm not holding back. Not really. I just don't think you'll believe it. I was a bit taken aback myself."

"Okay, I'm seriously curious now." Sarah nudged her with her elbow. "What did he do?"

"Promise you won't laugh?"

"That might be hard at this point. You've got a bit of a buildup going here."

"I know. I'm making way too big a deal of this." Maggie turned and took Sarah's hand. "He took my hand in his, like this, and said he'd had a wonderful evening. And then he lifted my hand up and kissed it."

Sarah smiled. "Very gallant."

"I know. Right? I didn't know what to make of it. I was totally tongue-tied."

Now Sarah laughed. "Well I can't even begin to imagine that!"

"Well it's true. I barely got out a very lame 'me too.'"

"How did he leave it?"

"The usual. 'I'll call you.' But you know how that goes."

"Oh, come on. Don't be so pessimistic. I have a good feeling about this one."

"Yeah. Actually, I do too," Maggie said as they walked through the front door of the school. "Just don't want to get my hopes up too much."

Sarah's week had flown by and she left school feeling excited that Robert was going to make it home early. Kate had offered to pick Lizzy up so Sarah could have some time alone to make a nice dinner. She just needed to make a quick stop at the market to get the fish and maybe some fresh-cut flowers. She planned to use the good china in the dining room, and the flowers would make a nice centerpiece. Robert would be surprised and, she hoped, pleased. It had been a long time since they'd had a nice meal in their own dining room. Her fallback was always the more casual approach of eating at the table in the kitchen, but she knew Robert preferred a more formal meal. She wanted to try to do that for him more often.

After a week of feeling unusually tired, she now felt a bounce in her step as she walked to her car. The sun was shining for the first time in days and she could see Mt. Rainier rising majestically up into the sky. It was one of those rare gorgeous days in Seattle. Robert would have some wonderful views flying in. She was glad his flight was on time. Hopefully he didn't drink too much. Her stomach clenched at the thought, but she forced herself to stay positive. It was early. She was sure he'd be fine. But he'd probably want something with dinner. She made a mental note to get a nice bottle of wine too.

"Hey Sarah. Wait up."

Maggie's voice pulled her out of her thoughts. Sarah turned back just as her friend caught up with her.

"So now you're leaving me without even saying good-bye?"

"Sorry. Just a little preoccupied. Robert's coming home early so I'm in planning mode. Besides, I thought you'd be rushing home to get ready for your hot date."

"And you would be right! He just called with a change of plans. We're going to see *The Maltese Falcon* downtown for Classics Night. Turns out he's a big Bogie fan. Imagine that!"

Sarah raised her eyebrows and smiled. "Sounds like you've found your soul mate."

"Well, it's a little early to be jumping to that. But it does bode well. You know how much I love old movies."

"Yes, I do," Sarah said, rolling her eyes.

"Oh, c'mon. Old movies are great. As they say, 'They just don't make 'em like that anymore.'"

"And some people are incredibly grateful for that!" Sarah chuckled.

Maggie frowned. "Hey, don't knock it 'til you've tried it. You might actually enjoy them."

Sarah felt instantly remorseful. She knew this was something that was near and dear to Maggie's heart. *Quit being so insensitive. Say something to fix this.* "I'm just messing with you," she said. "You know I grew up on *Gone with the Wind.* It was my mother's favorite movie. And I liked *Casablanca* when we watched it. It's just that Disney and Pixar seem to be my staples these days. And Robert doesn't really like watching movies."

"All the more reason for some more girls' movie nights."

"Sounds like a plan. If I can steal you away from your new boyfriend." Sarah winked.

"Don't be saying things like that. I don't want to jinx it. Besides, he's a new attorney, remember? I'll be lucky to see him once a week. We'll still have plenty of time for girls' nights."

"Good," Sarah said. "We'll have to plan one soon." She glanced at her watch. She was starting to feel anxious about getting things ready before Robert got home and wanted to leave, but didn't want to offend Maggie. "I should really get going . . ." she said tentatively.

"Yeah. Me too." Maggie reached out to give her a hug. "Have a great weekend."

"You too," Sarah said, hugging her back. "Especially tonight."

Maggie smiled as she pulled away. "You know it. I'll give you the update on Monday. Want to do lunch?"

"Sure thing. It's a date," Sarah said, already sliding into her car. She waved to Maggie as she drove out of the lot, her mind racing. She hoped the traffic wasn't bad on the way to Pike Place. What kind of fish should she get? She could see what looked good. She was in the mood for halibut or sea bass. But Robert always seemed to prefer salmon. She'd better go with the salmon . . .

Sarah stood back and took in the overall effect. The table looked beautiful and the candles she'd added were the perfect finishing touch. She straightened a napkin in its ring, dimmed the lights slightly, and smiled to herself. She was sure Robert would be surprised. And pleased. She was turning away from the table when she heard the front door open and Lizzy's voice call out, "Hi Mommy! Guess who's here?"

Sarah walked into the foyer as Robert was closing the door.

"Kate and I nearly collided coming into the driveway," he said, leaning in to give her a kiss.

"Well your timing is perfect. Dinner is almost ready."

"I can tell," he said, inhaling deeply. "It smells great. Do I have time for a quick shower?"

"Sure," Sarah said, tamping down her annoyance. *Don't get upset. He'll be happier if he takes a shower. Don't say anything to upset him. You can lower the temperature of the oven to slow the potatoes down a bit. You don't want to blow this.* A gnawing tension crept into her body. She told herself to take a breath and relax.

"Great," Robert said as he started upstairs. "I'll be quick."

"Sounds good," Sarah called after him. She really hoped that was true. She'd worked hard on this dinner and needed it all to be perfect. She wanted Robert to be happy with her. A fleeting sense of fear made her breath catch in her throat, but she quickly reassured herself. She knew his moods and he seemed okay today. No reason to get all stressed out. *Just stay calm and get the food ready.*

When Robert came downstairs twenty minutes later, Sarah had uncorked the wine and was plating the food. He glanced at the counter and into the dining room.

"Wow. This looks wonderful," he said. "I can't remember the last time we ate in the dining room. What's the occasion?"

"No occasion. I just wanted to make you a nice meal for your homecoming!"

"Well, thank you!" He picked up the wine bottle to look at the label. "Good choice," he said, smiling. He leaned in to kiss Sarah's cheek and then tipped the bottle to pour himself a glass.

Sarah's heart leapt. "I'm glad you like it."

Robert smiled broadly. "I do. I'll come home more often if you promise me feasts like this." He carried his glass and the plate of food Sarah handed him to the table.

Sarah followed him with the other two plates and set them on the table. "Lizzy, dinner's ready!" she called down the hall as she returned to the kitchen for the wine bottle and another glass.

Lizzy scampered into the dining room, crawled up into the chair next to Robert, and excitedly started talking about the play date she'd had with Emma that afternoon. Robert didn't ignore her—in fact, he was being playful, and far more attentive than usual. Sarah beamed. This was how she wanted them to be all the time. Having dinner together, talking about their days. It was nice.

Robert lifted his wine glass. "To my beautiful wife and this wonderful meal."

Sarah smiled and raised her glass to his.

Lizzy lifted her cup of juice. "Me too."

"Of course," Robert said as he tapped the rim of her cup. "And I'm glad you had such a good time with Emma today."

Lizzy bounced happily in her seat and took a big bite of scalloped potatoes.

"Umm. Delicious," Robert said after taking his first bite. "Don't you agree, pumpkin?"

Lizzy bobbed her head up and down, her mouth full of potatoes.

"Well good," Sarah said. "It's really nice to all be together like this." She flinched as the words left her mouth. *Don't push it. He's going to feel pressured. You know that's a trigger for him. Why did you say that? Do you want to completely blow this nice evening? Ask about him. Shift the focus back to him.* "So, how was your week?"

"Good. I closed a big deal that I've been working on for several weeks. My biggest this year. I was worried it might fall through, but I was able to make some adjustments and they accepted. And more quickly than I anticipated. It was nice to finish a little early. I know it's hard when I don't get home on the weekends. It can't be easy for you. But you've been a real trooper."

Sarah smiled and her whole body melted into the chair. This was the Robert she fell in love with. She said a silent prayer of gratitude. She hadn't realized how much she needed to feel that they were in a good place again.

"How was your week?" Robert asked.

Sarah launched into a story about one of her students, and they finished their dinner with an easy flow of conversation. When their plates were empty, Sarah rose to clear them. "Would you like some coffee with dessert?" she asked Robert.

He reached out and took her hand in his. "That would be great."

She squeezed his hand and smiled.

"What's for dessert?" Lizzy asked.

"Fresh-baked apple tart and vanilla ice cream."

"My favorite," Robert said. "Boy, this just keeps getting better!"

Sarah's whole body was humming with happiness as she retreated to the kitchen to make the coffee and ready the dessert.

When she came back into the dining room, Lizzy was telling Robert about making snowflakes at school.

"Did you know that every snowflake is different?"

"I did know that," Robert said as Sarah placed the tart and ice cream in front of him. "Just like people are all different. Like you. There is only one Lizzy Jenkins in the whole world."

Lizzy's eyes popped open. "That's what Mrs. Johnson said!"

Sarah sank into her chair, surprised but happy to see Robert acting so paternal. Maybe now that Lizzy was older he'd want to spend more time with her. The thought thrilled her. Maybe this would be a new chapter for them. She surreptitiously watched

Robert and Lizzy as they gobbled up their desserts. This was the family portrait she wanted to capture; this was the feeling she wanted to hold on to.

When they were done eating, Sarah refilled Robert's coffee and helped Lizzy carry her dishes to the sink. "Good job! Now into the bathtub with you and then I'll come read you a story."

Lizzy skipped out and Sarah walked back to the dining room to finish clearing the table. She hesitated, watching as Robert sipped his coffee and leafed through a magazine, wondering whether to say something or leave well enough alone. Her impulse pushed her forward.

"Lizzy's teacher asked me about her birthday today. I can't believe it's only five weeks away."

"Five weeks, huh?" Robert said without looking up. "Our little girl is growing up."

"She is," Sarah said as she picked up the last of the dishes from the table. "You know, she's been asking about a puppy again."

"Well, we both know that's not going to happen," he said without looking up. "You know how I feel about pets."

"I know. But maybe a small dog would—"

"Sarah," Robert said, all the soft playfulness in his voice gone. "No dog. End of conversation, okay?"

Sarah nodded. "Okay," she said quietly. A lump caught in her throat and she felt suddenly spacey. *Stupid. Why did you say that? You know how he feels about this. Why do you always have to screw things up? You were having such a nice evening. Why can't you ever just leave well enough alone?*

Robert smiled and returned to reading. Sarah swallowed hard and tried to ignore, without much success, the sudden flicker of anger smoldering just under the surface. She continued cleaning, noisily stacking dishes and slamming doors. It was as if their nice evening had never happened; all her frustration with Robert had come surging back. Why was everything always on his terms? Didn't her wants and needs ever count? She glanced into the dining room and realized that Robert was oblivious to her upset. He always seemed to be able to completely tune her out whenever he wanted. Clearly, she wasn't going to get his attention this way.

She decided to try a different tack. She walked back into the dining room.

"I started planning her party," she said.

"Huh?" Robert said without looking up.

"Lizzy's birthday. I started planning her party."

"Party? She's turning six not sixteen!"

"She's so excited," Sarah said, ignoring his negativity. "And she wants you to be there. It'll be fun."

"Oh, yeah. A bunch of screaming six-year-old girls. My kind of fun!"

"Robert, come on . . ."

"Don't worry," he said, getting up from the table with his magazine in his hand. "I'll be there." He kissed her on the top of her head.

"Thank you," Sarah said, and her anger and tension eased. She'd been afraid he might say he couldn't come and she knew Lizzy would be devastated. "She'll be so happy to have you there."

"I'm sure it'll be wonderful," he said. He left the room without a backwards glance.

Sarah continued cleaning up and thinking about the party. She could do an Easter theme. Easter was early this year. March 23. Just a couple weeks after Lizzy's birthday. She should ask Kate to help; she always had the most creative ideas. Robert needed to be in LA two weekends from now. That would be a good time to do the party planning—they could have a girls' pizza night with Kate and Emma. And she'd ask Maggie to come too. She smiled. Lizzy would love it. It would be a great party. And Robert would be there. *It will be perfect.*

Chapter 8

When Sarah asked Kate about a party-planning pizza night, Kate had jumped on it. She'd even offered to pick up the girls from school and go with them to get the pizzas, a plan for which Sarah was currently very grateful. She hadn't been feeling well most of the past week and was exhausted now. She was looking forward to some downtime before everyone arrived. Maggie was coming too, although she'd made it clear that the girls' night with pizza and beer was the main attraction. When it came to planning a birthday party for six-year-olds, she said, she'd take a pass.

Sarah was lying on the sofa mentally reviewing her ideas for the party when the doorbell rang. *Must be Maggie*, she thought. *Lizzy would have come barging in!* She slowly got up and walked to the door, pausing briefly as a wave of nausea passed. She heard a quick double blast of a car horn and opened the door to see Maggie turn and wave at Kate, who had just pulled into the driveway. Lizzy and Emma rushed out of the car and came running for the door. Kate followed with two pizza boxes.

"Kid-friendly and adult cuisine, at your service!" she said as she handed the boxes to Sarah.

"Thanks for picking these up," Sarah said, trying to rally. She waved everyone into the kitchen. "Let's get this party started." She opened the boxes on the counter next to a stack of plates. "Lizzy, Emma, go wash your hands and I'll get your pizza ready."

Both girls squealed as they ran out of the room.

"I wish I could get that excited over pizza!" Maggie said.

"Ah, yes," Kate said, "to be a kid again!"

Sarah handed Kate a plate with two slices of cheese pizza on it. "Mag, there are some bottles of Juice Squeeze in the fridge. And some beers too."

"I'm on it," Maggie said as Lizzy and Emma rushed back into the room and jumped up into adjacent chairs at the table.

"Hey kiddos," Maggie asked as she opened the refrigerator. "What flavor Juice Squeeze do you want?"

"Pink Lemonade," Lizzy said.

"Me too," Emma said.

Maggie brought the girls their drinks. "Kate, Sarah—beer?"

"Sure," Kate said as she sat down next to Emma with her slice of pizza.

Maggie grabbed two beers and looked at Sarah, who still hadn't responded. "What about you?"

Sarah laid the final two plates on the table and shook her head. "I think I'll just have a Pink Lemonade too. My stomach is a bit upset. Maybe it will help settle it."

"I'm sorry to hear that," Kate said. "Do you think you're getting sick?"

Sarah frowned. "No. Probably just stress. I've been a little overtired."

Maggie raised her beer. "Well, time to relax and de-stress!"

Everyone raised their bottles, tapping each other's all around the table. The girls frantically dug into their pizza slices.

"Slow down," Kate said to them. "There's plenty more where that came from!"

"Mm, delicious," Maggie said after taking a bite. "I think this is one of my favorite pizza places in Seattle. Although I just went to that new place downtown—the one with the brick-fired, thin-crust, fancy stuff. I have to admit, I was pretty cynical going in. I'm not generally a fancy food kind of person. But it was really good."

Kate nodded her head. "I know. Will and I went there on a date night a few weeks ago, and we were impressed."

Sarah nibbled at her pizza. No pizza sounded good to her right now. The smell alone made her feel like she was going to puke. She was exhausted and her boobs hurt; it reminded her of when she was pregnant with Lizzy. But she was sure it was just bad PMS; she often felt like this when she was late. She'd probably start her period any minute now.

"I was there on a date too," Maggie said. "I probably would never have gone, but Ryan convinced me."

Kate raised her eyebrows and smiled. "Is this a new love interest?"

Maggie smiled. "Yeah. A few weeks."

"And?"

Maggie shrugged. "It's been fun. I don't want to jinx it, but I think it's going well."

"That's exciting," Kate said. "I'm happy for you."

"Thanks."

"Sarah, why were you keeping this from me?"

Sarah was so busy thinking about the nausea and fatigue, she barely heard her. "Huh?"

"Are we that totally boring?" Maggie said.

"No." Sarah flushed. "I'm sorry. Just spaced out for a moment."

"Are you sure you're okay?" Kate asked.

"Yeah." Sarah stood up from the table. "Like I said, I'm just a little tired. Here, let me clean up these plates and then we'll do some party planning."

Lizzy clapped her hands. "Yay!"

Sarah started gathering plates—and then another wave of nausea rose up. She put the dirty plates down and braced herself against the counter until it started to recede. She quickly grabbed a pad of paper and pen and sat back down.

"So, we have the date and a guest list. And I was thinking we would have an egg hunt. Any other ideas?"

"Balloons!" Lizzy said. She jumped out of her seat to get close to Sarah's face. "I want balloons!"

"Great idea," Sarah said motioning to her to sit back down. "Lots of colors. Like the Easter eggs."

Emma turned to Kate. "Mommy, we should have your bunny cake!"

"Bunny cake?" Maggie asked.

"You cut and decorate the cake to look like an Easter bunny head," Kate explained.

Sarah grimaced with apprehension. "Easy for you to say!"

Kate chuckled. "I'd be happy to do it if you want. What do you think, Lizzy? Would you like a bunny cake?"

"Yeah!" Lizzy jumped up and down. "Please, Mommy!"

"Okay then," Sarah said. "A bunny cake it is." She turned to Lizzy and Emma. "Now you two put your bottles in the recycling and then you can go play for a while."

Lizzy and Emma dropped their bottles into the recycling bin and scampered out. Sarah turned to Kate. "Are you sure about the cake?"

"Of course," Kate said. "I love doing stuff like that."

Maggie rolled her eyes. "More power to you."

The phone rang and Sarah got up to answer it.

"Hey there," Robert said when she picked up. "I wanted to check in and see how my girls were doing."

"We're good. Kate and Emma are here. And Maggie. We're having pizza and planning Lizzy's party."

"Great," he said, zero interest in his voice. "Can I say hi to Lizzy?"

"Sure, let me get her." Sarah covered the receiver and looked at Maggie and Kate. "Be right back."

"Ten bucks says he's a no-show for the party," Kate said after Sarah was out of earshot. She grabbed their empty beer bottles and dumped them in the recycling, then walked around the counter to start cleaning up.

"What makes you say that?" Maggie said as she got up to help Kate. "Sarah would be so bummed."

Kate shrugged. "It's classic Robert. He pretty much does what he wants, without much consideration for Sarah."

"No way! He's so attentive, always taking her out and sending flowers and gifts."

"Control tactics."

Maggie's eyes widened. "That's a bit harsh."

"I don't know," Kate said, shaking her head slowly. "Sarah's let a few things slip lately. Like he told her she couldn't go to that writing conference she was so excited about."

"She told me she changed her mind," Maggie said slowly. "She said she didn't want to leave Lizzy over spring break."

"See?" Kate said. "That's what I mean. It's probably more like *he* changed her mind. That's the scary thing; she convinces herself that he's right or something. She told me she was being self-ish and impractical. My guess is those words were straight from the horse's—Robert's—mouth."

Maggie shot Kate a warning look, and she turned in time to see Sarah walk back into the kitchen.

"What about Robert?"

Kate thought fast. "Just wondering if he'd be home for the party," she said, hoping her casual tone was convincing.

Sarah nodded. "He's gonna fly home the Friday night before the party."

"He's in LA again?" Maggie asked.

"Yes. Where it's sunny and warm. And I'm stuck here in this cold, endless rain!"

"You and Lizzy should go down for spring break," Maggie said.

"I thought about that, but Robert's really busy and it would be too distracting for him. He has a lot of responsibility; he needs to stay focused on work."

Sarah turned away to finish cleaning up the counter and Kate raised her eyebrows at Maggie and nodded her head toward Sarah, thinking, *What did I tell you?* This was exactly what she was talking about. There was a term for it. What was it? Gaslighting. That's what she thought it was called.

"Why don't we move to the livin' room," Sarah said, turning back to them. "Y'all want some coffee?"

Maggie frowned. "What's with the Southern accent?"

Sarah shrugged. "Guess it still slips out now and then."

"Yeah." Kate frowned. "Usually when you're stressed."

"You're from Southern California," Maggie said. "When did you ever have a Southern accent?"

"We moved there when I was eight," Sarah said. "I was actually born in Savannah. And my mother had a Southern drawl like no other!"

"Wow, I can't believe I never knew that," Maggie said. "That explains a lot."

"What is that supposed to mean?" Sarah asked, a slight edge to her voice.

"Nothing bad," Maggie said. "I just never saw you as the Southern California type. But the Southern part . . . That I can see. Accent and all!"

"Yeah, well, I'm not terribly proud of it. I got really teased in school when we moved to San Diego. So I tried to talk without an accent at school, but then I had to talk with an accent at home or my mother would get upset."

"Sounds challenging," Maggie said.

"Tell me about it. I never knew if I was coming or going half of the time!"

"So now when you're stressed you slip back into the accent?" Maggie asked, glancing at Kate.

"Sometimes."

"So what's bothering you now?" Kate asked.

"Nothing," Sarah said quickly. Then, purposely accentuating the accent, she said, "Now, if y'all would kindly retire to the sittin' room, I'll fetch y'all some coffee."

Kate and Maggie both snickered.

"Coffee sounds great, Scarlett, but first we'll help you clean up," Maggie said.

Sarah pushed them both toward the living room, shaking her head and continuing her drawl. "No. Now y'all go relax and I'll be there directly."

"Okay! Okay!" Kate threw her hands up and scooted away toward the living room.

"Yes ma'am!" Maggie said. She followed quickly behind Kate, laughing.

In the middle of preparing the coffee, Sarah stopped and slumped over the sink, holding herself up with one arm while holding her stomach with the other hand. She suddenly felt like crying. She needed to pull herself together. She was being such a baby; worrying about nothing. It was just a bad case of PMS. She took a deep breath and slowly regained her composure. She put the coffee pitcher and three cups on a tray and went into the living room where Maggie and Kate were seated on the sofa, talking.

". . . we had such a great time," Kate was saying. "We were even able to take a hike before we left in the morning." Kate turned as Sarah came in. "I was just telling Maggie about my date night with Will to Bainbridge Island."

"It sounds wonderful," Maggie said. "I could use a weekend away."

"Well maybe that's in the cards with this new man of yours," Kate said.

Maggie smiled. "Maybe so."

Sarah put the tray on the coffee table. As she picked up the first cup and started pouring, she spilled hot coffee on herself. She reflexively dropped the cup to grab her burnt hand and it shattered as it hit the glass coffee table.

"Shit!" Sarah cried out as she sank to the floor, still holding her hand. She slumped down and started to cry. *You are such a klutz. What is your problem? You need to get a grip. Pull it together.*

Kate was at Sarah's side in seconds, putting her arm around her. "What's going on?" she asked.

Kate's comforting touch only made Sarah's sobs deepen. "It's really terrible," she managed to say between gasps. "I don't know what to do."

Maggie, who was now sitting on the floor on Sarah's other side, frowned. "What do you mean?"

"I . . ." She hesitated, then blurted out quickly, "I think I might be pregnant."

"Wow," Kate said. "I didn't even know you were trying."

"I wasn't," Sarah said and started crying again.

"Why are you so upset?" Maggie asked. "This sounds like great news. You love being a mom."

Sarah curled up slightly, hugging herself. "It's just that Robert's gonna be really angry."

"That's ridiculous," Kate said.

Sarah got more agitated. "No, it isn't. He doesn't like kids. He didn't want Lizzy. He wanted me to get an abortion."

Kate's eyes widened. "I . . . didn't know that."

"But he must have changed his mind," Maggie said.

Sarah calmed slightly. "Sort of. We talked. He agreed to one child. To make me happy. To get his mother off his back about marriage and grandchildren. But he was very clear: only one." She started to get agitated again. "And I've been so careful not to get pregnant and then he . . ." She stopped herself and began to cry more strongly again, hugging her knees and rocking back and forth.

"He what?" Kate asked, but Sarah just shook her head and continued crying.

Maggie and Kate sat quietly on either side of her until she began to calm down. When she did, Kate finally broke the silence. "Maybe things are different for Robert now. Maybe he won't be as upset as you think he will be."

Sarah remained curled up, hugging her knees. Even she could hear how childlike her voice was when she spoke. "No. He'll be mad. I'll be in big trouble."

"In trouble?" Maggie said, jumping up. "For God's sake, Sarah! Who the hell made Robert the king of you?" She couldn't stand it anymore. Why was Sarah being such a wimp?

Sarah looked at Maggie, surprised, and Kate frowned.

"Oh, come on. Don't look so shocked. This is ridiculous. You're so focused on what Robert wants or doesn't want. But what about you? What do you want?" She couldn't keep her mouth shut about this. Sarah needed to stand up for herself.

"Touché," Kate said. "A bit blunt, but point well taken."

Sarah smiled weakly through her tears and looked up at Maggie. "Is this one of those cheer-bully moments?"

"Absolutely. It's about time you thought about yourself for once."

Kate turned back to Sarah and put her hand on her forearm. "Maggie's right, Sarah," she said. "How do you feel about this? What do you want?"

Sarah was briefly quiet and then her eyes filled with tears. "It would be great for Lizzy. I always hated being an only child."

"So?" Kate asked.

"So, I'm scared because I know Robert won't—"

"Mommy, what's the matter?"

All three women's heads swiveled around. Lizzy was standing behind them.

Sarah wiped the tears from her face. "Nothing, honey. I was just thinking about something that made me really happy."

Lizzy looked at Sarah with a puzzled look on her face.

"I know." Sarah smiled. "Grown-ups don't always make sense, do they? How are you and Emma doing?"

"Can we have some ice cream?" Lizzy asked, seemingly satisfied with Sarah's explanation.

Maggie shook her head in wonder. "Kids," she muttered.

"Sure," Sarah said.

Lizzy raced out. "Emma. She said we can!"

Sarah stood up and picked up the coffee tray. "Either of you want some ice cream?"

"I'm game," Maggie said and followed Sarah to kitchen. She was glad for the distraction. She hated seeing Sarah so upset.

"Sure, why not," Kate said, bringing up the rear.

Sarah pulled two cartons of ice cream out of the freezer as Lizzy and Emma hurried back in and crawled up into their chairs.

"Rocky Road or Cookies 'n Cream?" Sarah asked.

"Cookies 'n Cream," both girls said simultaneously.

"I think I'll take the Rocky Road," Maggie said.

"Yeah, me too," Kate said, grabbing another serving spoon. "I'll work on the Rocky Road."

"Thanks," said Sarah as she carved out a scoop of Cookies 'n Cream and dropped it into one of the bowls.

The girls chatted excitedly as they ate their ice cream. Maggie watched how attentive both Kate and Sarah were to their daughters, but she didn't miss Kate's occasional furtive glances in Sarah's direction. She wondered if her fears about Robert were really true. Maggie still couldn't quite believe it. Her image of Robert and Sarah's relationship had always been that of the perfect couple. She was having a hard time wrapping her head around Kate's perspective. But Kate had spent more time around Robert; maybe she knew something Maggie didn't.

Sarah was quiet and slowly picked at her ice cream, lost in thought. Maybe Kate and Maggie were right. Maybe Robert would be okay with it. He loved Lizzy. Surely he would see that having a sister or brother would be good for her. She started to think about the best way to tell him, then stopped herself. She needed to be sure first. She should go get a pregnancy test. Or better yet, just stop worrying about it for a while. Her period would probably start soon. She'd never been all that regular anyway. She'd been late plenty of times before. *You're just being a drama queen again. You never should have said anything. You made such a fool of yourself. Think how stupid you'll look when you find out you aren't pregnant.*

Kate's voice brought her back into the room. "Emma, it's getting late. We need to get going."

"Nooo . . . Pleeease . . . We want to play some more."

"Ten minutes," Kate said. "Then we go."

"Yay!!" Emma and Lizzy shouted in unison as they held hands and skipped out of the room.

Sarah stood up and absentmindedly began clearing the table. Maggie and Kate stood up to help.

"Sarah, you seemed pretty worried earlier about Robert's reaction," Kate said. "You want to talk about it more?"

"No. I'm fine. I might not even be pregnant. It's probably just bad PMS. Or maybe I have a tumor or something."

Maggie frowned. "That's a positive thought."

"I'm not serious," Sarah said. "I just mean there could be some other reason I missed my period—like stress or something. I'm going to stop thinking about it for now."

"There you go, channeling Scarlett again," Maggie said.

Sarah smiled.

Maggie smiled back. "At least I got a smile out of you."

Sarah raised the back of her hand to her forehead and said in her best southern drawl, "Yes, my dear Maggie. Tomorrow is another day."

Kate laughed. "Okay. Appreciating the humor. But I do want to help if I can. Let me know if you want to talk more or if you want me to go with you to the doctor."

Why wouldn't she let this go? Sarah kept her tone light. "Thanks, but I probably don't even need a doctor. Besides, I'm a big girl. I can take care of myself."

"I know you are." Kate looked her in the eyes. "I'm just saying it's okay to lean on your friends now and then."

"Seriously," Maggie said. "No need to take this Scarlett thing all the way to martyrdom!"

"All right, I get it," Sarah said, putting up her hands in surrender. "Thank you both. I will keep that in mind. Now let's get these girls to bed."

Chapter 9

Sarah somehow made it through the week, staying busy with work and after-school playdates for Lizzy. But every day that passed without her period nudged her anxiety up a notch. She couldn't bring herself to do a home pregnancy test. She'd done that when she was pregnant with Lizzy and it had been negative. She remembered how relieved she'd been at the time, only to find out later that she actually was pregnant. She didn't want to go through that again.

Kate had tried to convince her that the false home test was probably a fluke, but she wouldn't budge. She needed to know for sure this time. So she'd made a doctor's appointment for Thursday and arranged a sub for her classes that day. She'd even agreed to let Kate take her.

She and Kate had dropped the girls off at school that morning and then stopped for coffee to kill some time before her ten o'clock appointment. Now in the waiting room, Sarah shifted uncomfortably in her chair. She glanced at Kate, sitting next to her reading a magazine, and felt grateful to have her as a friend. She was so competent and self-assured; nothing seemed to faze her. Sarah wished she could be more like that. She never felt very sure of herself. She felt like an imposter most of the time, trying to look normal on the outside but feeling like a freak on the inside.

"Thanks again for coming," she said aloud.

"Sure," Kate said. "I told you I'm happy to help."

Sarah gave her a watery smile and returned to her inner thoughts.

"Worried?" Kate asked.

"Huh?" Sarah said blankly.

"You seem quiet. I just wondered if you were worried."

Sarah shook her head. "No. Just thinking about a weird dream I had last night. It left me feeling kind of unsettled."

"What was it about?"

"I was married to my college boyfriend. I was telling him I was pregnant and he was really excited and happy." Sarah smiled, remembering how good she'd felt in the dream.

"Did you guys ever talk about kids when you were together?"

Sarah thought back to her conversations with Matt and nodded. "Yeah. He knew he wanted to be a dad. There were times we'd be doing something, like flying kites at Kite Hill or wandering around Pike Place, and he'd make a random comment about doing this with our kids one day."

"So, the dream makes sense to me. I'm sure it's hard to think that Robert might not be excited about the baby."

"We don't even know that there is a baby," Sarah said, feeling suddenly uncomfortable and wanting to change the subject. *You are so stupid sometimes. Why did you tell her about the dream? You should have kept your mouth shut.*

"Well, even so, there's Lizzy. I know you wish Robert were around more for her."

Sarah's eyes welled up briefly and she looked away. She hated how Kate always seemed to see right through her. She did wish Robert was around more. She was tired of feeling so alone. Why did it have to be such a fight with him all the time? He always turned it back on her, as if their struggles were all her fault. She thought back to his response when she'd tried to talk to him at her birthday dinner. He worked hard and provided well for them and thought she was being unappreciative.

Well, he's right. You should be more grateful for what you have. You know he was clear with you when you got married and had Lizzy. You just never believed him. You and your own stupid fantasy. And now you're upset all the time about something that's never going to change. So just buck up. Quit your whining and just accept the reality of it all.

Sarah composed herself and turned back to Kate. "I knew when I got pregnant that work was his priority. I can't feel sorry for myself."

"Sure you can. It's always okay to let yourself feel whatever you are feeling."

Sarah looked at Kate and felt her throat tighten again. She turned away and swallowed hard to choke back the tears. She was determined not to cry. Why couldn't Kate just stop talking?

"Sounds like you and this boyfriend were good friends."

"We were," Sarah said without looking at Kate. "I never really had that with Robert." Her words caught her by surprise. It wasn't something she'd really thought about before, but it was true. Things were different with Robert than they had been with Matt. She and Robert had never been friends. Lovers, yes. Husband and wife, yes. But not friends.

"You mean friendship?"

Sarah startled slightly and turned toward Kate. "Huh?"

"Boy, you are in another world today! I was asking if I heard you right—that you were saying you aren't really friends with Robert."

"No. I didn't mean that." *You're doing it again, just saying things without thinking. Kate already seems to be down on Robert. Don't make it worse!* "Sure, it would be nice if we had more time together, but that's just not possible." She shifted in her chair, sitting up stiffly. "He's a good provider. I could do a lot worse."

A medical assistant appeared at the door between the waiting room and examining rooms. "Sarah Jenkins?" she called.

"Well, here goes," Sarah said as she got up out of her chair.

Kate gave her hand a squeeze. "Good luck!"

Kate watched Sarah disappear through the door. She was such a puzzle. She seemed in her own world much of the time. Withdrawn. Guarded, even. As if she was hiding something. Kate wasn't sure what that might be, but her gut was telling her that something was definitely off. She shook her head and returned to her magazine.

About twenty-five minutes later, Sarah came back out.

Kate stood up to greet her. "Well?"

Sarah held up an ultrasound picture. "I'm pregnant!"

Kate considered how to respond. She couldn't tell if Sarah was happy or not. Tentatively, she asked, "And how do you feel about that?"

Sarah grinned. "I'm happy. I wasn't sure all week. I've been feeling so many different feelings. But when I saw the ultrasound, even though it doesn't really look like much, I knew I wanted it. I want another baby."

Kate reached out to hug Sarah. "That's fantastic. Congratulations!"

"Thanks," Sarah said, hugging her back.

"How far along are you?"

"Six weeks and two days."

"Well, this calls for a celebration." Kate threw an arm around her shoulders. "I'm treating you to lunch. Where would you like to go?"

"Somewhere outside to take advantage of this amazing weather!"

"I agree. I know just the place," Kate said.

They reached the elevator as the doors were opening. Two people from the rear pushed their way through the jam-packed car to get out. Sarah and Kate stepped aside until they passed and then squeezed into the spots they'd left open, on opposite sides of the elevator.

Kate was excited for Sarah and glad she'd realized that she did want the pregnancy. But she was also feeling a little uneasy about the whole Robert thing. Sarah had seemed genuinely scared last weekend when she first told them. Was that just the pregnancy hormones at play or was there really some threat from Robert? From what she could tell, he was a bit controlling at times, but she'd never considered that he would be violent. She needed to find some way to ask Sarah more about it.

On the other side of the elevator, Sarah's feelings churned. The joy she'd felt when she saw the ultrasound had caught her off guard. She really wanted this. But a sense of dread quickly crept in on the heels of her excitement. How would Robert respond? How should she tell him? She wanted to tell him in person, but he wasn't going to be back for two weeks. And that was the weekend of Lizzy's party. What if he was angry? Maybe she should tell him out somewhere, like in a restaurant. He wouldn't let himself get angry there. But that would mean waiting until after Lizzy's party.

The elevator jolted as they reached the garage, interrupting her thoughts.

"Boy, talk about sardines," Kate said as the entire car emptied out.

"No kidding! A claustrophobic's nightmare."

They walked in silence to Kate's car. When they were both settled into their seats, Kate looked at Sarah. "How are you feeling about telling Robert?"

Sarah hesitated. "He'll be home in two weeks for Lizzy's party. I'll tell him then."

"I didn't ask *when* you would tell him. I asked how you feel about telling him. Are you worried about his reaction?"

Sarah's cheeks started to heat up. She shook her head. "No, it'll be fine."

"But you were really upset and scared last weekend. What was that about?"

"I don't know," Sarah said, trying to stay calm. She wanted Kate to stop questioning her. "Probably just pregnancy hormones. You know what that's like."

"I do, but are you sure that's all that it was? What about everything you said about when you were pregnant with Lizzy? How he wanted you to have an abortion? Some part of you must be worried that he'll say that again."

"I don't know." Sarah felt her irritation building. She'd never really had a fight with Kate and she didn't want to start now. But she was really starting to piss her off. "I don't want to think about that right now. It's a beautiful day and I'm happy and I just want to go have lunch and celebrate."

Kate wasn't buying it. She was sure Sarah was avoiding something and wanted to press her more about it. But her gut told her to back off. Sarah was clearly not ready to think about it yet. Robert wouldn't be home for two weeks. She'd find another time to talk to her.

"Okay then," she said as she turned the key in the ignition. "Celebration lunch here we come."

It was well into the second week before Kate finally had another opportunity to talk to Sarah. Sarah had come to pick up Lizzy from a playdate with Emma, and the girls were halfway through an hour-long video. It was an unseasonably warm day, so she'd offered Sarah a cup of tea and they'd settled into chairs on the deck.

Kate was pondering how to broach the subject of Robert and the pregnancy when Sarah started talking about final preparations for Lizzy's party that weekend.

"I want to thank you again for making the cake. It is really generous of you."

"My pleasure," Kate said. "Really. I love baking. I've always had the fantasy of owning a little bakery."

"Really? You never told me that."

"Yeah. I've played with recipes for years and even imagined what the store would look like inside, right down to the sample baskets and hand-written menu board!"

"Why don't you do that?" Sarah said, lighting up. "I can totally see you doing that! We should all do something we love that much."

"Like you with your writing?" Kate said, surprising herself with the quick comeback.

"Maybe . . ." Sarah glanced down into her tea. "But I love teaching and that's what I'm doing now. But you should really look into the bakery thing. Especially now that Emma and the boys will be in school all day."

"Maybe I will," Kate said. She appreciated Sarah's support, but she wanted to shift the conversation back to the party and Robert.

"You really should," Sarah said.

"Totally." Kate nodded. "So, back to the party. Do you have everything else ready?"

"Other than a couple of last-minute things, I think I'm good to go. I've been trying to pace myself. I've been so tired and the nausea has gotten worse. It's more than just morning sickness. It's more like all-day sickness. But I'm not throwing up, so I guess I should be grateful."

"I don't know. Sometimes I think it's better to throw up every morning and be done with it rather than feel nauseous all day."

"Yeah. It's so draining. I just want to go to sleep to get away from it. I'm having a hard time finding anything appetizing."

"I remember it well." Kate shuddered slightly, revisiting her own pregnancies. "I was so glad it only lasted until twelve weeks."

Sarah moaned. "Ugh! I'm barely eight weeks and feel miserable! I didn't have it this bad with Lizzy."

"Maybe that means it's a boy!"

Sarah smiled. "I've thought that too. I'd like a boy. And that might make Robert happy too."

Kate saw her opening. "I wanted to ask you about that. The last time we talked you didn't really want to think about what Robert would say. How are you feeling about all that now?"

Sarah's body tensed. Not again. Why couldn't Kate just leave it alone?

"Oh, I've been so busy, I haven't really given it much thought," she said. What a lie. It was all she'd been thinking about. How to tell him. When to tell him. Whether to tell him. He was never around. It would be another month or two before she started to show. Maybe she should just wait until then.

"But he'll be home for the party this weekend, right?"

"Yes. Of course. He wouldn't miss Lizzy's party."

"So, you must have thought about when to tell him. You've made some kind of plan, right?"

The anxiety she'd been suppressing boiled to the surface and Sarah wrestled to keep the looming panic at bay. Why was Kate pushing her so much? Why didn't she just mind her own business? She wasn't helping. Sarah didn't know what she was going to do. And she couldn't think about it right now. She needed to stay focused on the party. It had to be a nice party. She wanted everything to be perfect for Lizzy.

"I really don't know, exactly," Sarah said, looking Kate squarely in the eyes. "But I'll figure it out." Kate frowned and Sarah looked away. "Really," she said, her voice wavering slightly. "It's no big deal. Right now, the party is what I need to be thinking about."

"I'm sorry," Kate said softly. "I didn't mean to upset you. I've just been worried. You seemed so stressed and scared that night at your house. I'm just trying to be a friend and be supportive."

Sarah's chest tightened. *Don't be such a bitch. Kate has been really good to you. She's just being a good friend. It's not her fault your relationship is so fucked up. Why do you have to be like this? You should apologize.* "I'm sorry, Kate. I'm just tired and hormonal and nauseous. I appreciate your concern, but I'm fine. Really. It's no big deal."

"And you would tell me if it were?"

"Of course," Sarah lied. "But now I'm fine. And I want all your energy focused on making a wonderful bunny cake!"

Kate smiled. "Okay then. But I'm holding you to your promise. You will talk to me if you need to, right?"

"Yes," Sarah said. "I promise."

Chapter 10

Sarah turned off the overhead lights as the last student rushed through the door. She paused for a moment, enjoying the natural light filling her empty classroom. She was grateful the sunshine was forecasted to last through the weekend. She had been worried they might be stuck inside for the party. Robert would not have handled that well! Nice weather definitely made everything easier. She would center most of the activities outside. Robert would probably retreat to his study, but at least he would be there. That was all that mattered.

She hummed cheerfully to herself as she packed up her things to leave. She'd carefully planned all the details; she was sure it would be a wonderful party. Lizzy was beside herself with excitement. Sarah had barely been able to get her out the door to school this morning. Thinking about this made her smile and helped her push away the nagging unease that had been with her all week—especially since her conversation with Kate.

Kate was right. She needed to talk to Robert about the baby. But she couldn't think of any good way to tell him. The longer she waited the worse it would be, but she was afraid of his reaction. Her stomach clenched and she struggled to reassure herself. He might be upset at first, but he'd come around to see it as a good thing. Just to be safe, she'd wait until after the party.

Maggie bounced into the room. "Hey, preggo!"

Sarah jumped. "Jeez, Mag. You scared the shit out of me."

"Sorry. I'm just excited for the weekend!"

Sarah smiled. "I know. Friday afternoons always rev you up!"

"So true. Better than even a triple espresso! And I'm ready to party! How about you?"

"Ready as I can be. You're getting the balloons, right?"

"I'm on it. Thirty helium balloons to the rescue."

"Great. And quit calling me preggo." Sarah said, her eyebrows drawing together. "Remember, Robert and Lizzy don't know yet."

"No worries. Your secret's safe with me. Do you need some help out?"

"Sure." Sarah handed her a box of student essays.

Maggie took the box. "You'll have loads of time for these this weekend."

Sarah smiled. "I know. Ever the optimist, right? But they need to get done. So, I imagine it will be a late Sunday night!"

"Every day I count my blessings I'm not an English teacher. Thank God for Scantron! Test scores in the blink of an eye."

"Oh, but you don't know what you are missing."

"Oh, I think I do! Those once-a-semester term papers are more than enough reading for me!" Maggie said. She cocked her head. "By the way, when are you going to tell Robert?"

"I'm not sure," Sarah said, fighting back a wave of irritation. Not Maggie too. She'd had enough of this with Kate. Why couldn't they both just leave her alone? "I've been so busy with the party that I haven't been able to think about it much."

Maggie frowned and looked at Sarah as she continued to gather up her things to leave. Knowing how her friend obsessed about things, she found it very hard to believe that she wouldn't have been thinking about this, regardless of how busy she'd been. That just sounded like a lame excuse. Something definitely felt off. Should she say something? She wanted to be supportive, but she didn't want to upset Sarah. And it was often a fine line with her. She had learned to read her fairly well, but at times she still got it wrong. She decided to risk it this time.

"Are you worried?" she asked cautiously.

"Nah," Sarah said. "I think I overreacted before. He'll be fine with it—excited, even." She grabbed her bag and headed for the door. "Let's get out of here. I have a list a mile long of things I need to get done!"

Maggie opened her mouth to press Sarah more as she followed her out of the room—and then stopped herself. Robert was Sarah's husband. If she thought he'd be fine with the news, worrying about it was silly. Besides, as down on Robert as Kate was, as far as Maggie could tell, he was basically a dream come true. Still, she made a mental note to watch him more closely at the party.

She fell into stride with Sarah. "So, what's on this long list of yours? I thought you had everything handled."

"Just the last-minute stuff. I'm going to get some groceries before I pick up Lizzy and the cake at Kate's, and then I'm heading home to stuff Easter eggs, put up decorations, and prep food."

"Are you sure you don't need any help?"

"No. I'll be fine and Robert will be home tonight, so he can help.

You getting the balloons is a huge help, believe me. That will make my day so much easier tomorrow."

"Happy to do it," Maggie said as they reached Sarah's car.

Sarah popped the trunk and Maggie put her box of student papers inside.

"See you tomorrow," Sarah said.

Maggie gave her a hug good-bye and started walking backwards toward her car. "Yes, you will. I'll be there! With bells on!"

"I sure hope not," Sarah said.

Maggie's smile drooped a little. What did that mean?

"On the bell part," Sarah clarified.

Maggie perked back up. "Well, now that you mention it . . ." She turned toward her car and waved over her shoulder. "See you tomorrow!"

Oh my God, Sarah. What an idiot! When will you learn to keep your mouth shut? Why do you give her ideas like that? And with Robert and his mother coming.

Sarah felt panicked. She regretted telling Maggie about the pregnancy. She was her best friend and she adored her, but she was a bit of a loose cannon. Sarah couldn't ever be sure what she might say or do, which was why she had always kept her away from Robert. Should she call her to make sure she didn't do anything weird? What could she say? Maggie hated snobs with a passion. If Sarah said anything, it might fuel the fire even more. She'd have to take her chances and just hope Maggie behaved.

Sarah's inner dialogue continued and didn't stop until she pulled into Kate's driveway. Lizzy and Emma were drawing with chalk on the sidewalk out front, and they jumped up when they saw Sarah's car.

Lizzy ran to the car. "Mommy, Mommy!" She said breathlessly. "Come see my cake! Come see my bunny cake!"

Lizzy's excitement was contagious, and Sarah chatted happily with her as they drove home from Kate's, the bunny cake safely wedged between grocery bags in the trunk so it wouldn't slide around.

"Is Daddy home yet?" Lizzy asked when they turned onto their street.

Sarah smiled. Thinking about Robert coming home and seeing their daughter's excitement to see him made her happy. Everything was right with the world. She was going to enjoy the moment and not worry about anything else.

"Not yet," she said, glancing over her shoulder at Lizzy. "But he should be home in about an hour. I think he is going to love your cake!"

"Me too!"

Sarah pushed the garage door opener as she pulled into the driveway, but nothing happened. She tried again with no luck and made a mental note to change the battery. She popped the trunk, then reached back and handed Lizzy her keys before exiting the car.

"You go open the door for me and pick up the mail and I will bring in the cake."

"Okay." Lizzy quickly unbuckled herself, jumped down out of the car, and ran for the front door.

Sarah grabbed the bags of groceries and carried them in through the front door. Lizzy was on her knees, gathering the mail up off the hardwood foyer floor. Sarah left the groceries on the kitchen counter and hurried back to the car. She carefully lifted the cake out of the trunk and used her elbow to close the lid. *Be careful,* she coached herself. *No klutziness allowed today. Go slow. The last thing you need is to mess this up.* She carefully carried the cake through the door that Lizzy was holding open for her.

"Thank you, ma'am," she said to Lizzy.

"You're welcome, ma'am," Lizzy said, following her cue.

Sarah carefully walked into the kitchen and gently lowered the cake onto the counter. Lizzy followed her in, mail in hand.

"Wasn't it nice of Kate to make this for you?"

Lizzy nodded. "Here, Mommy," she said, holding up a mass of envelopes.

"Thanks, sweetie. Now hop in the bathtub and when you're done we'll fill up these eggs." Sarah pulled three bags of multicolored plastic Easter eggs out of a bag and laid them on the kitchen table.

"Okay!" Lizzy skipped out of the room.

Sarah counted her blessings that Lizzy was in a good mood today. She couldn't deal with one of her meltdowns with so much still to do. And it would make things a lot easier with Robert. She needed his help to put up the decorations outside, a task he hated. If Lizzy was being whiny or bratty on top of it, she knew Robert would retreat to the den or his office and leave her to deal with it all on her own. And he would make Lizzy's mood her fault. As he'd pointed out many times before, Lizzy's behavior was a reflection of her failings as a mother. *Never mind that she has an absent father,* Sarah thought, and a brief flicker of hurt and anger rose up. She quickly pushed it away. Robert wasn't absent today. He would be here, he would help, and they would have fun as a family. She reminded herself of their weekend together three weeks ago. It would be like that again.

She quickly flipped through the mail and dropped it on the counter, her mind going a mile a minute. Filling the eggs would occupy Lizzy long enough so she could start to prep some of the food. She'd work on the deviled eggs first, then the *crudité* and dips. She'd left her grocery list on the kitchen counter that morning; she hoped she hadn't forgotten something important. *It was pretty lame to forget your grocery list. Not thinking. As usual.*

She got an oversized bowl out of the cupboard, filled it with the plastic eggs, and placed it in the center of the kitchen table. She rummaged in one of the grocery bags and came up with several bags of jelly beans and foiled chocolate Easter eggs, which she carefully arranged on either side of the bowl. Finally, she added a pile of Easter stickers and stepped back to look at the display. Perfect! She couldn't wait to see the expression on Lizzy's face. She'd love it!

She emptied the vegetables out of the last grocery bag and started to open the refrigerator when she noticed the red blinking message light on the phone. She took the phone out of its cradle and hit the voicemail button. The automated voice announced that there were two new messages. Robert's voice was the first to come through.

"Hey Sarah. It's me. I can't make it back this weekend. Tell Lizzy I'm sorry to miss her party. I'll call tomorrow night so she can tell me all about it. I'll give my mom and sister a call too. I'm sure they can come early and help if you need it. Big hugs to both of you."

"No . . ." Sarah said aloud before the next message started.

"Hi Sarah. It's Carol. I just got a call from Robert. I don't know how you put up with him sometimes. He's so much like Dad, a complete workaholic! Anyway, I talked to Mom and we'd both be happy to come early to help. Just give me a call and let me know what time."

Sarah let her hand and the phone drop onto the counter and stood stunned for a moment. This couldn't be happening. He needed to be here. He couldn't do this to Lizzy. She took a deep breath, fighting back the tears, then grabbed the phone and dialed.

Robert picked up on the second ring. "Hello."

"How can you do this?" Sarah said. "Lizzy's gonna be so upset. You can't do this. You need to be here. Don't you ever think about her—or me, for that matter?"

"Sarah, calm down . . ."

"Don't tell me to calm down," Sarah said, tears spilling down her cheeks. "This is terrible. I need you here. You've known about this party for weeks."

"Sarah, I'm sorry, but it can't be helped. We're behind on this installation and under the gun from the client. I have to be here."

"Can't someone else do it?"

"You know better than that. It's my project. I can't just leave it to someone else."

"But what about Lizzy? What about your mother?" Sarah asked, her voice steadying slightly.

"I already talked to my mother. And Lizzy will be fine. She'll have all her friends there. She won't even know I'm missing."

"That's not true—"

"Sarah, stop. We'll celebrate next weekend. It'll be like a second birthday. She'll love it. But right now, I'm late for an important dinner, so I need to go."

Sarah felt like she was floating. This couldn't be happening. She needed to do something. Make him understand. There had to be a way.

"Robert, please! You have to be here. You know how much it means to Lizzy. Can't you get a flight in the morning and be here for a couple hours and then go back?"

"Sarah, that's nuts. I'd lose a whole day's work and I can't afford to do that. You're being unreasonable and dramatic. This is not a big deal. You need to take a few breaths and get a grip."

Sarah felt something snap inside. The good Robert was gone and the jerk was back. "You are so fucking dismissive. Seriously. Do you really believe your own bullshit?"

"For Christ's sake, Sarah. I don't have time for this. I'll call tomorrow. Good-bye." He hung up before Sarah could respond.

Sarah stood at the counter, her body trembling. She held the receiver in front of her face and yelled, "Fuck you, asshole!" She couldn't believe he was doing this. He knew how important this was to her and Lizzy. He knew how much planning and work she'd put into it. And to say his mother would help? What a joke that was. She would just point out all the things Sarah had done wrong and make her feel worse than she already did.

The thought of Cynthia's inevitable criticism melted Sarah's anger into tears. She dropped the phone and slumped over the counter, her chest heaving. She couldn't handle Cynthia without Robert. And she needed his help with the outdoor decorations. She couldn't do this alone; she'd never get everything done in time. Everything would be ruined. She felt so tired and overwhelmed. It felt hard to breathe.

Lizzy's voice calling from down the hall startled her. She had momentarily forgotten all about her.

"Mommy, I can't find my pajamas."

Sarah stood up, wiped the tears from her face, and tried to take a deep breath. Her shoulders felt weak and she couldn't inhale fully. She felt numb.

"They're still in the dryer," she called out weakly.

"What?" Lizzy shouted back.

Sarah tried again to inhale and called back more loudly, "Just a minute. I'll get them."

She started for the garage—and then she remembered Maggie's offer to help. Since Robert wouldn't be here, it would be fine to have her come over. She picked up the phone and dialed her number.

The phone rang several times with no answer. Sarah was about to hang up when Maggie picked up.

"Hello?"

"Hey Mag, it's me. You sound out of breath."

"Yeah. I ran for the phone. I was just getting out of the shower and I thought it might be Ryan. We have a date tonight."

"Oh," Sarah said, surprised. "You didn't tell me."

"I know," Maggie said. "I never really had a chance. You've been so busy with the party and the whole pregnancy thing."

"I'm sorry . . ." *You're such a horrible friend. Not even thinking to ask Maggie about Ryan. No wonder you're alone. That's what you get for being so self-centered.*

"No worries. I knew we'd catch up once things settled down a bit for you. Besides, you know I want to keep this thing low key for now. Until I know if it really is a thing."

"I don't know," Sarah said. "It sure seems like a thing to me."

"Maybe. But that's not what you called to talk about. What's up?"

Sarah racked her brain for something plausible to say. She couldn't ask Maggie for help now. She had to think of some other reason for calling.

An idea popped into her head. "About the balloons. Could you also see if they have a nice 'Happy Birthday' Mylar? Something big and colorful?"

"Sure thing. Sounds like a great idea. I'll actually call now so they can have it ready when I pick up the others. I'm gonna have fun getting all this into my car!"

"Great," Sarah said, trying to be upbeat. "Thanks so much. And have a great time tonight. I can't wait to hear more."

"Oh, you will. Every gory detail! See ya tomorrow."

"See ya."

After hanging up the phone, Sarah sighed. She felt drained. Maybe she could try Kate. But she had helped so much already. Besides, she probably had plans. *You shouldn't bother her. Just get a grip. Quit being such a loser and pull it together.*

The phone rang, disrupting her thoughts. Her heart leapt. Maybe it was Robert. Maybe he'd changed his mind. She picked up the phone to look at the caller ID. It was Kate.

"Hi, Kate. I was just thinking about you."

"How funny! Great minds and all that."

"Yeah. Definitely. What's up?"

"I forgot to give you the candles for the cake. I found some cool tall thin pastel ones."

"They sound perfect. I meant to look for something different like that, but then forgot." *As usual.*

"Well, it's taken care of," Kate said. "So, was there something else?"

"Not really." *Don't bother her. They probably have things they want to do tonight. You're not helpless. You can handle this.*

"Somehow you aren't convincing me. Is everything okay?"

Sarah felt her throat tighten and the tears welled up in her eyes again. "I'm just freaking out a little," she said in a rush. "Robert can't come home and I have food to prep and eggs to fill and decorations to put up outside and—"

"Sarah." Kate's voice was measured and soothing. "Slow down. Why don't I come over?"

"No, I can't ask you to do that."

"You didn't ask. I offered."

"But you've done so much already. I'm okay, really. I'll get it all done. And I'm sure you-all have plans for tonight."

"Hang on a second."

Sarah waited. She hated the idea of imposing, but she had to admit that she would be very relieved if Kate came to help.

Kate came back to the phone. "The boys are camping with their Boy Scout troop, so we were just about to order pizza and watch *Totoro* with Emma for the one hundredth time. As much as she loves that damn movie, I know seeing Lizzy will be much more exciting. And you've saved Will and me! We'll pick up pizzas and be over in about a half hour."

"It's really not—"

"Sarah, we're coming. End of conversation. It'll be fun. See you in a few."

Kate hung up the phone and turned to Will. "Thanks for doing this."

"Anything to avoid *Totoro* again," Will said. He tilted up his chin and held the back of his hand up to his forehead. "I was feeling a sudden headache coming on. The kind that can only be cured by crawling into bed with my laptop."

"Yeah, like I'd really let you get away with that!"

Will chuckled. "Don't I know it! So . . . what's going on with Sarah?"

"More than I think we know," Kate said.

Will smiled. "What's this? A bit of dramatic flair from my normally calm, cool, and collected wife? Say more."

Kate frowned. "I'm not sure. Just my gut talking to me again."

"Well, my experience with your gut is that it's usually pretty accurate."

"Yeah," Kate said. "That's what I'm afraid of." She generally trusted her instincts and knew something was off with Sarah—something that had to do with Robert. She just wasn't sure what that was.

"My curiosity is piqued," Will said. "Is it about the pregnancy? Or something else?"

Kate nodded. "I think that's part of it. She seems really scared to tell him about it. I mean, more than scared. Like, terrified."

Will frowned. "Maybe something's going on with her—like she's hormonal and overreacting or something. I mean, it doesn't make sense for her to be terrified to tell him about a pregnancy."

"I know. That was my first reaction. But now I think she might be underreacting—or hiding something." Kate bit her lower lip. "Something has been bugging me for a while. She completely defers to him all the time. She'll want to do something, but when he says no she acquiesces and then acts like it was her idea or something."

"Interesting," Will said thoughtfully. He rubbed his chin with his thumb and index finger. "Sounds like I need to learn some of his technique."

"Very funny," Kate said, whacking him lightly on the chest. "I think you learned a long time ago not to tell me I couldn't do something."

"Yes, I did." Will wrapped his arms around Kate and pulled her toward him. "And I've been a much happier man ever since!"

"And I've been happier too." Kate smiled and kissed him, but she wasn't done talking about Sarah and Robert. "I know their age difference might be part of it, but I get a creepy *Stepford Wives* feeling at times."

"That's a bit extreme. I mean, I know he's kind of pompous, but I just write that off to his family. He has a different worldview than us common folk!"

"I know. I've thought about that too. And I know my feelings aren't rational. But something just feels really off. And then there's the whole piece about him working in LA all the time and hardly ever being home. What's that about?"

"Sounds like you might have some thoughts on that," Will said, smiling. "Out with it, woman!"

"Okay," Kate said. "Yes. I admit it. I wonder about another woman. Is that such a stretch?"

Will shook his head. "No. Not at all. Or he could just be a workaholic or something. I mean, look at his old man. You don't get where he got without living and breathing the company."

"Maybe. But I know Sarah has suggested several times that they move to LA and he always makes excuses. He won't even let them come down and visit. He says it will distract him from his work."

"Okay. Maybe a bit more suspicious. So, he's got a mistress. Or he's a workaholic. Or both."

"You can add 'controlling jerk' to that list."

"Boy, you really don't like the guy, do you?"

"I don't know. I've tried to give him the benefit of the doubt, but my gut is screaming on this one. And now to call last minute to say he's staying in LA this weekend? Sarah's pretty freaked out. He was supposed to be home to help her get everything ready for tomorrow."

Will shrugged. "It's a six-year-old's birthday party, not a wedding. What's the big deal?"

"I know," Kate said. "I don't disagree. But that's what I'm saying. Her reactions seem really off sometimes and it makes me wonder what is really going on inside that house."

"So, you think there's more to it than an absent husband and a lonely wife?"

Kate shrugged. "I don't know. She doesn't seem very sure of herself. She's guarded. She doesn't talk about much and seems to put on a happy face, if you know what I mean. I think she needs support, but I'm never sure how to help."

"Well, right now we can bring pizza and hang party decorations!" Kate smiled. "Always the voice of reason."

"At your service," Will said, taking an exaggerated bow. "And now for the really important question: What kind of pizza should I order?"

Sarah stood quietly at the counter, phone still in hand, relief flooding her body. She wouldn't be alone tonight. Will and Kate would be with her to help. And Emma would distract Lizzy and soften the blow of Robert not coming home. Everything would be okay.

"Mommy! I'm cold!" Lizzy called out again. "Where are my pajamas?"

"Change of plans," Sarah called back as she laid the phone down and headed toward Lizzy's room. "Emma and Kate and Will are coming over with pizza to help us get ready for the party." She reached the door of Lizzy's room in time to see the towel-covered ball on the floor bounce up and transform into a standing, naked child.

Lizzy squealed with glee. "Really?"

"Yep! So go ahead and get dressed, and then you can come help me in the kitchen."

Sarah knew she should tell Lizzy that Robert wasn't coming home, but she quickly talked herself out of it. No need to upset her when she was so happy. Besides, she'd be occupied playing with Emma and probably wouldn't even notice. At least for a while. Sarah could avoid telling her until later. Dealing with one of Lizzy's meltdowns tonight, in front of Kate and Will, would be humiliating. Waiting was definitely the best plan. She'd wait until after they were gone.

"When will they be here?" Lizzy asked. "What kind of pizza are they bringing? Can we have ice cream for dessert? Can Emma help me fill the eggs?"

"Whoa, girl," Sarah said, putting up both hands. "Hold your horses! First things first. You need to get dressed and I need to finish putting away the groceries. I'm sure they'll be here before you know it!"

"But Emma can help fill the eggs, right?"

"Of course. But first you need to get some clothes on!"

"Okay." Lizzy went to her dresser and pulled out some underwear.

Sarah smiled and let out a sigh as she walked back to the kitchen. Lizzy was excited and happy. Not a word about Robert. Maybe this would all be okay. Maybe she could get through the night and not have to deal with it.

Her thoughts continued to swirl as she put away the groceries. She'd have to tell Lizzy at some point. But when? She didn't want her to be so upset that she wouldn't sleep. As tired as Sarah was, she knew she couldn't deal with that tonight. But she also didn't want to tell her right before the party. That would be a disaster. The party needed to go perfectly. There just didn't seem to be any good time.

Lizzy skipped in just as Sarah was folding the grocery bags and putting them in the bag holder in the pantry.

"Wow," she said, seeing Lizzy fully dressed. "That was fast."

"Are they here yet?" Lizzy asked.

"Yes," Sarah said, matching Lizzy's excitement. "They're hiding in the garage."

Lizzy gave her mother a puzzled look and started toward the garage.

"I'm teasing! No, they aren't here yet. I just got off the phone with Kate a few minutes ago. And they need to pick up the pizza first."

Lizzy scowled and Sarah caught her breath. *Stupid idiot! Are you trying to trigger her? You better find some way to distract her.*

"I'm sure they'll be here any minute. Why don't you go pick out a movie for you and Emma to watch while you have your pizza?"

Lizzy's face brightened. "Okay." She skipped out of the room.

Sarah relaxed slightly, knowing she'd dodged a bullet. She needed to stay a step ahead of Lizzy if she wanted to avoid the Robert conversation. Once Emma was there, it shouldn't be a problem. In the meantime, though, she needed to keep Lizzy busy.

She pulled a pan out of the cupboard, filled it with water and put it on the stovetop to boil. She'd get the eggs cooking and then start cutting the vegetables for the *crudité*.

She was slicing celery when Lizzy came bopping back into the room with a video in her hand.

"We can watch *Totoro*! It's Emma's favorite."

"Great choice," Sarah said, smiling. Kate and Will would get a good laugh from that! "Why don't we open the bags of candy and put them in bowls so they'll be ready for you and Emma?" Sarah grabbed two bowls from the cupboard. "You can put the jelly beans in one bowl and the chocolate eggs in the other." She got the scissors from the drawer as Lizzy crawled up into one of the chairs at the table.

Sarah had just cut open the first bag when the doorbell rang.

"They're here!" Lizzy jumped down from the table and ran for the door. Sarah said a silent prayer. Thank goodness. Saved by the bell. Literally! She smiled and quickly emptied the candy into the two bowls, put the scissors back in the drawer, and threw the candy bags into the trash. She turned to follow Lizzy to the front door, only to be nearly knocked down by her and Emma running back into the kitchen.

"Come see," Lizzy was saying breathlessly. "We get to fill the eggs with candy and stickers for our Easter egg hunt tomorrow."

"Slow down," Sarah said good-naturedly as she turned to greet Will and Kate. Will was carrying two large pizza boxes.

"So, where should I put the grub?" he asked.

"Right here on the counter would be great," Sarah said, clearing a spot.

Sarah was ready to drop, but the evening had gone fantastically, and for that she was grateful. She and Kate had prepped all the food and Will had hung the decorations outside. He'd even fixed a loose rail on the deck. Emma and Lizzy had had a great time filling the eggs after they'd finished the movie. Lizzy hadn't mentioned Robert.

The only stress in the evening had been when Kate asked her how she was feeling about Robert not coming back for the party. Sarah knew she couldn't talk about it. She was afraid she'd start crying or get upset. She didn't want to risk it. Besides, they were having a good time, talking and laughing. Why dampen the mood? So she'd just put Kate off and changed the subject.

She loved hanging out with Kate and Will. They were everything she thought a couple should be. And how parents should be. She wished she and Robert were more like them. Even though they'd all been working, they'd also had fun and Sarah had actually relaxed and enjoyed herself. But now, as they prepared to leave, she felt some of her anxiety and sadness creep back in. She was afraid that Lizzy would ask about Robert, and she didn't know what to do if she did. She was so exhausted. The thought of handling one of Lizzy's meltdowns right now sent her into a panic.

"So, I'll come a little early tomorrow to help with the last-minute stuff," Kate was saying. "What time is Maggie coming with the balloons?"

"She's picking them up at noon, so she'll probably be here about twelve thirty."

"Great," Kate said. "I'll plan on the same. That will give us an hour and a half to tie up the balloons and hide eggs and put out the food. Should be plenty of time. I think you're in good shape."

"Yeah, I think it's all good. Thanks to you guys. I couldn't have done it without you. I can't thank you enough."

"It was our pleasure," Will said as he turned and smiled at Kate. "Much better than what we had planned!"

"That's for sure," Kate said, smiling back at him. "And the girls had fun. I think they will both sleep like babies tonight."

"I hope so," said Sarah. "I could use a good night's sleep. As long as she doesn't realize Robert's not here, I should be in good shape."

Shit. Why did you say that?

Kate glanced at Will. "She doesn't know—"

"Oh, I almost forgot," Sarah said. "I still have Emma's jacket from the other day. Let me grab it for you." She quickly rushed out of the room.

Kate leaned in toward Will as soon as Sarah left the room. "See what I mean?" she whispered. "It's stuff like that that seems off to me."

"A little, I guess. Seems like she doesn't want to tell Lizzy that he isn't coming. I can understand, if she thinks Lizzy will be upset and it will keep her up all night."

"So you just wouldn't tell her?"

Will shrugged. "I don't know. I'd tell Emma, but she's not Lizzy. Sarah knows better than we do how she will react."

"Maybe you're right. I just feel bad for Lizzy. I'd hate to have her blindsided by it tomorrow."

Will frowned and shook his head as Sarah came back carrying Emma's jacket.

Kate knew it was a warning, but she couldn't contain herself. "So, you didn't tell Lizzy that Robert wasn't coming?"

Sarah looked coolly at Kate as she handed her Emma's jacket. "There's a chance he'll be able to fly up in the morning. I don't want to upset her unnecessarily."

"Well we should round up our young'un," Will interjected playfully, before Kate could say anything more. "It's past her bedtime."

"Yeah. For Lizzy, too. Hopefully we can tear them apart for a few hours!" Sarah said. "I'll go let them know."

Chapter 11

Sarah had managed to get Lizzy to bed without any mention of Robert last night. She'd been so excited and exhausted that for once Sarah's suggestion that the sooner she went to sleep, the sooner morning would come, had worked. Lizzy was in bed and asleep within a half hour of everyone leaving.

The morning was more of the same. Lizzy woke up excited and singularly focused on getting ready for her party. She tried on half of the dresses in her closet before settling on a pastel floral sundress with a lime green jacket. She couldn't have looked more like an Easter egg if she'd tried, but Sarah knew to keep that thought to herself. She needed to bite her tongue and avoid saying anything that might upset Lizzy, including telling her about Robert not coming. So, she didn't. No need to rock the boat.

Shortly before noon, Lizzy came downstairs dressed and ready for a party that didn't start until two o'clock. Sarah smiled. Miracles never cease. Miss Perpetually Late was actually ready early.

"Well don't you look beautiful!" she said as she continued to unload the dishwasher, wondering what she could do to occupy Lizzy while she got everything ready. "Are you hungry? I could fix you a little lunch."

"How soon will they be here?"

"Well, we still have two hours 'til the party, but Emma, Kate, and Aunt Maggie are coming early. They should be here pretty soon."

Lizzy plopped down into a chair at the table. Sarah struggled to come up with a distraction—and then an idea came to her. "You and Emma could watch the video from your birthday party last year. What do you think about that?" Sarah congratulated herself. Good thinking. That would give her, Kate, and Maggie time to hide the eggs and tie the balloons around the deck.

Lizzy clapped her hands together. "Yeah! Where is it? Let's put it on."

"Don't you want to wait for Emma?"

Lizzy frowned. "Well, we can get it ready."

Sarah smiled. She couldn't argue with that logic. "Okay. Better go find it then. It should be in the TV cabinet in the den."

Lizzy ran ahead as Sarah dried her hands. She was laying the towel down on the counter when the doorbell rang.

At the sound of the bell, Lizzy came running back and beat Sarah to the door. She pulled it open and was greeted by a huge bouquet of pastel-colored balloons. A pair of legs extended down like a tree trunk; Maggie's face was nowhere to be seen. Sarah burst out laughing.

"Lizzy, you and the balloons match! You could hide in there and nobody would even find you!"

Lizzy giggled and Maggie leaned sideways to peek out from around the balloons. "Well by George, I do declare she's right! How did you know?" she asked Lizzy.

Lizzy shrugged and reached for the balloons. "I want to hold them."

"Okay," Maggie said stepping into the foyer and handing the

clump of ribbons to Lizzy. "I have more in the car, so you take these and I'll go get the rest."

"Look, Mommy!" Lizzy said, staring up at the balloons. "Aren't they pretty?"

"They sure are. I'd say Aunt Maggie did a great job picking them out for you. Let's put them in the living room for now. Then we can help Aunt Maggie bring in the rest." She herded Lizzy into the living room, then took the balloons from her and gently let them float up to the ceiling in the corner. Relieved of her cargo, Lizzy sprinted outside.

When Sarah got outside, Maggie was kneeling on the backseat of her Pathfinder, grabbing at the floating ribbons in the back of the car. She handed the big Mylar "Happy Birthday" balloon out to Sarah, who wrapped its ribbon around Lizzy's hand several times.

"You can take this one and Aunt Maggie and I will bring the rest."

Maggie handed Sarah a bunch and crawled out of the car with the final few in her hand. They were following Lizzy back into the house when Lizzy suddenly turned around.

"Mommy," she said, looking up at Sarah. "Where's Daddy?"

Maggie stopped in her tracks. "He didn't—"

"I'm sure he'll be here soon," Sarah said quickly. "But right now, we need to get these balloons inside so we don't lose them."

Lizzy squealed and ran back toward the house, the balloon in her hand dancing gently behind her. Sarah turned to see Kate's car pulling in off the road.

"He didn't come?" Maggie said.

"No, he didn't," Sarah said under her breath. She didn't like Maggie's accusatory tone. "And I'd appreciate you keeping your voice down. She'll forget about him now that Emma is here. It's better if I just deal with it after the party."

Maggie shrugged. "If you say so . . ."

Once they had Emma and Lizzy settled in with last year's birthday party video, the adults went to work on the last-minute details. Sarah began plating the food, Maggie took on the task of tying balloons around the deck, and Kate offered to hide the Easter eggs in the backyard.

With Sarah inside the house and out of earshot, Maggie whispered to Kate, "She still hasn't told Lizzy about Robert not coming."

"Really? How do you know?"

"Because Lizzy asked her and Sarah said he'd probably be here soon. Then she told me that she just wants to deal with it after the party."

"Another Scarlett moment, I guess. It probably feels like too much to deal with right now."

"I guess. I suppose she's thinking of Lizzy." Maggie tied another balloon to the railing. "I mean, I'm not a parent so what do I know. Maybe it is better this way." It didn't seem better, though. It seemed wrong.

"I . . ."

Whatever Kate had planned to say, she didn't get a chance. Sarah had just come out of the house.

Sarah walked out of the house with eight small Easter baskets of different pastel colors looped over her arms. "We definitely have a theme going here. Mag, I'm so glad you thought to get the pastel balloons. I didn't think to tell you that."

"Well," Maggie said, "I'd like to take credit, but it was actually the store clerk who suggested it when I told her about the Easter theme."

Sarah smiled. "Then I'm glad you listened to her!" She lined the baskets up on a table dressed with a pale-yellow table cloth. Lilies in a Waterford vase—a gift from Robert's mother, Cynthia—served as the centerpiece. One of the many small touches Sarah had added in an attempt to please her mother-in-law. She gazed up at the sunny sky and then around at the decorations, grateful for the beautiful day. She looked at her friends and realized that she felt relaxed and happy. She was surprised to admit it, but she was actually glad Robert wasn't coming. He would have silenced some of Cynthia's criticism, but being attentive to his mood would have been stressful for her. She'd be able to relax more without him here.

"Hello there," a familiar voice called out.

"Hi Carol," Sarah called back as she went inside. Maggie and Kate followed her in. As she greeted Carol and Cynthia at the door, Sarah could see several other guests coming up the walk after them. "Kate," she said turning back to face her, "could you get the girls for me?"

Kate nodded. "Sure thing." She turned and disappeared down the hall.

Sarah greeted Carol and Cynthia with hugs and offered to take their purses and coats.

"Maggie, I think we'll use the den for everyone's things," she said, holding out the contents of her arms toward her.

Maggie stepped up to help. "Sounds good." She took the coats and purses and headed for the den.

As more guests arrived, Sarah directed the girls to a table on the deck that was covered in butcher paper and buckets of crayons for drawing and encouraged the parents to help themselves to *hors d'oeuvres*.

Once all the guests had settled in, Sarah took a minute to stop and catch her breath. All the girls were at the coloring table and the adults were talking in pairs or groups. They all seemed to be enjoying themselves. She checked her watch, calculating her timing. Most of the adults were slowing down on the food and a couple of the girls had stopped drawing. Probably time to move things along.

Sarah went to the table with the baskets and called out to the girls, "It's time for the Easter egg hunt!"

All the girls came running except for one determined artist who was putting the finishing touches on an elaborate bunch of multicolored flowers.

"Erin, honey," Sarah said, "we don't want to start without you. You can draw some more later if you want."

Erin looked up and reluctantly left the table to join the other girls, who were excitedly squirming and talking over each other. Sarah quieted them and gave instructions as she handed out the baskets. "Wait here until everyone has a basket. The eggs are hidden on the deck and in the yard." She handed the last basket to Emma and then yelled, "Okay. Go find 'em!"

All the girls squealed and scattered.

Maggie walked over to stand next to Sarah. "You lucked out with the weather. This is the clearest I've seen Mt. Rainier in a long time."

Sarah glanced out at the mountain, framed by a cloudless blue sky. "I know." She lifted her face up to feel the warmth of the sun on her skin. "This is the most beautiful day we've had in months."

"Alert," Maggie whispered, glancing over Sarah's shoulder. "Mother-in-law approaching."

Sarah turned. Cynthia was walking gracefully across the deck. As always, she was stylishly dressed, with impeccable makeup and hair and an air of pretentiousness. Carol, more relaxed and casually dressed, walked alongside her.

They stopped in front of Sarah and Maggie.

"The girls all look so nice in their dresses," Cynthia said.

"They do," Sarah said, surprised but pleased by Cynthia's pleasantness.

"I hope they don't ruin them with this egg hunt."

Sarah felt instantly deflated. *You're such a fool. Why do you even get your hopes up with her?*

"Mom, relax," Carol said. "They're having fun."

"I'm just saying it would be a shame to—"

"Let's go get you a drink." Carol moved closer to her mother and took her arm to steer her back into the house. She glanced at Sarah and rolled her eyes.

"I don't care for a drink. Or for being patronized." Cynthia forcefully pulled her arm away from Carol and strode back into the house.

Carol grimaced. "Sorry about that."

"It's okay," Sarah said.

"No. It really isn't okay. But it's sweet of you to be so accepting." Carol turned to go after her mother. "I'd better go do some damage control."

Maggie stepped closer to Sarah once Carol was out of earshot and erupted. "What's with her today? Can you say woke up on the wrong side of the bed? And in a major way!"

"It's not just today," Sarah said. "That's how she always is."

"Seriously? That sucks. Brings to mind Jane Fonda in *Monster-in-Law*."

Sarah smiled. "I know. I keep hoping she might actually mellow with age, but I'd probably have better luck with hell freezing over!" As soon as the words were out of her mouth, she realized she could say the same thing about Robert. Like mother, like son.

"Yeah, that's probably a lost cause. I sure hope Robert protects you from her when he's around!"

"Yeah," Sarah said slowly, choosing her words carefully. She couldn't tell Maggie that he was just like her. She'd lose all credibility. "One of the many reasons I wish he were here today."

"I hear you," Maggie said. "But I'm here. I can be his stand-in. She messes with you again and I'll give her a piece of my mind."

Sarah felt her stomach clench. The last thing she needed was Maggie creating a scene. "Thanks for the sentiment. But it's fine. I really don't let it bother me." She hated lying to Maggie. In fact, she longed to tell her the truth, but at the moment, it wasn't an option.

"If you say so. Just let me know if you change your mind."

"I'll do that," Sarah said. She was pretty sure Maggie wouldn't do anything, but she'd try to keep them apart, just in case.

"So, what's next?" Maggie asked.

"We'll serve the cake and then I'm gonna tell them a story here on the deck. After that we'll go inside and open presents."

"Great. You cut and I'll serve."

"Thanks." Sarah began to cut small pieces from the bunny's ears. "I feel bad cutting into this. It's such a work of art!"

"A work of art that's meant to be eaten!" Kate said as she joined them. "Let me take over. I have no problem cutting it up!"

Sarah smiled and handed her the knife. She wiped her hands on a napkin and called out to the girls, who were finishing up their egg hunt.

"Okay, girls. Bring your baskets and come sit up here on this blanket. It's time for cake and then I have a special story for you."

She felt a little nervous. She hoped the story went over okay. Maybe she should have tried it out on Lizzy first. But she wanted to surprise her. And Robert. And now he wouldn't even be here to hear it. *Shit, listen to yourself. Stop moaning and just tell the story. This is about Lizzy, remember? Quit being such a baby. Besides, he probably would have thought it was stupid.*

Once the cake was served and the girls were settled on the blanket, Sarah began to tell them the story of a little brown rabbit who felt different because all the other rabbits had beautiful white fur. He kept to himself and was very lonely until something happened that changed everything for him. The girls, and even the adults who had come closer to listen, were captivated until the very end.

"... and the little rabbit never had to be alone ever again. The end."

The girls and adults clapped and Sarah curtsied. "Now, let's go into the living room so Lizzy can open her presents!"

The girls all jumped up excitedly and ran for the house. Kate approached as Sarah was picking the blanket up off the deck. "Great story," she said, reaching out to help Sarah fold the blanket. "Where did you find it?"

"I made it up."

Kate raised her eyebrows. "Seriously?"

"Yeah. I was just gonna read something. But then I woke up with this idea the other day so I decided to go with it."

"Well I'm glad you did. It was great. Really creative and sweet."

Another mother approached and said, "Nice story Sarah."

"She wrote it herself!" Kate said.

"Really?" The mother turned from Kate back to Sarah. "I didn't know you were a writer. It was really wonderful."

"I'm glad you liked it." Sarah smiled as they all walked into the house together. It was the first time someone had acknowledged her as a writer for a while. She had to admit that it felt good.

∽

Sarah quickly scanned the living room. All the girls were huddled together on the floor, playing with Lizzy's newly opened gifts, and the adults were sitting around the room on the sofa and chairs, watching and talking. She smiled when she saw six-month-old Cody in his baby carrier, periodically sucking his pacifier in his sleep. She remembered Lizzy at that age, and how precious those moments when she would finally fall asleep had been. Cody's mother, Jane, looked relaxed as she sat at the end of the sofa, engrossed in a conversation with another mother.

"Can I get more coffee for anyone?" Sarah asked the room.

Several mothers nodded.

"Yes, dear, that would be lovely," Cynthia said. "I'll take one sugar and a small amount of cream, please."

Carol got up and motioned to Sarah. "Stay put. Sit down for a bit. I'll get it."

"I'll help you," Maggie offered.

Sarah saw the look on Maggie's face and knew she was trying to hold herself back from telling Cynthia off. At least she had the good sense to get out of the room before she said something she regretted.

"Pompous old biddy," she said under her breath to Sarah as she passed her. "Why doesn't she get her own frickin' coffee?"

Sarah suppressed a smile as she watched Carol and Maggie leave. She sank down into a chair, relieved for a little break. Adrenaline had been pouring through her body since she'd woken up that morning, and now she was exhausted. At least the party was winding down and everything had gone just as she'd envisioned it. In fact, it had been perfect. Lizzy seemed really happy.

The only thing missing was Robert. These were the moments she wanted to share with him. Why didn't he get that? How could she make him understand that he was missing out on so much? If they could all just spend more time together, he would see what he was missing.

Jane waved to Sarah from across the room to get her attention. "May I use your bathroom?" she asked in a loud whisper.

Sarah nodded. "Sure. It's right down the hall. Second door on the right."

Sarah looked around the room as she watched Jane gently tiptoe through the mass of girls on the floor. Everyone seemed to be enjoying themselves. Everyone except Cynthia; she looked quite dour. But then, nothing ever seemed to please her. Especially when it came to Sarah. Sarah was sure she was missing Robert, who was clearly her favorite of her three children. The oldest and the only boy. Sarah wondered how Carol could stand it. She knew she would have taken the path of Robert's youngest sister and moved across the county. The farther away the better.

Cody dropped his pacifier and began to whimper. Sarah started to get up, but Lizzy beat her to it. She scooted over to him, put the pacifier back in his mouth, and rubbed his head.

"Here Cody," she said sweetly. "Here it is. It's okay."

Cody quieted and began sucking the pacifier.

Tears filled Sarah's eyes as she watched their interaction. Kate walked over and gently put her arm around her. "She's going to be a great big sister," she whispered.

Sarah turned to Kate and smiled through her tears. "She sure is." She gave her a quick hug. She was glad Kate knew she was pregnant and was seeing in Lizzy what she was seeing.

Maggie and Carol came back with a tray of coffee and began handing out cups as Sarah drifted into thoughts of Lizzy and the new baby. This was a good thing. Lizzy would be a great big sister. It would be wonderful for her. Surely Robert would see that. She chided herself for worrying; she was just being silly. It would be okay. Better than okay. It would probably bring them closer together.

"Carol, dear," she heard Cynthia say. "Could you get me some more cream? This is a bit dark for me."

"Sure Mom," Carol said, taking the cup from Cynthia and rolling her eyes as she passed Sarah. Sarah smiled at her, wondering how she did it. Carol had the patience of a saint—a quality Sarah didn't possess, especially when it came to Cynthia. She knew when to keep her mouth shut, but her truer instincts were more in line with Maggie's. It would feel really good to just tell her off.

She looked over at Cynthia and wondered what she would be like at her age. Cynthia didn't seem happy—but then, Sarah had never been close enough to her to ask. She knew that Cynthia had friends; she played bridge and had lunch with them at the country club. Maybe she was content with her life, but it seemed very lonely to Sarah. She knew how lonely she was with Robert gone so much, and she at least had work. Cynthia didn't even have that. She seemed to live vicariously through her children, especially Robert. But her affection had never extended to Sarah—and Sarah knew why. She was a big disappointment to her mother-in-law. Cynthia had always expected to have a daughter-in-law from her world. And Sarah was definitely not that girl.

"Bye. Thanks for coming," Sarah said to the last of the guests as she closed the front door. She walked back into the living room just as Carol and Maggie entered from the kitchen. Kate was on the floor with Lizzy and Emma, playing with Lizzy's gifts, and Cynthia was sitting close by on the sofa, still cradling her coffee cup in her hands.

"The food is put away and the dishes washed," Carol said. "Anything else we should do?"

Sarah shook her head. "No, not at all. You've done plenty." She was truly grateful for all the help, but now she just wished everyone would leave so she could take a nap.

"No problem," Carol said. "It was fun! My boring big brother definitely missed out!"

"He might beg to differ!" Sarah said and then frowned. "I'm surprised he hasn't called yet."

"Well, feel free to give him my two cents' worth for not being here!" Carol said.

"I ditto that!" Kate said, looking up from her play with the girls on the floor.

"Mom, about ready to go?" Carol said, turning to Cynthia.

Sarah turned away to hide her grin. She knew Cynthia had been ready to leave for a while.

"Yes," Cynthia said. "I'll just need my coat and purse."

"I'll get it," Maggie offered, and she rushed out to get her belongings.

Sarah chuckled inwardly. Maggie was just as eager to get rid of Cynthia as she was.

Cynthia put her cup down on the coffee table, pushed herself up off the sofa, and walked to stand under the archway that opened into the foyer. Sarah was still thinking about Robert and wondering why he hadn't called, so she missed the look Cynthia flashed her way.

"Sarah," Cynthia said sternly. "I'm leaving now."

Her tone jolted Sarah back to reality. *Earth to Sarah. Why weren't you paying better attention? You know how important these formalities are to her.*

"Lizzy," she said, standing up. "Nana is leaving. Please come say good-bye."

Lizzy ran to her grandmother. "Bye Nana." She gave her grandmother a hug.

"Good-bye Lizzy. You had a very nice party. Do you have a thank-you for your Nana?"

"Thanks, Nana."

"It is politer to say 'thank you,' Lizzy," Cynthia said, her irritation apparent.

Sarah felt her stomach clench. She knew Robert would hear about this. She could hear Cynthia's words now. *The girl has no manners. Like mother, like daughter.* She should have prepped Lizzy. Or at least prompted her. Just more evidence for Cynthia of her shortcomings as a mother.

"Thank you," Lizzy said, looking to Sarah for direction. Sarah smiled and put her hand on Lizzy's upper back to reassure her.

"You are very welcome, my dear," Cynthia said.

Carol stepped up. "Hey, what about your favorite aunt?" She kneeled and reached out to give Lizzy a hug.

Lizzy smiled and hugged her back. "Thank you, Aunt Carol."

"Sure thing, munchkin. You had a really great party!"

Lizzy beamed. "Yeah! It was the bestest party ever!"

"It was the best party, Lizzy," Cynthia said. "Bestest isn't a word."

Lizzy looked up at her grandmother, but Carol quickly stood up between them and took her mother's arm.

"Let's go, Mom," she said as she directed her toward the door.

Sarah joined them just as Maggie returned with their coats and purses. She helped Cynthia into her coat. "Thank you both for coming," she said. "And thanks for all your help, Carol."

"My pleasure," Carol said. "It was a great party. I think Lizzy loved it, thanks to all your work and planning!"

"Yes," Cynthia said. "It was very lovely." She held her cheek out and Sarah responded with the expected perfunctory peck.

Carol gave Sarah a hug before taking her mother's arm again and heading for the car.

"Thank goodness that is over," Cynthia said when they were out of earshot. "The noise of all those children was getting on my nerves. I should have taken two Valium before I came instead of one."

"So why did you even bother coming?" Carol said.

"Well I certainly didn't want to, with Robert not here. He would have made it more bearable—enjoyable, even. But you know damn well I couldn't have stayed home. How would that have looked?"

Carol rolled her eyes. "Well, if you're so concerned about appearances, what about Robert not being here? How do you think that looks? I think Sarah was pretty upset about it."

"Naturally. The girl doesn't understand our world. She never has. Robert's work comes first. He's focused and driven, just like your father was." She paused to take a breath. "Just yesterday at the club, Molly Sheridan came up to me expressly to acknowledge Robert's accomplishments. I'm very proud that he has become so successful. He certainly doesn't need to waste his time at a child's birthday party."

"Well, I sure would have liked it if Dad had shown up to some of my birthday parties. He never even knew when it was my birthday."

"Oh, don't be ridiculous," Cynthia said as they reached the car. "I always made sure he signed your card."

Carol shook her head as she opened her mother's car door. "Yeah. Thanks, Mom."

Sarah waited at the door until Carol and Cynthia were in the car and waved to them as they backed out of the driveway. She wondered how Cynthia would respond when she found out about the baby. She'd probably be really happy if it was a boy. She might even be nicer to her. And that would make Robert happy too. She sighed and said a silent prayer for a boy before turning and going back into the house.

Emma and Lizzy were playing quietly, dressing her Barbies in the new clothes she'd gotten. Kate and Maggie had cleared all the gift wrap and ribbons from the living room and gone into the kitchen. Sarah joined them in there.

"Thank you so much again for all your help," she said. "I couldn't have done it without you."

"Of course," Kate said.

"Time to take a load off," Maggie said, pouring herself more coffee and motioning to the table where Kate was already seated, cup in hand. Sarah poured herself a cup and plopped down into a chair. Maggie raised her cup.

"A toast: To the best sober party ever!"

"Hear, hear," Kate said. "Great job, Sarah."

They all clinked their cups.

"Cynthia might beg to differ," Sarah said.

"Oh, the hell with her," Maggie said. "I was ready to deck her a few times. What a miserable, arrogant, sad sack she is."

Kate laughed. "Boy. You don't hold anything back, do you?"

Maggie shrugged. "I just call it like I see it. She takes wet blanket to new levels."

"Well, I'll agree she was a bit remote," Kate said. "But everyone else seemed to have a wonderful time, especially Lizzy. Which is what matters. All in all, I'd say it was a huge success!"

Sarah smiled weakly. "Thanks. But like I said, I couldn't have done it without both of you. I can't thank you enough."

Kate placed her hand on Sarah's forearm. "Our pleasure. Really."

"Absolutely," Maggie said. "It was fun!"

"It was," Sarah said wearily, closing her eyes and sipping her coffee. The phone rang and her eyes popped open.

"That's probably Robert," she said, already moving toward the phone.

"Hello," she answered, and then glanced over to Maggie and Kate and nodded. "Yeah, we're all done. Carol and your mom just left." Sarah hesitated, listening to Robert and then said, "She had a great time, but let me put her on so she can tell you herself."

She mouthed "Be right back" to Kate and Maggie before turning to leave the room.

Kate was glad to see Sarah so cheerful. She turned to Maggie. "She seemed pretty happy today."

Maggie nodded. "I agree. More so than I've seen in a while."

Kate smiled. "I know. You should have seen her when Lizzy was taking care of Cody. She just melted. She is so ready for another baby!"

"Yeah. She really seems to have warmed to the idea. I was little worried at first."

Kate nodded. "I was too. But something shifted when she saw the ultrasound. Now I just hope Robert can embrace it."

"Amen to that!"

The two women sat quietly. Kate continued to think about Robert and the baby, as well as what to say to Maggie. She felt protective of Sarah and convinced there was something going on with Robert. She was worried about Sarah getting hurt. But she didn't want to dump all that out onto Maggie. What if she was wrong?

"Boy, I'm beat," Maggie said. "This kid party stuff takes a lot out of you!"

Kate laughed. "Welcome to our world! This is nothing. Imagine doing it 24/7!"

Maggie screwed up her face. "I don't think I want to. Being the fun aunt might be my path in life!"

Kate smiled. "I hear you."

Sarah came back into the kitchen and put the portable phone back on the base. "Well, the girls are begging for a sleepover, but I'm not sure I can handle any more."

"Wiped out?" Maggie asked.

Sarah nodded and slumped into a chair. "I've been feeling tired and queasy the past few days. Welcome to the first trimester!"

"Why don't I take Lizzy tonight?" Kate said.

Sarah shook her head. "No. I don't want to impose. You've already done so much. You've got to be beat too."

"Tired, yes. But pregnant I'm not. C'mon. You need some rest. I won't take no for an answer."

"Well, if you're sure . . ."

"Good," Kate said. "It's settled. They'll probably fall asleep as soon as I get them home anyway."

"Everything okay with Robert?" Maggie asked.

Sarah nodded. "Yeah. He couldn't talk long, but he said he might make it back as early as Wednesday or Thursday."

"Are you still gonna wait until he gets back to tell him about the baby?" Kate asked, aware that she might be pushing too much again but unable to restrain herself.

"I don't know." Sarah picked at the edge of the table. "It's hard to wait. Today made me feel excited to tell him. I might call him back tonight."

"Rest a little first," Kate said, worried that a negative reaction from Robert would be even more devastating after the high of the day. "Maybe a hot bath."

"Great idea," Sarah said. "That would feel luxurious right about now. Just what the doctor ordered!"

Chapter 12

Sarah felt rejuvenated after the bath. She hadn't realized how much tension she'd been holding all day or how in need of some alone time she'd been. She felt grateful, yet again, to Kate for coming to her rescue. Lizzy would have been so wound up from the party. She wouldn't have gotten a moment's peace. And she needed to be calm to call Robert. Fears that he would be angry about the pregnancy lingered just under the surface, but she pushed them away. She knew what she needed to do. Be positive. Upbeat. Excited. Then Robert would be excited too.

She came out of the bathroom in a towel and went into the walk-in closet to look for her cozy flannel nightgown that Robert hated so much. It was just what she wanted to wear tonight, and he wouldn't be here to complain about it. When she pulled open the dresser drawer, her black dress and the plastic cleaner's bag were still where she'd stuffed them the night of her birthday dinner. She'd forgotten all about that. She took them out, threw the bag in the trash, and started to shake out the dress. She stopped and hesitated. She wasn't going to be wearing this for a while. *Sorry, Robert.* She wondered if it could be fixed. Or if she'd ever fit into it again. She started to hang the dress on a hanger, but as she did her inner dialogue intensified. *Why*

*would you want to? You're not nineteen anymore. It's embarrassing
how ridiculously short it is. What were you thinking even then? You
should be ashamed of yourself.*

Sarah thought about the dress and Robert and felt conflicted. It
was true: she did feel embarrassed wearing it. Robert had picked it
out and always wanted her to wear it, but truth be told, she'd never felt
comfortable in it. It really wasn't her. She never would have chosen it
for herself. She should just get rid of it. But what would Robert say?
Maybe she should just save it for now. She reached for a hanger—
and then Maggie's comment about Robert not being the king of her
jumped into her mind. She smiled. Maggie was right. Why did she
always do what he wanted? She needed to stand up for herself for a
change. She took hold of the dress on either side of the broken zipper,
firmly ripped it in half, and tossed it into the trash can.

"Good riddance!" she said. She pulled her nightgown out of the
drawer and pulled it over her head.

In the bathroom, she stopped to look at her reflection in the
mirror. She hadn't noticed before, but her face was looking slightly
fuller. She touched her belly and smiled. She really couldn't wait
much longer to tell him. The changes in her body were already starting to show. She reached for her toothbrush, feeling a new resolve.
No time like the present. She would brush her teeth and then go call
him.

Sarah glanced at the clock after crawling into bed. Eleven sixteen. He
should still be awake. She paused briefly, then excitedly picked up the
phone and hit the speed dial.

"Hello. This is Robert Jenkins . . ." Robert's voice recording started immediately. Sarah hung up the phone and held it in her lap, feeling frustrated. Why did he have his phone turned off? He couldn't possibly be asleep already. He never went to sleep this early.

She closed her eyes and let her head sink back into the pillow for a few moments, feeling the depth of her exhaustion. She was so tired she could fall asleep sitting up.

She forced her eyes open and dialed Robert another time, but again the phone went to voicemail. She started to feel anxious. She really needed to talk to him tonight. She was ready. Tomorrow wouldn't be good. He'd be working, and he'd made it very clear she shouldn't call when he was at work unless it was an emergency.

The urgency she felt was overwhelming. She made a decision. She'd call the landline. He had told her to only use it in emergencies, but surely this was a good enough reason. She got out of bed to get the number from her address book and then crawled back in bed and dialed.

"Stephanie McAllister, you were amazing tonight," Robert said as he unlocked the door to his beach house. "Have I ever told you how smoking hot you are when you are wheeling and dealing?"

Stephanie smiled. "You might have mentioned it."

"Well it's true. You go in for the kill in a way that leaves them thinking you've just given them a wonderful gift!"

"Yeah, I got skills."

"Yes, you do," he said. "And I've got champagne. This definitely calls for a celebration. It's in the fridge. Go ahead and pull it out. I need to get the remnants of my steak out of my teeth!"

He took off his suit coat and headed to the bathroom. Stephanie kicked off her heels, took off the crimson print wrap hanging loosely around her shoulders, and draped it over the back of the leather sofa. Her sleeveless black dress hugged her shapely body.

"That was a delicious dinner," she called out to Robert as she opened the refrigerator. "And nice atmosphere. We should make that a regular client restaurant." She lifted the bottle of champagne— and then almost dropped it when the kitchen wall phone next to her rang.

"Steph, can you grab that?" Robert called from the bathroom. "It might be Sam calling to see how tonight went."

Stephanie closed the refrigerator, champagne in hand, and picked up the phone with the other hand.

"Hello," she answered.

"Oh. I'm sorry," Sarah stammered. "I must have dialed the wrong number."

"No problem," Stephanie said pleasantly and put the phone back in the cradle on the wall. "Just a wrong number," she called to Robert as she began twisting the cap off the champagne.

Sarah felt her stomach tighten, but she pushed the fear away. *You stupid klutz. You must have dialed it wrong. Try to be more careful.* Sarah slowly re-dialed the number, saying each one aloud as she pressed the corresponding button. She listened as the phone began to ring.

"Hello," a woman answered.

Sarah felt flustered at hearing the same woman's voice again. "I'm sorry," she managed to spit out. "Is this 310-555-3258?"

"Yeah, that's right. Who were you trying to reach?"

"I'm sorry. I was trying to reach a Robert Jenkins. I thought this was his number."

"Yeah, it is. He's right here . . . Robbie, it's for you."

Sarah's mind raced. Robbie? Who called him Robbie? She'd never heard anyone call him that before. Who was this, anyway? And what was she doing at his place so late?

"Hello?" Robert's voice said.

"Robert?"

"Sarah. Why did you call this number? I told you to always call me on my cell phone."

"I tried, but it went straight to your voicemail." Sarah could hear the irritation in Robert's voice. She didn't want to upset him, but she wanted to know who had answered the phone. She felt confused. She couldn't think.

"My battery died. Why are you calling so late anyway? Is Lizzy okay?"

"Yeah . . . she's fine." Sarah hesitated. "Who . . . who answered the phone?"

"Sarah, why are you calling?"

"I . . . I wanted to talk to you about something," Sarah said, feeling suddenly small and scared.

"At this hour? Can't it wait until tomorrow?"

"Uh . . . yeah . . . okay," she managed to say.

"Good. I'll talk to you tomorrow. Good night."

Robert hung up the phone and began loosening his tie. He'd been having such a great evening. Why did Sarah have to call and ruin it all? And why was she calling? Whatever it was about, he wasn't looking forward to the conversation.

"Everything okay?" Stephanie asked.

"Fuck no," Robert said as he pulled off his tie. "You shouldn't have answered the phone."

"Don't get pissed at me," Stephanie shot back. "In case you don't recall, you asked me to answer it."

Robert sighed and dropped his shoulders. He didn't want to take this out on Stephanie. "I know. I'm sorry. I'm just tired of having to lie and come up with more stories and excuses."

"Maybe it's time to just tell her the truth."

Robert shook his head. "It's complicated."

"I know you think it is."

Robert knew Stephanie's opinion. He should come clean with Sarah. But that would also mean coming clean with his parents. And he wasn't sure he was ready for that. Not yet.

"Right now, I don't want to think about it at all." Robert reached for the champagne bottle. "What I do want to think about is the big deal we closed tonight. We are an awesome team!" He poured two glasses and lifted one up. "To us," he toasted.

Stephanie picked up the other glass and gently tapped the rim of Robert's glass. "To us!"

Maggie sat up in bed with a start when her phone rang. She automatically reached for it, her eyes still closed.

"Hello?" she said, her voice groggy.

"Maggie," a tremulous voice said. "I'm sorry to wake you."

"Sarah." Her eyes flew open. "What's wrong? Are you okay?"

"I called Robert a while ago and a woman answered."

"Shit . . ."

"I don't know what to do," Sarah said between sobs. "I don't know who it was. It's so late. Why would she be there?"

Maggie shook her head, trying to wake up. She was having a hard time understanding what Sarah was saying. She wasn't making any sense. "Did you talk to Robert?"

"Briefly," Sarah said, her voice wavering. "He thought something had happened to Lizzy and then was mad that I called him on his home phone."

"Why the hell would he be mad about you calling on his home phone?" Maggie wondered aloud, feeling more confused by the second. This all seemed so convoluted. Was Sarah having a bad dream or something? Then she remembered what Kate had said about Robert's control tactics. Was this an example of what she meant?

"I don't know," Sarah said, her voice steadier. "He told me that I should call his cell because he always has it with him. To only use the landline in an emergency. But tonight, I guess his battery died. It kept going straight to voicemail. And I really needed to talk to him about the baby. So I called the home phone."

"What did he say when you told him?"

"I didn't get a chance," Sarah said, and she began crying again. "He said it was late. That it could wait. That we would talk tomorrow."

Maggie was waking up and her mind was slowly kicking into action. She didn't know what to think or what to say. There might be a logical reason that a woman would be there, but she had to admit that it did look suspicious. Was Robert having an affair? It didn't seem possible. He was always so romantic with Sarah. But maybe that was a guilt thing. Like that episode of *Friends* when Joey's dad was being extra nice and loving with Joey's mom because he was having an affair.

"And she called him Robbie," Sarah continued through her sobs, pulling Maggie back from her mental meanderings.

"What?" Maggie asked, trying to catch up.

"The woman who answered the phone. She called him Robbie. I've never heard anyone call him Robbie before."

Maggie didn't know what to say. Why on earth had Sarah called her? She should have called Kate. Kate was good at this kind of thing. She'd probably say something reassuring. What would be reassuring right now? She didn't have a clue.

"Are you still there?" Sarah asked.

"Yeah. I'm here. Just still waking up."

"I'm sorry." Sarah sounded like she was hyperventilating. "I shouldn't have called. I know it's late. I just didn't know what to do. I feel really shaky and scared, like I'm going crazy or something."

Maggie continued to feel at a loss for words. She didn't understand why Sarah was having such a strange reaction to this. Maybe this was some of the pregnancy hormone stuff Kate had talked about. She could call her in the morning and ask—but what should she do now? She felt totally out of her element. Maybe she should just go over there. It might help Sarah to have someone with her.

"Why don't I come over?"

"No. I can't ask you to do that."

"Sure you can," Maggie said as she crawled out of bed. "I'll take a quick shower to wake up and then I'll be right over."

"Okay," Sarah choked out. "Thanks."

Maggie poured a cup of coffee and sat down at the kitchen table with a heavy sigh. She felt incredibly weary, not just from the lack of sleep but also from the emotional drain of supporting Sarah, who had been beside herself the previous night. It had taken her a long time to finally fall asleep. Maggie had dozed after that, but never fully slept. She would give anything to be home in her own bed right about now.

She took a long swig of coffee, closed her eyes, and swallowed slowly, willing her body to relax into the chair. She was sitting quietly with her eyes still closed when she heard a short knock and the sound of the front door opening.

"Hello," Kate called out from the front hall.

"Hey Kate," Maggie called back. "I'm in the kitchen." Relief flooded her body. She was ready to pass the baton.

Kate came in and put her purse down on the counter. "How's she doing?"

"She's in the shower. She didn't go to sleep until about three thirty. She was pretty wiped out."

"I imagine. Any idea who the woman was?"

Maggie shook her head. "She wasn't very coherent last night. I was hoping she might be a bit clearer after some sleep." She lifted up her cup in the direction of the pot on the counter. "Coffee?"

"Sure," Kate said and helped herself to a cup.

Maggie thought of Lizzy. "Where are the girls?"

"Will took them out for breakfast. He'll come by when they're done."

"That was nice of him."

"Nice of who?" Sarah asked as she dragged herself into the room.

"Hey, kiddo," Kate said as she moved to give Sarah a hug. "We were talking about Will. He took the girls out for breakfast."

Sarah dropped down into a chair at the table. "Oh. That was nice."

"How 'bout a cup o' joe?" Maggie asked.

"Okay. That would be good."

Maggie got up and poured Sarah a cup, then watched as Sarah

absentmindedly added cream. She stared into the cup, slowly stirring it with a spoon. Maggie glanced at Kate, but neither of them spoke.

Sarah finally broke the silence. "I feel like I'm in the middle of some horrible nightmare that can't possibly be happening and at the same time I feel like a complete idiot for not realizing how obvious it all was. All those weekends working. All the reasons why Lizzy and I shouldn't visit."

"Sarah, don't beat yourself up," Kate said. "You trusted him. You weren't looking for something like this. Whatever this is."

Sarah looked up. "Exactly! What is it? Is it a fling? A one-night stand? Or something more? Maybe he's living a whole separate life like in the movies or something?"

"I say we string him up by his balls," Maggie said.

"Whoa," Kate said, shooting Maggie a stern look. "Let's slow down. It's probably better to talk to Robert before jumping to any conclusions." She turned to Sarah. "What exactly did he say last night?"

Sarah frowned. "That's what's been bugging me. I was totally caught off guard, but I did manage to ask him who had answered the phone. But he completely ignored the question. As if I hadn't even asked it."

"Well, hell, then you just ask him again!" Maggie said. The coffee was kicking in and she felt her sense of outrage swelling.

Kate nodded. "Exactly. You need to get some answers from him before you jump to any conclusions."

"Right now, I have no desire to talk to him at all," Sarah said. "Maybe I'll just wait until he comes home."

"Are you nuts?!" Maggie shouted—and immediately regretted it.

"Yes," Sarah said, turning abruptly to Maggie. "I'm completely fucking nuts! Can't you tell?!"

"I'm sorry. I didn't mean it like that. It's just, if I were you, I couldn't stand to wait. I'd want some answers right away."

"Well you're not me, are you?"

"No, I'm not." Maggie felt a little sheepish. She knew she needed to be more sympathetic. Sarah was really stressed and sleep-deprived. Time to keep her mouth shut.

Sarah stared into her coffee. Maggie glanced over at Kate with a guilty look. Kate shrugged and mouthed, "It's okay."

After several minutes, Sarah spoke again. "I had another dream about Matt last night," she said without looking up.

"The college boyfriend?" Maggie asked. "I didn't know you had a *first* dream about him."

Sarah didn't react; she just kept talking, as if to herself. "This dream was different. In the first one we were married and he was really excited about the baby. This dream was more like reliving all the things we did together."

"Like what?" Kate asked.

"Just having fun. It was comfortable and easy. Not that we didn't have disagreements, but we always worked things out pretty well. We were a team. And we had fun."

"Sounds like a nice relationship," Maggie said.

"Yeah." Sarah got up without saying more and went out into the garage.

Kate frowned and looked at Maggie. "Where's she going?"

"I'm not sure," Maggie said, "but I think I might have an idea." She got up and followed Sarah.

"What . . ." Kate said, shaking her head. She had no idea what was going on, so she shut her mouth and headed for the garage. When she walked in, Sarah was up on the counter, moving boxes around on the top shelf.

Kate tilted her head and looked up at Sarah. "What are you doing?"

"Looking for something."

"That's kind of obvious," Maggie said. "Mind cluing us in?"

"Remember me telling you about the letter that I never opened?"

Maggie shook her head. "Yeah. I thought that might be it."

"I'm a little lost here, guys," Kate said, but neither Sarah nor Maggie acknowledged her.

Sarah pulled a large box labeled "COLLEGE" out from behind several other boxes. "Here. Help me," she said to Maggie.

Maggie scooted up onto the counter and helped her pull the box down from the shelf and onto the workbench.

Kate couldn't figure out what had gotten into Sarah. Or Maggie, for that matter. "Would someone mind telling me what is going on?"

Sarah began opening the box. "When Matt broke up with me I was really hurt and I wrote him a crazy dramatic letter. He was in Africa, so by the time I heard back from him I was already dating Robert. And still pretty pissed at Matt. So I didn't read it. I just threw it in this box without opening it."

"And you're choosing now to read it? When you suspect your husband is cheating on you?" Kate shook her head. None of this was making sense. What was Sarah thinking?

"He's showing up in my dreams for some reason. Maybe I'm supposed to read it now."

"But—"

The doorbell rang—and rang again, and again, cutting Kate off.

She heard the sound of the front door slamming, and the patter of feet.

"Mommy! I'm ho-ome!" Lizzy yelled.

"I'll look for it later," Sarah said. She quickly closed the box and turned to go back into the house. Kate made it into the kitchen just as Lizzy and Emma ran in. Will sauntered in after them.

Lizzy barreled directly over to Sarah, who knelt down and wrapped her arms around her. "Hi, sweetie. Did you have a good sleepover?"

"Yeah! And we just had waffles!" Lizzy said.

"With whipped cream!" Emma said.

"And strawberries!"

"Sounds very yummy," Sarah said. "Thanks for taking her to breakfast, Will."

"My pleasure," Will said. "We had fun. And I got to hear all about the party. Sounds like a good time was had by all!"

"Thanks to Kate and Maggie. I couldn't have done it without them!"

Robert glanced out the wall-length sliding glass doors at the sunny beach and gentle waves. He was on his third beer and halfway through the game, but he still couldn't shake the feelings that had haunted him since Sarah's call last night. He knew he should call her but couldn't bring himself to do it. He rationalized that it would be good to give her some time. Maybe she would let it go.

He watched Stephanie walking up from the beach, her tanned body moving gracefully toward him. She hadn't pushed him more last night about coming clean with Sarah, but he knew where she stood. He appreciated that about her. She was direct. She stated her opinion and then let it go. Nagging was not in her repertoire.

He smiled as she came through the door, beach bag in hand. "How was it?"

"You're missing some great beach time staying cooped up in here," she said. "It's gorgeous out there."

"Who are you kidding?" Robert muted the TV and waved his beer toward the beach. "I've got the best of both worlds. Great views of the beach and the Lakers on TV."

"You are such a total basketball bum!"

"Look who's talking, Little Miss Beach Bum."

"Guilty as charged. It's my happy place! There's nothing more relaxing than feeling the sun on my skin and listening to the waves." She tossed her beach bag on a chair and pulled the scrunchy off her ponytail, letting her dark hair cascade down over her shoulders. "I'm going to take a shower."

"Sounds good. I just checked Sam's flight status. He's due in on time at five thirty."

"Perfect," she said as she started toward the bathroom. "We can stop and get fish tacos on the way home. If I know my big brother, he will be craving Mexican food after two weeks in China!"

"Or we could actually go to a Mexican restaurant and have a real meal!" Robert said. He would push for that. He wasn't a big fan of the taco truck.

"Whatever," Stephanie said over her shoulder. "I say we let Sam decide. It is his welcome home dinner, after all."

"Sounds good to me. But he might surprise you and want a nice steak. You better dress accordingly."

"So, what you're saying is that I should dress for anything from a taco truck to a five-star restaurant?" she called from the bathroom.

"Exactly."

"You realize that's an impossible task, don't you?"

"Oh, come on. You're the fashion goddess. I have complete faith in you."

"Well, I guess that kills the flip-flops idea," Stephanie said as she closed the bathroom door.

Robert smiled and unmuted the TV.

Chapter 13

Maggie wove her way through the throng of students in the hallway. She'd been avoiding Sarah all day, unsure of what to say. Honestly, she felt a little creeped out by how quickly Sarah's demeanor had changed yesterday when Will and the girls got back. It was as if nothing had happened. Maggie had left before Kate and Will so she hadn't gotten a chance to talk to Sarah more, and when she'd tried to call later in the evening there'd been no answer. Now it was the end of the day and she knew she needed to at least make an effort to check in.

She warily walked into Sarah's classroom as Sarah laid down a paper to wipe her eyes.

"You okay?" Maggie asked.

"Yeah, I'm fine. Just got a little emotional reading these essays."

"Boy, I know just how you feel," Maggie said as she sat on top of a student desk in front of Sarah. "I was grading Civil War term papers last night and crying my eyes out."

Sarah rolled her eyes. "Very funny." She lifted up the student's paper she had been reading. "Josie Fischer. She was describing what it feels like when she paints. Sitting with the blank canvas, waiting for the color or shape to show itself. It's exactly the way my mother used to describe it."

Maggie's eyes opened wide. "I didn't know your mom was a painter."

Sarah nodded. "It was her passion. But I never knew that until I was in high school. She started telling me a lot of things then. Maybe it was the depression talking. My dad was a mean son of a bitch and I think she felt completely beaten down."

"So she was too depressed to paint?"

"No, not at all. It was my dad. He wouldn't let her. Six months after I was born she came home to a bonfire in the backyard. All her canvases, brushes, easels, everything."

"You're shitting me! That sounds totally medieval."

"Tell me about it."

Maggie was having a hard time imagining anyone doing such a thing. "Why would he do that? What did he have against her painting?"

Sarah shrugged and shook her head. "I tried asking her, but she was pretty vague. Something about my dad thinking it was too expensive and frivolous, and that it took her away from being a housewife and mother."

"That's ridiculous! What a jerk!"

"Yeah. No argument there." Sarah said. She stood up from her desk and began getting ready to leave.

Maggie quietly watched Sarah packing up for a minute and then said, "So, she never painted again?"

Sarah slowly shook her head no.

Sarah could feel Maggie's eyes on her as she gathered her things. Broaching this subject with her made her self-conscious. Thinking about it always took her down a dark rabbit hole—stirred up her personal demons. *It was your fault. You took her away from all that she loved. You know she regretted having you. She could have been happy if it weren't for you.* Suddenly Sarah felt overwhelmed. She had to leave. Focus on something else. Pack up her papers and get away from Maggie.

"No wonder she was depressed," Maggie said. "How did she handle it?"

Sarah shoved her students' papers into her bag. "She killed herself. Six weeks after I left for college. That's how she handled it."

"Holy shit!" Maggie looked horrified. "Sarah. I'm sorry. You never told me."

"It's in the past. I don't like talking about it."

"Maybe you should talk about it. That's a pretty heavy thing." Maggie paused for a moment and then continued. "And her painting. I may be stating the obvious, but it's a little like Robert and your writing."

Sarah felt something break loose inside her. She stopped putting her papers in her bag and turned to face Maggie.

"It's not at all like that. Robert is not stopping me from writing. I work full time, in case you haven't noticed. And I have Lizzy. I don't have time to waste on writing right now."

"Bullshit! You sound like your father."

Sarah glared at Maggie. "That's a horrible thing to say. He was an awful person. I'm nothing like my father."

"That's not what I meant. What I meant is that writing is your passion, just like painting was your mom's passion! It pisses me off to see you give it up just because of Robert. You can write and still be a mother. That's no excuse."

"Being a mother means making sacrifices sometimes. Something you wouldn't understand." Sarah felt so shaky. She had to get out of there.

"Maybe a good mother models taking care of herself and doing what she enjoys in life."

"Oh, so now I'm a bad mother?" Sarah yelled. "Should I add that to the list right after 'lousy wife'? You know, I really don't need this from you right now, Maggie. I thought you were my friend." She grabbed her bag and stormed out the door.

Maggie went to the door and called after her. "Sarah! That's not what I meant . . ."

Sarah didn't look back. Maggie was being a total bitch. She was nothing like her father or her mother. Her father was an abusive, controlling asshole and her mother was a spineless wimp. Never standing up for herself. Letting Sarah's father walk all over her. How could Maggie say such mean things to her? She felt claustrophobic. She couldn't breathe. Why did she feel so shaky? She rushed through the front door and broke into a run.

Maggie watched Sarah speed walk around the corner at the end of the hall, then slowly walked back to her classroom. She had really done it this time. When would she ever learn to just keep her mouth shut? But then again, how could Sarah not see the connection? It seemed so obvious.

Her cell phone was ringing when she reached the door to her room. She ran to grab it and answered without bothering to see who was calling.

"Well hey there, gorgeous!" a voice greeted her. It was Ryan. Maggie felt her body immediately relax and her mood brighten.

"Well hey there to you! What a nice surprise." She hadn't expected to hear from him until their date later in the week.

"Are you up for some spontaneity?" he asked.

"Well, that depends. What did you have in mind?"

"Well, unfortunately nothing all that exciting! But I just dropped some documents off down the street from you and have about an hour before I need to be back. Want to grab a quick beer at the Rusty Hub?"

Maggie felt elated—both to see Ryan and to have someone to talk to. "That actually sounds like just what the doctor ordered. I just had a big fight with Sarah and I could use a friendly ear."

"At your service! See you there in a couple minutes?"

"Perfect." Maggie grabbed her purse. "I'm walking out the door as we speak."

"Sounds good. Last one there treats?"

"You're on!" She hung up her phone and broke into a run. She would easily get there first. He would need to drive and find a parking space, and she could be there in a minute or two at the most. She smiled as she thought about how much she was enjoying dating Ryan. For a sometimes-serious lawyer, he could be fun and goofy and spontaneous. Definitely another mark in the plus column for this relationship.

She ran the block to the pub, pulled open the door, and headed for the bar—only to see that Ryan was already there and paying for two freshly poured beers.

"Hey!" she said, breathing heavily. "That wasn't fair."

"Oh, but look how quickly it got you here. I wanted to have every minute that I could with you. Besides, I did already pay for the beers." Ryan winked at her.

Maggie chuckled. "Yeah, well maybe I'll forgive you this time. Just don't let it happen again."

"Wouldn't think of it," Ryan said as he picked up the two beers and motioned her toward a booth near the back.

Maggie slid into the booth as Ryan put the beers down on the table. Once he was seated across from her, he held his glass up to Maggie. "To spontaneity."

"Yes," Maggie said, smiling broadly as she lifted her mug to his. "To spontaneity."

"So," he said, taking a sip of beer. "What was this big fight about?"

"Well, it's a little complicated to explain." She paused briefly, thinking about what to say. "I think I should give you a little background first. I haven't really talked to you about Robert at all. There's stuff you need to know to be able to understand the fight."

"Fire away," Ryan said, "I'm all ears."

Maggie described Sarah's relationship with Robert, detailing her initial impressions of their marriage as well as more recent events and Kate's observations, which had given her a very different picture. Ryan listened attentively as he sipped his beer.

"I totally get why you would draw that comparison," he said when Maggie was done recounting the fight. "It does seem rather obvious from the outside. But is sounds like Sarah wasn't ready to hear it."

Maggie sighed. "Clearly. My timing was really off, wasn't it?"

Ryan smiled and shrugged one shoulder. "Maybe a little."

Maggie put her face in her hands. "Oh, I'm so lame. Why I can't learn to keep my mouth shut? I just blurt out the first thing that comes into my mind without really thinking about it first."

Ryan reached out and took her hand. "That's not always a bad thing," he said, looking into her eyes. "It's one of the things I really appreciate about you. You're authentic and real. No PC BS with you!"

"That's for sure. I think I was out to lunch when they handed out the political correctness handbook!"

"Lucky for me!" Ryan said. "I get so much of that at work. You're a wonderful breath of fresh air!"

"Yeah, sure. In a total Bridget Jones–esque, verbal diarrhea sort of way."

"Well, Bridget does have her charms. But I was thinking more Lauren Bacall in *To Have and Have Not*."

Maggie thought back to the old Bogie-Bacall film they'd watched the previous weekend, one of the many in Ryan's extensive collection. "Well," she said, "two lines come to mind. One is my personal favorite, but I think you're referring to another one."

Ryan raised his eyebrows. "Do tell."

"'What are you trying to do, guess her weight?'" she said, giving her best sultry impression. "And, 'If you want me, just whistle. You know how to whistle, don't you, Steve?'"

"Both work," Ryan said, smiling broadly. "Strong, confident, no-nonsense. And not afraid to tell it like it is."

"Well, I guess it's lucky for me that you see it that way! I'm not sure Sarah would say the same thing right now."

"Give her time. You spoke a truth that may be hard for her to swallow. But from what I've heard, your friendship is strong. I know it can handle it."

"I hope you're right." Maggie shook her head and took another sip of beer.

Sarah glanced at the clock. Two more hours before the final bell. Her skin was crawling. She felt more anxious than she had all week. And that was saying a lot, given the stressful events of the past seven days. She hadn't talked to Maggie since their fight on Monday, she'd been

dealing with daily intense meltdowns with Lizzy about Robert missing her birthday, and she still hadn't been able to talk to Robert about
what happened. They'd traded phone messages, but neither of them
had mentioned the woman on the phone. She knew he was counting
on her to ignore it. To not bring it up. That was their dance. Just
pretend it didn't happen. He would play his part by doing something
nice to pull her back in and then life would just go on as it had before.
But she couldn't do that. Not this time.

She was struggling to focus and hold it together. She knew her
students found it odd when she gave them a free period to work on
homework, but it was the best she could do today. On a Friday afternoon, she knew she wouldn't get any complaints. What kid doesn't
want to get their homework done before the weekend?

She busied herself straightening and organizing. Normally this
kind of activity would distract her and steady her nerves, but today
it wasn't working very well. The minute hand on the clock dragged
mercilessly and her anxiety was barely containable. She played out
different scenarios in her mind. What kind of mood would Robert be
in? What if he brought her something nice and acted as if it never happened? Would she be able to confront him? And what about Lizzy?
She didn't want her to hear them fighting. But maybe they wouldn't
have a fight. Maybe Kate was right. She shouldn't make assumptions.
She just needed to ask him calmly and he would explain. There was
probably a perfectly reasonable explanation. She was worrying over
nothing. She could get herself so worked up sometimes. Better to
focus on everything being okay. She imagined telling Robert about
the baby, showing him the ultrasound picture, telling him the story
of Lizzy and Cody, and then the two of them telling Lizzy together.

She was smiling when the final bell rang, jolting her back to reality. She felt momentarily self-conscious—then realized her students

were oblivious. They were singularly focused on getting out of school. And she'd already packed up everything she was taking home, so all she needed to do was close up the room and she would be on her way to get Lizzy.

Sarah was pulling in a big pane window to latch it when she heard a familiar voice behind her.

"Are you talking to me yet?" Maggie asked.

Sarah glanced around. "Yes, of course," she said as she continued closing windows. She didn't want to talk to Maggie, but she wasn't about to tell her that. She would just keep it short and try to get out quickly.

"I wouldn't have known. You've been avoiding me all week."

"Oh, I've just been really busy," Sarah said, avoiding eye contact. "Lizzy's been a challenge and I've had things to do after work every day."

"We could have had lunch."

Sarah knew Maggie wouldn't believe her excuses. But she didn't care. She was still angry with her. "I've been working through lunch," she said, pointing to a stack of student essays next to her desk. "I've had a lot of grading to do with these term papers."

Maggie wasn't buying Sarah's explanation, but she knew pushing her more wouldn't be a good idea. She decided to try another tack. "Well, I've been thinking about you," she said. "I was wondering how you were doing after all the Robert stuff."

Sarah shrugged. "I'm fine. I made too big a deal out of it. I'm sure there's probably a simple explanation."

"Oh, come on," Maggie blurted before she could stop herself.

Sarah looked up at her and Maggie quickly tried to backpedal. "I mean. . . I guess that's possible."

"Of course, it is," Sarah said. "In fact, I'm surer of it all the time."

Maggie didn't know what to say. She thought Sarah was full of shit, but telling her that wasn't going to help. She decided to keep it simple. "Well good," she said and left it at that. "So, he's coming home today, right?"

"Yes," Sarah said, glancing at the clock. "In just a few hours. So I better get going." She turned her back to Maggie and gathered her things to leave. "Why don't we have lunch on Monday?" she said. "We can get caught up then."

"Sure," Maggie said. "Do you need any help with anything?"

"Nope. I'm all set." Sarah reached out to give Maggie a quick hug. "I'll see you on Monday."

Maggie returned the hug. "It's a date."

"Great." Sarah pulled away and headed out the door.

Maggie followed, closing the door behind her. As she watched Sarah disappear around the corner, she realized that she felt worried, though she wasn't sure why. Just a nagging feeling that something was really off.

Sarah rushed down the hall and out the front door toward the parking lot. Her heart was racing again and her stomach felt tight. Damn Maggie. Why couldn't she ever leave well enough alone?

She got in her car and drove several blocks before pulling the car over to the side of the road. She leaned her head on the steering wheel and broke down crying. What was going on with her? She felt overwhelmed but wasn't sure why. She'd been feeling good until Maggie came in. What had she said? Sarah couldn't remember. Something about Robert. That she was sure there was a simple explanation. Sarah heard her own voice as if it were someone else's: *What a crock! You don't believe that for a second. Yeah. Maybe it is a possibility. But that's not what your gut is telling you.*

Sarah took a deep breath, trying to calm herself. She needed to talk to Robert. To find out who that woman was. But she was scared to ask. What if it was something serious? Maybe she didn't want to know. It might be better to just pretend it hadn't happened. But she knew she could never do that. She did want to know. She coached herself to be strong. *Don't chicken out. You can't be like your mother. You're not your mother. You need to figure out how to ask him. But do it right. Don't screw it up.*

She thought of Lizzy. She couldn't talk to Robert with her there. She needed to be gone. Things would go more smoothly if it was just the two of them. A plan formed in her mind, and as it did she felt calmer. She grabbed her cell phone and dialed Kate.

Kate answered on the first ring. "Hey Sarah."

"Hi Kate. I was wondering if you could do me a huge favor." Sarah struggled to steady her voice.

"Yeah. Sure. Are you okay?"

Sarah tried to take a deep breath. "Yeah. I'm just having an emotional day. I think the pregnancy hormones are surging. And Robert's due home in a few hours. I feel nervous about talking to him. It might be better if Lizzy wasn't there."

"Say no more. I'll pick her up when I get Emma and just keep her overnight. They'll love it."

"Thanks so much," Sarah said, relieved. "I owe you."

"Don't worry about it. Just go home and take care of yourself. And good luck with Robert. Call me later if you need to talk."

"Will do," Sarah said, knowing she wouldn't.

Chapter 14

Sarah pulled into her driveway and realized that she didn't remember driving home. She'd been on autopilot again. Not a good sign. It frightened her to lose time like that. Robert called it "checking out." "Earth to Sarah," he would say.

You need to get a grip. You can't be checking out now. You only have a few hours before Robert gets home. Think about your plan. Make sure the house is clean. Cook some food for him. Make yourself presentable. Don't do anything to set him off. Do you think you can do that without screwing up this time?

Sarah rushed into the house and started checking off items on her mental list. She scanned the foyer, living room, dining room, and kitchen. The house was already relatively clean. That was a good start. She would just do a quick run-through of the rest of the rooms for any last-minute things that might be out of place. And she had leftover lasagna from last night. That would be perfect. She would just throw a salad together and make some garlic bread to go with it.

She glanced at the clock. She needed to get some laundry started and then she would tidy the rest of the rooms before taking her shower. She hoped Lizzy's room wasn't a mess—that would throw her timing off. She soothed herself with the thought that she could always just throw everything in the closet. As long as the room looked clean from the hall, Robert would never know the difference. She walked out into the garage, turned the washer on, and began adding the dirty clothes. She thought about what to wear. She needed something that looked nice but not too sexy. She didn't want to go there until she was able to talk to Robert and get some answers. She hoped he hadn't been drinking. That would definitely complicate things.

She finished putting the laundry in the washer and closed the lid. As she put the empty basket on the workbench, she noticed the box labeled "COLLEGE" still sitting where she had left it the previous weekend. She pulled open the lid and rummaged through the top layer. She found a magazine folded open to her short story "The Window Garden" and skimmed through it, remembering how proud she'd felt when it was published. She put it down on the counter and continued looking through the box until she found Matt's letter. She picked up the magazine and carried it and the letter back into the house.

She glanced at the clock as she walked through the kitchen and realized she'd lost time rummaging through the box. *Stay focused. You don't have time to be taking trips down memory lane right now. You need to concentrate on Robert. Check the house, shower, and get ready. This needs to go well. You really can't afford to screw this up.*

She quickly tidied the den and went upstairs to check Lizzy's room before going into the master bedroom. She resisted the urge to read the letter, and instead laid it and the magazine on her bedside table. She picked up some dirty clothes she'd left on the floor, made the bed, and quickly wiped down the bathroom surfaces. Then she got in the shower.

~

Sarah looked at her outfit—a pair of slacks and a sweater—in the mirror. She looked nice but not overtly sexy. Robert had complimented her the last time she'd worn this, saying she looked sophisticated. She thought it would be a good choice for tonight. She put her hair up and put on some light makeup. She didn't want to look like she was trying too hard. She glanced at the clock and her body relaxed. She was ready for Robert, and with time to spare.

She picked up Matt's letter off the bedside table and sat down on the bed. The familiarity of his handwriting triggered a barrage of memories. She saw images of things they'd done when they were together, and it felt as if it was all happening now. They were hiking together on Mt. Rainier on a beautiful, rare sunny day, stopping for a loving kiss and embrace. Then the scene shifted and he surprised her with a kite that they took to fly on Kite Hill. And then they were sharing an ice cream sundae and Matt playfully dabbed whip cream on her nose. She felt relaxed and loved. Everything was comfortable and easy. And fun. She had so much fun with him.

She jumped when she heard Robert's voice call from downstairs. "Sarah. Lizzy. I'm home."

"Shit!" she said aloud. She'd been so lost in her thoughts that she hadn't even heard the front door. *What are you doing? You're going to screw this up. You need to focus. Now!* Sarah quickly put the unopened letter and the magazine in the drawer of her bedside table and got up to go downstairs. *Don't mess this up. You know what you need to do. Stay calm. Be nice. Don't upset him. And don't fight.*

~

Sarah found Robert in the den, already surfing through stations on the TV. He glanced up when she came in.

"Hey there. Why is your car in the driveway?"

Damn. She hadn't thought of that. Cars in the driveway were another one of his pet peeves. "The battery died in my opener and I didn't have any replacement here."

"Well, be sure to get one tomorrow," he said turning back to the TV. "Where's Lizzy?"

"She's sleeping over at Kate's tonight."

"Well that was poor planning on your part, Sarah," he said looking back at her with a scowl. "You know I like to see her when I come home."

Since when? Sarah thought but bit her tongue. *Don't aggravate him.* He must feel caught off guard; he had probably been counting on Lizzy as a buffer. She could use that to her advantage.

"I know," she said levelly. "But tonight, I thought it would be important for us to be alone to talk."

"That's ridiculous," he said, continuing to scowl at her. "We can't talk with Lizzy here?"

So, he *was* going to pretend as if nothing happened. Sarah was prepared for that. Part of her even wanted to go along with it. But she braced herself. She couldn't act as if nothing had happened. She needed to be strong and tell him how she felt. And she needed to get some answers.

"Well, it's been a hard week for me. I've been really upset and I wanted to have some alone time to think before you got here."

"And did you?"

"Did I what?"

"Have time to think? Since it is such a hard thing for you to do with our daughter in the house." He turned back to the TV.

Sarah felt momentarily deflated. She was no match for Robert. How could she be so foolish as to think she could have a reasonable conversation with him? She considered that it would be easier to just let it go. But a voice crept in and told her to be strong, to ignore his jabs, to not let him get to her. If she got angry, things would get bad, and she didn't want to go there. She needed to stay calm.

"I'd appreciate it if you could stay focused on the issue," she said.

"What issue?" Robert asked as he continued flipping through channels.

"The issue of who answered the phone when I called."

"Oh that," he said, waving the remote slightly. "Just a work colleague."

"Why was she with you so late?"

"Sarah, what's with the third degree?" His voice was stern now. "It's not really any of your business."

Sarah stepped in front of Robert. "What do you mean it's none of my business? There's a woman in your house at eleven at night and you say it's none of my business?" She was angry now, and tired of his patronizing attitude. She had a right to some answers. She'd be damned if she was just going to sweep this one under the rug.

Robert stood and reached out to hold Sarah's upper arms. "Sarah, calm down. This really isn't something to get upset about."

Sarah flailed and broke out of his grip. "Not something to be upset about! You are so full of shit." Her blood was boiling. How dare he be so dismissive and condescending?

"Sarah, lower your voice. You're screaming."

Sarah hated how cool he seemed. It was as if the angrier she acted, the more composed he got.

"I don't give a shit if I'm screaming. I'm going to keep screaming until I get some answers. Who the hell was she and why was she in your apartment? Is she your girlfriend? Some bimbo? Or maybe just one of your many one-night stands? Maybe you're fucking all of LA?"

She regretted the words the second they came out of her mouth. *Great job, Sarah. Way to hold it together. You're acting like a crazy person. You're such a mess. Can't you do anything right?*

Robert picked up his car keys and turned toward the door. "I'm not going to talk to you when you're like this." He started to walk away.

Sarah became frantic. She couldn't let him leave. He had to talk to her and give her some answers. And he still didn't know about the baby. The words came before she realized what she was saying: "I'm pregnant."

Robert stopped and turned around slowly. "What did you say?"

"I said I'm pregnant."

"How did that happen?"

"What, you need a lesson in sex ed?" *What the fuck! Are you trying to make this worse? Be an adult.*

"Cut the sarcasm, Sarah," Robert said as he turned away. He put his hand up to his head and then turned back to her. "I don't know how you could let this happen. How could you be so careless? I'm not going to do this again. Just get it taken care of."

"Taken care of? What the hell are you saying?"

"You know damn well what I'm saying. Have an abortion. End of conversation. I won't have another child."

"No! I won't. I want this baby. I want Lizzy to have a brother or sister." Sarah's voice trembled and her lower lip quivered.

"Give it up, Sarah. You can't manipulate me by crying. You did this to me last time and I went along with it. But not again. I won't do it again."

Sarah lunged at Robert, fists up. He grabbed her arms and pushed her onto the couch.

"You are so fucking childish. I'm sick of it and I'm sick of you." Robert turned away from her and stormed out. She heard the front door slam shut and she curled up in a ball on the couch and sobbed.

Sarah was drained and chilled from crying. She'd taken a shower to warm herself and was now curled up on a chair by the window wearing a thick robe and warm socks. Robert had been gone for hours and he wasn't picking up his phone. After six messages, she'd stopped trying. She anxiously glanced at the clock on the mantle. It was after midnight and she was starting to feel panicked. Where was he? Maybe something had happened. Maybe he'd gotten drunk and crashed his car.

You're a terrible wife. This is all your fault. Why do you always do this? He's right. You're a spoiled brat. You can't blame him for being sick of you. You're sickening. You need to make this up to him. You need to find a way to fix this. Maybe you should just get the abortion. Maybe that would make things better.

"Oh, Robert. Please be okay," Sarah said aloud, her tears returning. "I promise I'll do better. I really will. Please come home to me. Please be okay." She sat quietly for what felt like an eternity, her eyes glued to the driveway. Her heart leapt when she finally saw the flicker of his headlights. She jumped up, waiting at the wide doorway between the living room and the foyer. *Breathe. Be cool. Don't be a bitch. Be nice.*

Robert came in the front door and jumped slightly when he saw Sarah standing there.

"You startled me," he said, his voice flat. He looked away from her as he slipped out of his overcoat.

"I've been worried about you," she said, struggling to keep her voice low and steady. "Where have you been? I have been trying to call you."

"I know. I got your messages. All twenty of them."

"I didn't leave twenty messages," Sarah said, wounded.

He sighed. "I was being sarcastic. I didn't answer because I didn't want to talk. I thought that would have been obvious to you."

"But we need to talk."

Robert shook his head. "No, we don't. Not tonight. I'm going to take a shower and go to bed. We can talk tomorrow." He turned and started up the stairs.

Sarah stood motionless for a moment. She didn't know what to do. She felt desperate. She'd been waiting for hours to talk to him. She knew she'd never be able to sleep. She was too scared and shaky. They needed to talk things through. She ran up the stairs after Robert.

"Robert! Wait!" She grabbed the back of his suit coat. "Please talk to me about this now. I'm sorry. I feel really terrible. You were right. I was being childish. I'll do whatever you want. Please just talk to me. We'll both feel better if we talk through this."

"No, Sarah. We're both tired. We can talk tomorrow. After we've had some time to cool off."

"No! We need to talk now!" She felt frantic and she pulled harder on Robert's coat, trying to stop him.

"Stop pulling on me!" He twisted his body forcefully to try to shake Sarah off, and her thick socks slid on the hardwood floor. She struggled to keep her footing, but her left foot slipped off the stair. She let go of Robert's jacket, flailing, and reached for the banister.

Her fingertips grazed the wood, but she couldn't grab on. She fell backwards and tumbled down the stairs.

"Sarah!" Robert cried out, and he ran down the stairs to where she was lying on the floor.

Sarah felt him put his hand to her head.

"Sarah?"

She moved a little and winced, her eyes still closed.

"Don't move. Just lie still for a minute. Where does it hurt?"

Sarah opened her eyes and tried to move again, but even the slightest movement made her grimace from the pain. "All over. My back. My arm."

"I think we should call 911," he said. "Don't move. Just lie still." He covered Sarah with a blanket and put a pillow under her head before dialing for help.

Robert stretched his neck, trying to release the pent-up tension as he thought back over the events of the night. This was his fault. Maybe he should have talked to her. But he'd been so tired and emotionally drained. He'd known that he needed sleep and hadn't known what to say to her. He still didn't. He knew he should tell her the truth, but that would change everything. He wasn't sure he was ready for that. The alternative, though, was to keep creating lies. And he was so tired of all the lies.

Sarah had been so agitated while they'd waited for the paramedics, rambling about things he didn't understand. He'd tried to keep her still and comfortable, but she'd seemed terrified. And, frankly, a little crazy. The paramedics had given her something to settle her before moving her onto a gurney and putting her in the ambulance.

He'd followed in his own car and spent most of the night in a hard-plastic chair in the hospital waiting room.

It had given him plenty of time to think. He was ravaged with guilt. It had been horrible explaining what happened to the paramedics, the nurse, and finally the ER doctor. He knew how it looked—how it made him look. And he knew it wasn't who he was. But it was who he'd become recently with Sarah. Not that he was blaming her. He knew it wasn't her fault. He was to blame for not being honest. First with himself, and then with her.

He'd been watching her sleep for several hours now, sipping the latest of many cups of vending machine coffee. He was grateful she was okay. It could have been so much worse. He knew this was a wakeup call. Stephanie and Sam were right. He couldn't continue like this.

Sarah shifted in the bed, muttered something, and opened her eyes. She looked around, confused by the unfamiliar surroundings, before seeing Robert sitting in the chair next to her bed.

"Good morning," Robert said.

"Hey," Sarah said groggily. She attempted to sit up, and winced. "Ow." She fell back into the softness of the bed.

"You got bruised up pretty good. They gave you some pain medication and something to sleep, but I imagine it's worn off by now." Robert put his coffee cup down on the bedside table and stood up. "I'll see if I can find the nurse to get you something more." As he moved toward the door, Sarah called after him.

"Robert . . ."

He turned back toward her.

"The baby?"

He'd been dreading this. He walked back to the bed, sat down next to Sarah, and gently took her hand. "I'm sorry, Sarah . . ."

Sarah felt her throat tighten and her eyes fill. Robert must be wrong; he had to be wrong. She put her hand on her belly, and the tears began to pour. "No," she almost screamed. "That can't be true."

"I'm sorry. I know how much you wanted this baby." Robert hesitated before continuing. "But maybe this is for the best."

Sarah looked at Robert, stunned. What did he say? *This is for the best?* How could this be for the best? He couldn't possibly mean that.

"How can you say that?" she finally said, the agitation apparent in her voice.

"Maybe we shouldn't talk about this now. You should stay calm. You need to rest."

She pushed herself up into a sitting position, bracing against the pain. "You just don't want to talk about it. You got what you want. The baby's gone. You don't care how I feel." Her eyes burned from the salt of her tears.

"That's not fair. I do care. I know this is hard for you, but another child probably wouldn't be the best thing right now. It's hard enough to care for one child, and to add a baby . . . It would have been too much to do on your own."

Sarah looked blankly at Robert. She wasn't sure she'd heard him right. Did he say 'on her own'? What did he mean by that? What was he saying? What was he telling her? She struggled to find her voice.

"On my own?" Sarah's voice quivered, betraying her anxiety.

"I've been doing a lot of thinking . . ." Robert stopped.

"About?"

He shook his head. "Nothing. We can talk later."

"No," Sarah said. "Tell me. What did you mean by that?" She

felt the panic pulsing through her body. Was he saying that he was leaving? He couldn't leave. What would she do? He was right. She couldn't manage alone.

"Not now. I shouldn't have said anything."

"But you did say it. So tell me what you meant!"

"You really need to calm down. This isn't good for you."

"I can't calm down until you tell me what you meant by doing this alone."

"Our . . . marriage," Robert said softly. "I don't want to do it anymore. I want to separate."

Sarah's heart was racing and she felt nauseous. This couldn't be happening. They couldn't split up. There had to be a way to fix it. Something they could do. "But we haven't even talked about all this. Maybe we should see a counselor or something."

Robert shook his head. "That wouldn't make a difference. I don't need a counselor to tell me what I already know."

Sarah watched him take a deep breath, not sure if he was going to say more or not. Her panic felt unbearable. She had to know. To understand exactly what he was saying. For him to be clear. She opened her mouth to ask, but Robert started first.

"I'm not in love with you," he said, his face impassive. "I'm in love with someone else. In LA. My life is there and that's where I want to be. No more secrets. No more lies." He exhaled. "There. I said it. Finally."

"What about our life here?"

"What life? Let's be honest, Sarah. We're just keeping up appearances. We need to stop pretending."

"Pretending? I'm not pretending anything. This is my life. *Our* life!" Sarah felt the tears well up again.

Robert shook his head, sighed, and took a deep breath. "Okay.

You're right. I need to own this and say that I need to stop pretending. *I'm* the one who has been pretending."

"This can't be happening." Sarah's face felt numb.

"It's been happening for a long time . . ."

"Maybe we just need to try harder. I know I can try harder. Please."

"Sarah, no. I can't. I told you. There's nothing we could do to make this different. I'm living a lie and I feel angry all the time when I'm with you. And I take it out on you and then feel shitty about myself." Robert looked away. "And to have it come to this, with you lying here in this bed today because of me . . . I don't want to keep hurting you. I can't keep doing this. That's all there is to it."

Sarah stifled a sob. "And you don't think leaving is hurting me?"

"I know it feels that way now. But it's for the best. With time, we'll both be happier."

"What about Lizzy?"

"Lizzy will be fine. The two of you can stay in the house and I'll come up and see her. Let's face it, it really won't be all that different for her. It doesn't need to create problems. We'll just work it out reasonably."

Robert's detachment frightened Sarah. She could feel the finality of his decision and it made her feel more panicked and overwhelmed than ever.

"*Reasonably?* Nothing about this seems reasonable to me!" She tried to moved closer him on the bed, but pain shot through her back and she crumpled again, crying more strongly now. What was she going to do? She felt lost. Her body hurt. Her chest hurt. She'd lost everything—first the baby, and now Robert. It was like a horrible nightmare. How could this be happening?

∾

"Sarah, please," Robert said. He reached for her hand, hoping to soothe her. "Something broke loose inside me when you fell. I was terrified. I knew we couldn't go on like this."

Sarah shook her head. "This is terrible. How can you do something so terrible?"

"It would be terrible to continue," Robert said. "You deserve better than this. We both do." He hated seeing her so upset. He knew he probably seemed callous to her, acting so composed, but he also knew he could never explain to her that the lack of emotion had been there for him from the beginning. He'd never really loved her. But to say that now would be cruel.

Sarah quieted some and stared out the window. Robert reached up and cupped her head in his hand. "I know it'll be hard for a while, for all of us. And there will be hell for me to pay with my parents . . ."

Sarah smiled weakly. "That's for sure. The perfect son, divorced. It'll be quite the scandal. A blemish on the Jenkins family name."

"But that's just it. I'm almost fifty years old. It's time for me to stop living my life to please them."

Sarah looked at him. "And what about me? Am I just some disposable pawn in all of this? Does my life even matter to you? You're such a self-centered jerk."

"Fair enough. I guess I deserve that." He looked down at the floor briefly before continuing quietly. "I've been lying to you and I've been lying to myself." He looked back up at Sarah. "I know you may not believe me right now, but I am sorry. I do care about you. And about Lizzy. And I am truly very sorry."

Sarah closed her eyes and let her head sink back into her pillow. "I don't know what to believe. I can't think. My head hurts and my arm hurts. I hurt all over."

"You need something to help with that." Robert stood up. "Let me find the nurse. And then I should check in with Kate. They want to keep you another night, so Lizzy and I will have some father–daughter time. I can make up for missing her birthday." He leaned over and kissed Sarah on the forehead. "I'll be back in the morning to pick you up. Try to get some rest today."

Sarah nodded but didn't say good-bye.

Sarah was showered, dressed, and ready to leave when Robert came back the next morning with Lizzy. The day of rest had helped, and it felt good to get out of bed and move around, but she still felt bruised all over. The doctor had told her that she'd be sore for a couple weeks, as well as some other things that she couldn't remember now. She felt spacey, like nothing was making sense and nothing really mattered. She didn't even feel happy when Lizzy came bouncing through the door with a big "Get Well" Mylar balloon that, she suspected, Robert had gotten from the hospital gift shop.

Lizzy ran to the chair Sarah was sitting in, the balloon bobbing and twisting just over the top of her head. "Hi Mommy! Look what we got for you!"

Sarah reached out to give her a hug. "It's beautiful."

"Do you like it?"

"Yes, I do," Sarah said. She kissed Lizzy on the cheek. "Thank you, my very thoughtful girl."

"Daddy said you fell down and got hurt," Lizzy said, her face suddenly serious.

"I did. But I am okay now and ready to go home."

"So, you saw the doctor and all is good to go?" Robert asked.

"Yeah. We just need to stop at the pharmacy downstairs and get a prescription."

"Do you feel up for lunch? Or would you rather just go home? I promised Lizzy we'd go to Joe's Diner for a burger and milkshake. It was her choice for a late birthday celebration. But I could take you home first if you'd like."

"No!" Lizzy said. "Mommy has to go too. Right Mommy?"

"Well, I'm still a little queasy," Sarah said. "But a vanilla milkshake actually sounds good. It might help settle my stomach a bit." She wasn't sure if the queasiness was from the medication or the pain or if it was leftover morning sickness. She still couldn't believe the baby was gone. Tears flooded her eyes.

"What's the matter, Mommy?" Lizzy said as she moved closer to Sarah.

Sarah searched for a reply that would satisfy Lizzy without revealing the truth.

Robert jumped in to respond. "Mommy's still hurting some. Remember when you broke your collarbone? Sometimes the hurt doesn't go away for a while."

Lizzy nodded. "I remember. I'm sorry you are hurting, Mommy."

"Thanks sweetie. It's not that bad. I'll be better soon." Sarah's sadness receded as irritation at Robert crept in. He knew damn well that her tears weren't pain related. Once again, the master of pretense. But of course, she couldn't confront him with Lizzy here. And he knew that. Sarah was sure he'd continue to use Lizzy as a shield to avoid talking to her. As if lunch at Joe's was really her idea. What a bunch of bullshit.

Robert clapped his hands together. "So, let's get going. I'm starving!"

Lizzy clapped her hands as well, a perfect mirror of Robert. "Me too!"

Sarah tousled Lizzy's hair playfully and pushed up out of her chair. "Okay. Let's go get that prescription and then get you some food."

As they left the room, Lizzy ran ahead to push the elevator button and Robert followed quickly after her, fueling Sarah's irritation. Was this how the day was going to go? He'd go out of his way to avoid her? To never be alone with her? They needed to talk. Sarah needed to know what all this meant for her and Lizzy. She felt the anxiety seep back in. How was all this going to work? When would Robert tell his parents? What would they say? How would they treat her? And Lizzy? Robert had said she and Lizzy could stay in the house. Did that mean he would pay for it? She couldn't afford it on her salary. She couldn't afford much of anything on her salary. Should she get a lawyer? She wasn't sure she could afford to get a lawyer.

She stepped into the elevator, thoughts still buzzing. Lizzy was chatting happily about her second sleepover with Emma last night, stoking Sarah's anger. Robert hadn't even bothered to keep her with him. *Worthless excuse for a father.* Sarah suspected Lizzy hadn't slept much at Kate's. The upside was that she'd probably crash later this afternoon. She'd be able to talk to Robert then. The elevator came to a stop at the garage level and Sarah followed Lizzy off as Robert held the door.

With Lizzy safely strapped into her booster chair in the back seat, Sarah voiced her thoughts to Robert. "I think she's in overdrive from all the excitement of the past couple days, and I imagine a lack of sleep last night. I'm sure she'll nap later. We can talk more then."

"We really don't have much to talk about right now." He stared forward, through the windshield. "Besides, I need to get back to LA. I'm booked on the last flight out tonight."

"You're leaving today?" Sarah couldn't believe it. "Is this some kind of bad joke?"

"Not at all," Robert said, giving Sarah an exacting look. "The flight has been booked since last week. We have an early meeting tomorrow that I need to attend."

"But I just thought with everything—"

"I have it all handled. We'll stop for groceries and anything you might need on our way home. And I talked to Kate when I picked Lizzy up and she said she could help out."

"We can't keep asking so much of her."

"She offered. Said she was happy to do it. She'll sleep over at our house tonight in case you need anything and then take the girls to school so you can sleep in."

"But—"

"Sarah, it's all set. Everything is covered for now. We can figure the rest out later."

Sarah quietly fumed the rest of the way to the restaurant. There really wasn't anything more to say. Robert had said it all. As usual.

Chapter 15

Kate had taken the girls to school and was back at Sarah's, enjoying a cup of freshly brewed coffee and reading the paper. Sarah hadn't wanted to get up before they'd left and Kate decided to let her rest. She knew she needed it. She was thinking of all that Sarah had been through in the past forty-eight hours when she heard a knock on the front door.

"Hello-o," Maggie called out as she opened the door.

"Hi Maggie. I'm in here," Kate called back. When Maggie walked in, she got up to greet her with a hug.

"How's she doing?" Maggie asked as they both sat at down at the table.

"Not great. She doesn't want to eat or get out of bed."

"I guess that's to be expected. She was really excited about the baby."

Kate raised her eyebrows. "That's not the half of it."

Maggie frowned. "What else?"

"Robert left her!"

"Are you shitting me?"

Kate shook her head. "I know. Impeccable timing! You want to go up and see her?"

"I'm not sure she wants to see me. She still seemed mad when she left school on Friday."

Kate frowned. "Why was she mad at you?"

"We had a big fight last Monday. I thought maybe she'd told you about it."

"Not a word," Kate said. "Do you want to talk about it?"

Maggie shrugged and played with the corner of the newspaper. Kate decided to just give her a minute. She quietly sipped her coffee and waited.

Maggie was thinking about the fight with Sarah. She did want to talk to Kate about it. It was nagging at her, and she needed a second opinion. She just wasn't sure where to start. "Did you know her mother committed suicide?" she finally said.

"No! I didn't know. When?"

"Right after Sarah went away to college."

"Wow," Kate said. "That must have been really hard on her."

"I would think so, but she didn't want to talk about it. And then I made a comment comparing her parents to her and Robert and she just went off on me." Maggie kept fiddling with the paper; it helped to have something to do with her hands. "Another classic example of my lame social skills."

Kate reached over and put her hand on Maggie's forearm. Maggie looked up at her.

"You're her best friend," Kate said. "With everything that's going on, you're probably the safest person to lose it with."

Maggie attempted a smile. "Maybe."

"I know it would do her good to see you."

Maggie hesitated. "Yeah. I guess." She knew Kate was right, but she dreaded talking to Sarah. She felt so inadequate when it came to things like this. She was the fun, happy one, always good at avoiding tough subjects. But she knew there was no way to avoid this with Sarah.

"Well, no time like the present," she said. She took a deep breath, got up, and headed upstairs to Sarah's room where she knocked lightly on the door before walking in.

Sarah was curled up in bed with the blinds closed. Maggie walked over and sat down on the edge of the bed with care.

"I'm really sorry, Sarah," she said. She reached out and gently touched Sarah's arm. Sarah slid her hand out without saying anything and Maggie held it in both her hands as she continued her apology. "I'm sorry about the baby. And about Robert. And I'm sorry for what I said last week. It was really stupid. I'm a total bitch."

Sarah pulled the covers down from her face, looked at Maggie, and shook her head. "No, it wasn't stupid. You were right. I just didn't want to see it. You were doing what friends do. Calling me on my stuff."

"Another cheer-bully moment?" Maggie said.

Sarah smiled and nodded, then reached out to Maggie. When Maggie leaned in and hugged her, Sarah started to cry.

Maggie felt helpless and inadequate. Why was she so bad at handling difficult emotions? Probably something for her to look into, she thought sarcastically, although she knew she'd rather not. She floundered, unable to think of something to say. Nothing seemed right. So she simply continued to hold Sarah while she cried.

After several minutes, Sarah pulled back and reached for a Kleenex. She wiped the tears from her face, blew her nose, and took a deep breath. Maggie thought she seemed calmer. Maybe this was her opening.

"Kate has a great pot of coffee downstairs. Why don't we go down and get some?"

Sarah nodded. "That would be good. Let me just take a quick shower and then I'll be down."

"Sounds like a plan," Maggie said, already up and heading for the door. She felt awful admitting it, but she couldn't wait to get out of the room.

"Thanks, Mags," Sarah called after her.

Maggie stuck her head back through the door and pasted on a smile. "Sure thing."

Sarah spent the next week at home, sleeping her way through most of each day. She managed to get up every morning to take Lizzy to school, but then she would come home and go back to bed until it was time to pick her up again. She felt exhausted. Sadness creeped in from time to time, but mostly she was numb. She couldn't imagine how she would ever have the energy to go back to work. Simple tasks seemed overwhelming; her confidence was gone. And Robert wasn't helping; his silence felt unbearable. Still, she refused to call him. *He* needed to call *her*. He couldn't avoid her forever.

Robert was acutely aware of the need for some kind of action, but he felt paralyzed, unsure of the best next step. There was so much more to discuss with Sarah. And he needed to talk to his parents. But what to say? How much to say? And when? And where? When he'd flown back down to LA Saturday night, Sam had picked him up at the airport. He'd told Sam what had happened, and that he'd told Sarah it was over. That he wanted a divorce. That his life was in LA, and LA was where he wanted to be. All this time, Sam had never judged him or questioned his choice to stay with Sarah, and Robert appreciated that. But he was also equally silent when it came to giving Robert advice—and that was infuriating. He wanted to know Sam's opinions, thoughts, suggestions. Especially now. He needed help sorting this all out.

Maggie felt a little lost without Sarah at school and wondered how long she would be out. Physically, she seemed pretty okay now; she was a little bruised up but nothing was broken. But then there was the miscarriage. She wasn't sure how much recovery time was needed for that. And, of course, the mess with Robert just added a whole other dimension to it. Sarah must be overwhelmed. Maggie didn't want to ask yet, but she was certain that all the questions that had been running through her head about money and logistics were running through Sarah's mind as well. She was doing what she could to help—she'd been calling Sarah every day after work, and had brought her food one day—but as upbeat and chatty as she'd tried to be, Sarah hadn't been in a very talkative mood. She just seemed really down.

Kate had been checking in with Sarah regularly all week, and it was clear that Sarah was depressed. Understandably so. She was grieving. Kate couldn't imagine losing a child. And to also find out your husband was in love with another woman and was leaving? Sarah must feel decimated. So she continued to help as much as she could. She brought Sarah and Lizzy food and took the girls out to the park. She even offered to pick Lizzy up from school, but Sarah insisted on doing it herself—said it was good for her to get out of the house. Kate took that as a positive sign. Maybe she wasn't that depressed after all.

Sarah tried to tell herself the same thing. Even in her numbness she knew that taking care of Lizzy was important. It was what she had to live for now. She had to be there for her daughter. This was going to be hard on her—it was going to change her life—and she needed someone to provide stability while the ground was pulled out from under her. Sarah needed to be the consistent parent, since Robert clearly wasn't going to play that part. So she continued to get up every day and get Lizzy to school, hoping that with time she would start to feel better.

Chapter 16

Sarah's alarm crept into her dream, mimicking the sound of a foghorn. It took her a moment to rouse herself; when she finally realized where the beeping was coming from, she reached out clumsily to turn it off before dragging herself out of bed and down the hall to Lizzy's room.

Lizzy was still sleeping soundly. Sarah opened the blinds and squinted, raising her hand up in front of her face to block the light. She went to Lizzy's bedside and gently shook her shoulder.

"Wake up, Liz. Time for school."

Lizzy pulled away from Sarah's hand. "No. I don't wanna go."

"I'm not gonna fight about this today," Sarah said as she turned to leave. "Just get dressed." She couldn't do this again. Every day this week Lizzy had resisted getting up, and Sarah's reserves were deeply in the red.

"When's Daddy coming back?"

Sarah turned back, irritated and discouraged. "I told you yesterday: I don't know. Now get dressed so we won't be late." When she was halfway out the door, Lizzy shouted after her.

"He left because of you! It's all your fault!"

"Lizzy, stop it. I can't handle this today."

"No! I won't stop! You made him leave!"

"I did not make him leave," Sarah said, her voice getting louder and more agitated. "Now quit being such an immature brat and get out of that bed and get ready for school. Right now!"

"Yes, you did! You did too make him leave. I know you did. It's all your fault. I don't want you for my mother. I want to be with Daddy."

"Well you can't be with Daddy! So shut the fuck up and get dressed!"

Lizzy threw several toys after Sarah as she stormed out of the room, barely missing her head. "I hate you! You're a horrible mother!"

Remorse washed over Sarah. *She's right. You don't deserve to be a mother. Who screams and swears at their kid like that? And you should have been a better wife. You should have done things differently. You should have worked harder to make him happier with you. She's right. It is your fault that he left. You really are a worthless piece of shit. You can't do anything right. You never should have been born.*

She dragged herself back to her room. *You really have fucked everything up. The world would be better off without you. Lizzy would be better off without you.* She slowly pulled on a pair of yoga pants and a sweatshirt. The heaviness in her body felt overwhelming. She couldn't do this today. She felt too tired to even stand up. She collapsed onto her bed, reached for her cell phone, and dialed Kate.

"Hey Sarah," Kate said after the second ring. "How are you doing?"

"Not great. I just had a big fight with Lizzy, and I feel so drained and tired. Would you mind taking her to school this morning?"

"Not at all. I should be ready to leave here in about five minutes."

"Thanks," Sarah said quietly. "I really appreciate it." She set down the phone, lay down on the bed, and fell asleep almost immediately.

Sarah didn't stir when Kate peeked in twenty minutes later. Kate decided to let her sleep. She wrote her a short note and left it on her nightstand, then went to check on Lizzy's progress.

Seeing Emma had hugely improved Lizzy's mood; she was already dressed and ready to leave.

"Have you had any breakfast yet?" Kate asked her, scouring the kitchen for something quick.

"Nope. But I could just eat a bagel in the car."

"Great idea!" Kate said. She grabbed a bagel and a juice box from the pantry for Lizzy. "You two go buckle in and I'll be right there." As the girls scurried out, she dug her phone out of her purse and called Maggie.

After several rings, Maggie finally answered. "Hi Kate. Is everything okay?"

"I'm not sure," Kate said. "Sarah called me to take Lizzy to school this morning and went right back to bed. She was asleep when I got here." She hesitated briefly. "I don't know. It's been over a week. I guess I'm feeling a little worried."

"Yeah, I don't know what's normal. I mean, I get that she's been through a double whammy here with the baby and Robert, but she seems really down. Sick, even."

"I agree. I'm worried that she's really depressed. It would probably be good for her to see a doctor, or even a therapist. I was going to check in with her this morning, but I'm doing a cooking demonstration downtown today so my time is tight to get the girls to school. I opted to just let her sleep."

"She probably needs it," Maggie said. "I could stop by after school and check in on her."

"That would be great," Kate said, relieved. "I left her a note that Will would pick Lizzy up from school. I'll have him take her home to play with Emma so you can have some time with Sarah."

"Sounds like a plan. Thanks Kate."

"Absolutely. I just want her to feel better."

"I know," Maggie said. "Me too."

Maggie thought about Sarah periodically throughout the day. She wanted to help but wasn't sure how. She knew better than to say this to Sarah, but she thought she was wallowing too much. It was time to get over it and come back to work. She'd feel better if she would just get back on the horse, so to speak. It couldn't be good to just be sleeping all the time. Kate mentioned that she might be depressed. Maggie made a mental note to ask her more about that. She'd never known anyone who was depressed, so she wasn't sure what that would look like. Or how to help. Maybe Kate was right. Maybe Sarah needed a therapist.

She left school just as the rain started coming down more heavily. She'd left her umbrella in the car that morning, seduced by the subtle sunshine peeking through the clouds. *So much for our sunshiny day,* she thought as she covered her head with her book bag and jogged to the parking lot. She tried to think of things to say to Sarah on the drive to her house, but she was still at a loss when she pulled into the driveway. She dreaded going in.

"You can do this," she said aloud as she got out of the car and sprinted to the front door. She rang the bell and waited, but there was no answer. She reached for the door handle and tried it; it was unlocked. She opened the door and found the house dark and still.

She went up to Sarah's room, tapped twice on the open door, and walked in.

The room was cluttered with clothes and used Kleenex. Sarah was sitting on the unmade bed looking at something in her hand. Maggie picked up a handful of Kleenex from the floor and tossed them into the trash can on her way to the bed. When she drew closer, she realized what Sarah was holding: a grainy, black-and-white ultrasound photo.

"I hate seeing you like this," she said as she sat down next to Sarah. "It scares me and I don't know what to do to help."

"I just feel so bad," Sarah said continuing to stare at the photo.

"I know." Maggie motioned to the photo. "But maybe you need to put that away for a while."

"I don't want to put it away," Sarah said looking up at Maggie with tears in her eyes. "It's all I have left of the baby to hold on to."

"But that's just it, Sarah. You can't hold on to it anymore. It's gone." She paused a minute, trying to think of what would be best to say next. Something that would help Sarah think and feel differently. "You have to focus on the positive," she said. "At least you have Lizzy."

Sarah stood up abruptly, flailing her arms. "Damn it, Maggie," she shouted. "I'm tired of everyone saying that. Is that supposed to make me feel better? Because it doesn't. It makes me feel worse. I look at Lizzy and see all that I've lost."

Maggie sat stunned, not knowing what to say and cursing herself for totally blowing it yet again.

"Every day I imagine them growing up together, playing and laughing," Sarah continued in a small voice. "I see birthdays and holidays. Picture after picture. I can't stop the pictures. I can't make the pictures go away." She dropped to her knees in front of Maggie and began to sob, still clutching the ultrasound picture. "I can't make them go away . . ."

Maggie knelt down next to Sarah and put an arm around her. Still not knowing what to say, she just held Sarah quietly until her sobbing subsided to a quiet whimper.

"I know this is really hard right now. But you won't always feel this way. It'll get better."

Sarah shook her head. "It won't get better. I've screwed everything up. The world would be better off without me. Lizzy would be better off without me"

"Don't say that. That's not at all true, especially not about Lizzy."

"She hates me."

"She doesn't hate you. She's just having a hard time right now. Kids always say things like that when they're mad. But it's not true. You're a great mother."

"Great mothers don't give their kids broken homes and absent fathers."

"Sarah, stop. You can't blame yourself for Robert."

"I married him, didn't I?"

Maggie didn't respond. She knew from Sarah's tone that anything she said right now would not be well received. Better to just keep quiet.

Sarah looked away from Maggie. "Everything sucks. I can't go on like this." She stood up and walked out of the room. Maggie sat there for a moment, feeling both sad and helpless. Tears rose up, stinging her eyes. She took a deep breath and exhaled forcefully through her mouth before pulling herself up off the floor and following Sarah downstairs. She found her standing at the kitchen counter, staring blankly into space.

"You okay?" Maggie asked.

"Yeah," Sarah said, and her voice did seem much calmer. "I'm sorry. I'm just really tired. Kate will be here in about an hour with the girls. I think I'll take a nap until then."

"I can hang out until they get here."

"Don't be silly. You've got better things to do than sit here while I'm sleeping."

"You sure? I really don't mind. I can read one of these wonderful periodicals you've got here." Maggie motioned to a stack of magazines on the side table.

Sarah nodded, smiling. "Yes. I'm sure. I just feel drained. A nap will do me good." She gave Maggie a quick, fierce hug. "Now go—get out of here." She gently pushed Maggie toward the front door.

"Yes, ma'am!" Maggie said. She felt relieved that Sarah seemed more serene now—even happy. She grabbed her purse from the counter and exaggerated her prancing toward the front door.

Driving home, Maggie thought about what Sarah had said. That she didn't understand what she had lost. She was probably right: she didn't get it. She didn't have children, so how could she understand? She scolded herself for being selfish and vowed to be more thoughtful.

She was starting up the final flight of stairs to her apartment when she heard her phone ring from the depths of her cavernous bag. Maybe it was Ryan! She leapt up two steps at a time and quickly unlocked the door before rummaging for her phone. She glanced at the screen. Not Ryan.

"Hi Kate," she said, as she dropped her bag on the floor.

"Hey Maggie. You sound out of breath."

"Yeah. I just ran up the stairs. I definitely need to do more cardio!" she said, still breathing heavily. "Are you at Sarah's?"

"No. That's why I'm calling," Kate said. "I got a voicemail from her asking me to keep Lizzy for the night. Something about being tired and also not wanting anyone to go out in the storm."

"Well, it is nasty out. The rain is really coming down, and it's pretty windy too. I can understand wanting to stay put."

"Yeah, maybe," Kate said. "But when I tried to call her back she didn't answer. I just wanted to check in with you to see how she was doing. She sounded really distant on the voicemail, but maybe that was just her tiredness."

"She was upset when I got there, but then she actually seemed better by the time I left. Calmer, and even joking with me a little. I offered to stay, but she shooed me out. She said you'd be there in an hour . . ." Maggie paused, her thoughts speeding up and her words slowing down. "She . . . wanted . . . to take . . . a nap . . ." She stopped, remembering Sarah's comments. That the world would be better off without her. That Lizzy would be better off without her. That she couldn't go on anymore. Maggie's stomach tightened. She felt like she was going to throw up.

"Maggie? Are you there?" Kate asked.

Maggie barely heard her. Her head was spinning with disparate voices. One was saying that Sarah would never do something like that, and another was berating her for being so blind. Sarah had just told her that her mother had committed suicide. And Maggie had been the one who had drawn the comparison to her mother. Why hadn't she put two and two together? Why hadn't the thought even occurred to her?

"Shit!" she muttered under her breath. She was having trouble thinking. She needed to get back there.

"Kate, I've got to go," she said, and hung up the phone without waiting for a response. She grabbed her keys, scooped her bag up off the floor, and rushed out the door.

Kate looked at the phone in her hand, puzzled by Maggie's behavior. She knew Maggie could be a bit flaky at times, but something seemed off. She'd hung up so abruptly. What had happened? She tried calling her back, but she didn't answer. She decided to try Sarah again, but no luck there either.

She felt a nagging in her gut but blew it off, sure that she was worrying over nothing. Sarah was tired. She was probably sound asleep. She might even have turned the phone off. A good night's sleep would be good for her. And the girls would have a fun night together. She'd go over and check on Sarah in the morning.

Sarah heard the phone ring as she climbed back up the stairs with a bottle of Robert's vodka, but she decided to ignore it. She felt amazingly peaceful. She took a big gulp straight from the bottle, then set it down on her makeup table, grimacing, before going to the bathroom. She opened the medicine cabinet and took out two prescription pill bottles. She looked at the bottles and then at her reflection in the mirror. Tears began to blur her vision, and she quickly looked away. She carried the pill bottles back to her makeup table. Her hands were shaking as she put them down. She picked up the vodka bottle with both hands and took another gulp.

It's okay. This is the right thing to do. Lizzy will be better off. Robert will step up and give her a good life. She deserves that, and you can't give it to her. It's clear how worthless you are. You're terrible for her. She needs stability, not a crazy person for a mother. She'll be better off without you. She'll forget all about you. Everyone will forget you. Nobody will care.

She sat down at the table, picked up a pen, and wrote, "For Lizzy—when the time is right" on the envelope in front of her. She carefully set it aside, took another swig of vodka, and grabbed a blank sheet of paper. She felt both resolved and numb as she began to write:

"Dear Lizzy—I know there is probably not anything I could say that would help you to understand . . ."

Maggie cursed loudly as she drove frantically through the heavy rain and wind. Her anxiety had now escalated to terror; she dreaded what she might find when she got to Sarah's house. She realized that she hadn't thought this through. Maybe she should have called 911. But what if she was wrong? She thought of all the times Sarah had accused her of being overly dramatic. Of overreacting. She tried to reassure herself that this was probably just one of those times. Sarah was probably sound asleep. If Maggie was wrong about all this, and paramedics came charging into her home for no reason . . . She would never let Maggie forget it.

This line of thought soothed Maggie for a brief moment, but the adrenaline surged again as she pulled into Sarah's driveway. She quickly turned off her car and ran through the driving rain to the front door. She tried the handle; the door was locked this time. She rang the bell and pounded on the door: no response. She ran around to the back of the house and up onto the deck, silently praying that the French doors would be unlocked.

"Shit!" she said out loud when the door wouldn't budge. She ran back to the front of the house, wondering if Sarah had a hidden key. She looked under the potted plants and ran her hand over the doorframe. Nothing. Her heart was pounding and her stomach churned. She fought back tears and shivered as the cold water dripped from her drenched hair onto her face.

"Think, Maggie, think!" she said aloud, searching for ideas. She started looking for a rock—if nothing else, she could break a window—and then she noticed Sarah's car in the driveway. *What are the chances?* She ran to the car. It was unlocked! She scanned the front seat and grabbed the remote for the garage door. Her adrenaline spiked again as she pushed the button. Nothing. She tried again. Still nothing.

"Shit," she said, realizing the battery must be dead. She returned to the idea of breaking a window—and then another thought occurred to her: maybe the battery in her remote was the same as Sarah's.

She ducked out of Sarah's car, grabbed the remote from her car, and ran back to Sarah's. She exchanged the batteries, pushed the button, and the door started to lift. "Thank God," she said aloud as she sprinted through the garage and into the dark house.

"Sarah?! Sarah?!" she yelled as she ran from room to room, flipping light switches as she went. She raced up the stairs two at a time, her heart pounding in her chest, and pushed open the door to the master bedroom.

Pills were scattered all over the floor, along with crumpled writing paper and a spilled vodka bottle. She heard the shower running through the closed bathroom door.

She burst through the door to see Sarah sitting on the floor of the shower, fully clothed and soaking wet, her arms wrapped around her knees. She was rocking and crying under the steady stream of water and seemed unaware of Maggie's presence.

Maggie dropped to the floor, tears of relief streaming down her face. She sat there for a few minutes, thinking Sarah would notice her, but Sarah just kept rocking and crying. Finally, she crawled into the shower and wrapped her arms around Sarah. She wasn't sure how she would react, but Sarah immediately leaned into her embrace, letting her head fall down onto Maggie's shoulder. They sat quietly in each other's arms until Sarah broke the silence.

"I couldn't do it," she said softy. "I couldn't do it to Lizzy."

"It's okay," Maggie said, holding her closer.

"I hated her for leaving me."

"I know," Maggie said. She reached up with one hand and turned the shower off and continued to hold Sarah. As Sarah's sobs began to ease, Maggie sat silently, as much out of respect as out of numbness. She felt at a complete loss for anything to say. She didn't understand. She loved life and couldn't begin to imagine killing herself. She felt completely out of her league and had no idea what would be helpful right now. She was afraid anything she might say would be completely wrong or even hurtful. So she waited.

"Maggie, I'm really messed up," Sarah finally said, her voice trembling. "I need some help."

"Okay. We'll find someone," Maggie said, trying to sound reassuring despite her own anxiety. She needed Kate. Kate would know what to do. Sarah shivered slightly and Maggie realized they were both ice cold.

"We should get some dry clothes for both of us," she said.

"Yeah," Sarah said, her teeth chattering. "I'm really cold."

Maggie helped her get up and handed her a towel before grabbing one for herself. Once they were in dry clothes, Sarah crawled under the covers of her bed, still shivering.

"Have you had anything to eat today?" Maggie asked.

"I can't remember."

"I think you could use something warm. Do you have any soup?"

Sarah nodded. "Probably. In the pantry."

"Okay. You rest and I'll go see what I can rustle up."

Sarah nodded again and closed her eyes. Maggie went downstairs and immediately called Kate.

"Maggie. Is everything okay?"

"Yes and no. Do you think you could come over?"

"Sure. As soon as Will gets home to watch the girls. He just left to take the boys over to their Scout meeting, but he'll be back in a few minutes."

"Thanks, Kate. I really appreciate it."

"No problem. See you in a few."

Maggie hung up the phone and found a can of chicken noodle soup in the pantry. *Perfect.* She felt the tension in her body recede and realized she was hungry too. She'd make Sarah's soup and then see what she could find for herself. While the soup heated up, she searched through several cabinets and found a bowl, some saltines, and a tray. When it was bubbling, she poured it into the bowl and carried the tray upstairs.

Sarah was sitting up in bed. Her color was better and she was no longer shivering. Maggie handed her the tray.

"Thanks," Sarah said. She took the tray without looking at Maggie. She was embarrassed, sure that her friend was probably thinking she was nuts. And maybe she was. What had made her get to this point? How could she have even considered killing herself after the torment she'd felt when her mother died? She would never want to put Lizzy through something like that.

"My pleasure," Maggie said. "Do you want anything else? Some tea, maybe?"

"No, this is good for now," Sarah said. She felt awkward. She needed to say something. Maggie was probably totally freaked out.

Maggie backed away slowly. "Sounds good. I'm actually feeling a bit hungry myself, so I'm—"

"Maggie, I feel really stupid . . ."

"Sarah, don't. You're just really hurting. It's going to be okay. I called Kate and she'll be over soon and we can all talk about it."

Sarah could tell Maggie was uncomfortable. She cringed internally. She hated them seeing what a weak, horrible, crazy person she was. It was bad enough that Maggie knew, but now Kate too? Why had Maggie even come back? She would have been okay. She never could have gone through with it. Nobody would have ever known.

"What did you tell Kate?" she asked.

"Nothing. I just asked if she could come over."

"Good," Sarah said. "I'm fine now and I don't want to make a big deal about this. I was having a bad moment, but I wouldn't have ever really done anything. So I don't want to talk about it with Kate."

"But Kate will—"

"Maggie. I'm okay. I admit I've been depressed and it would probably be good to talk to a therapist or something. So we can talk to Kate about that. But that's all. Okay?"

"Yeah. Okay," Maggie said. "But how am I going to explain asking her to come over? She's going to think I'm a total drama queen."

"No worries," Sarah said, smiling. "She already knows that about you."

Maggie frowned—and then returned Sarah's smile. "Yeah, guess so. Ever the drama queen. And right now, darling, I'm absolutely starving! So, you enjoy your soup. I'm gonna go get something for myself."

Sarah chuckled. "Sounds good."

Chapter 17

Kate had gotten Sarah a recommendation for a therapist from her couple's therapist. At the time, it had seemed like a good idea, but now, sitting in the waiting room, Sarah had an overwhelming urge to run. *This is stupid. Only weak, crazy people need therapists. Stop being such a wimp and just get over it.*

If she left now, the therapist would never even know she'd been there. She could write it off as a miscommunication. She started to stand up—and the door in front of her opened.

"Sarah?" A woman in business-casual attire greeted her. Sarah guessed she was in her mid-forties.

Sarah nodded.

The woman reached out her hand. "I'm Monica Richardson. It's good to meet you."

"Likewise," Sarah managed to say as she extended her hand to Monica.

"Right this way," Monica said, motioning her forward and moving back through the door. Sarah followed her down a hall and into a well-lit and nicely decorated office. There was a simple but elegant writer's desk sitting at a diagonal in one corner and a sofa and oversized upholstered chair on the other side of the room. Several abstract modern paintings in muted colors decorated the walls. Windows lined one side, opening the room to the canopy of lush green foliage outside.

Monica motioned to the sofa. "Have a seat," she said to Sarah as she sat down in the adjacent chair. Sarah sat down tentatively on the edge of the sofa. She didn't want to be here. She needed a way out. Maybe she could just tell her it was a mistake to have come, apologize, pay her for the session, and leave.

"You know," Sarah said, "I feel a little silly being here. I've had a rough time recently and a friend thought it was a good idea, but I'm okay. I'm not really sure I need this." *You are so full of shit. You can't even get out of bed. You scream at Lizzy. You can't get anything done.*

"Well, Sarah," Monica said warmly, "I don't know if you need this or not, but since you are here, maybe you'd be willing to tell me a little about what's been going on."

Sarah's throat tightened and tears sprang into her eyes. "Sure," she squeezed out. She settled back into the sofa, swallowing hard and blinking to try to keep herself from crying. "Although I'm not really sure where to begin."

Monica leaned forward slightly. "Why don't you start with what you are feeling right now?" she said as she picked up a box of Kleenex and handed it to Sarah. "What are the tears about?"

For the next thirty minutes, Sarah reviewed the past several weeks, pausing at times to cry more deeply, to blow her nose, or to compose herself. Monica listened attentively, and Sarah increasingly found herself feeling more at ease as she spoke. She was surprised that her words poured out so effortlessly. When she finally finished the story, she looked at the pile of Kleenex on the table in front of her and suddenly felt self-conscious. *What are you doing? Why did you*

*tell her all that? A complete stranger. She probably thinks you're totally
nuts. You never should have come. This was a huge mistake.*

Exhaustion took hold, sudden and complete. Sarah shifted
uncomfortably and looked at Monica.

"What are you feeling right now?" Monica asked.

"Tired."

"You've been through a lot in the past couple weeks. It makes
sense that you're tired."

"I just want to go to sleep and forget everything."

"That's completely understandable. You've suffered some big
losses. It's hard to make sense of it all."

Sarah nodded. "I just feel so lost. And I have thoughts sometimes
that scare me. Like I'll never get better and there's no point in going
on."

"That's the grief talking," Monica said. "It may not seem like it
right now, but you won't always feel this way."

Anger replaced exhaustion. This woman was just like everyone
else. She didn't understand. She didn't have a clue what she was
feeling. Coming here was a total waste of time and money. It wasn't
going to help her at all.

"What's going on for you right now?" Monica asked, breaking the
silence.

Sarah shrugged dismissively. *Oh my God, is that all she ever says?
She's like a fucking robot or something. Why should you tell her anything? She wouldn't get it.* Sarah had no desire to even try to talk to
her.

"I ask because I noticed a subtle change. You seemed less sad and
perhaps a little angry," Monica said.

Sarah looked away. Of course she was angry. She was tired of
everyone telling her how she should feel—that she should get over

this. And now this strange woman was just staring at her, expecting her to say something. The silence was unnerving.

"I hate when people say things like that," she said without meeting Monica's gaze. "'Things will get better. This too shall pass.' It's all bullshit."

"So, when I said you wouldn't always feel this way, you felt angry because I was just giving you the same line of bullshit that everyone else has been feeding you."

At this, Sarah looked at Monica. "Yes! I felt like you didn't understand what I was going through."

"Well, in some ways you're right. I can't ever fully know what you are going through. Everyone's experience of loss is uniquely their own. So I'll depend on you to tell me that." Monica leaned forward slightly. "What I do know is that there are stages of grief that are very universal. Different individuals have different time frames, but slowly, that grief does begin to resolve."

"How?" Sarah asked. Part of her was still screaming at herself to get the hell out of there, but she pushed the voice away. Some of what Monica was saying seemed to make some sense. Maybe she should hear her out.

"With time," Monica said. "And with the hard work of feeling all of the emotions that come with grieving."

"Yeah, well, I'm not sure I'm up to that."

"You're not. Not yet. First we need to do some simple things to get you stronger."

"Like what?" Sarah was afraid of what Monica was going to say next.

"I'd like you to start adhering to some simple routines every day," Monica said. "Would you be willing to try that?"

Sarah hesitated. "I guess. What do you mean by routines?"

"I'd like you to stay out of your bed except to sleep at night. Get up, shower, dress, have breakfast, and take Lizzy to school. Does that sound doable?"

"I guess so," Sarah said, not at all sure that she was telling the truth. "I just get so tired."

"I know. You'll probably still need some naps, but just don't go back to bed. You could sit in a chair or lie down on the sofa instead. And you should set an alarm so you don't sleep more than an hour at a time during the day. Do you think that could work?"

"Maybe."

"You sound like you aren't really sure. Should we come up with a different idea?"

Sarah shook her head. "No. I can give it a try."

"Okay." Monica tilted her head as if considering her options. "Also, do you have friends who could do something with you during the day? Maybe take a walk or go for coffee?"

Sarah nodded. "Yeah." She knew Kate would do that. And probably Maggie, too, after school was out.

"Great. So, I'd like you to try to do at least one thing out of the house with a friend each day. What do you think?"

Sarah nodded, feeling slightly more confident. "Sure, I can do that."

"Good. That will be your homework for the week." Monica smiled. "We are almost out of time, but I want to check in before we end. When we started today, you weren't sure you wanted or needed to be here. I think a lot of what you are feeling is very normal given all that has happened. And I'm also confident that you can move through this and feel better. I'd be happy to support you to do that, but I want to be sure that you would like to continue here."

Sarah thought for a moment. She still felt foolish being there, but she had to admit that she also felt a little better. It felt good to have a plan that might help her start to feel better. And she felt comfortable with Monica.

"Maybe we could meet again and see how it goes," Sarah said.

"That sounds fine to me," Monica said. She reached for her appointment book. "We can schedule an appointment for next week."

As she left Monica's office, Sarah thought back over the past hour. As much as she hated to admit it, she'd liked Monica and was glad she'd come. After being near panic in the waiting room, she now felt calm. And a little more hopeful. She wanted to feel better, and Monica seemed confident that she would.

She drove to Kate's to pick up Lizzy. As she pulled into the driveway, gratitude for all Kate and Maggie had been doing flooded through her. They'd both gone out of their way to help and she'd been such a pill, wallowing in self-pity and not showing any thankfulness. She was lucky they hadn't dumped her by now. She promised herself she would do better. And she could start by apologizing to Kate now.

She had barely pressed the doorbell when Lizzy and Emma threw the door open.

"Come see what we made," Emma said, waving for Sarah to follow.

"Yeah," Lizzy said, grabbing Sarah's hand and pulling. "Come see!"

Sarah smiled when she saw the huge fort that had been constructed in the living room. Dining room chairs had been strategically placed in the middle of the room to hold up the sheets and blankets that were draped over the sofa and chairs.

"Look inside!" Lizzy pulled Sarah down to the floor in front of the opening. Sarah peeked in through the gap in the sheets to see a string of small white Christmas lights wound around the perimeter and a dozen pillows piled up to create two cocoon beds. The rest of the floor space was covered with stuffed animals of all sizes and shapes.

"Wow!" Sarah said. "What a cool fort. Did you do all this by yourselves?"

"Yep! 'Cept Mommy helped with the lights," Emma said looking over at Kate, who had just come into the room carrying a plate of cut-up apples and string cheese.

"And a little with the blankets, 'cause they kept falling down," Lizzy said.

"Well you did a great job," Sarah said. "It looks really cozy in there!"

"It does," Kate said. "So why don't you both crawl in there and I'll hand you your snack?"

The girls quickly slithered into the fort. Kate handed them the plate and turned to Sarah. "How about some coffee or a cup of tea?"

"A cup of tea sounds great." She followed Kate back to the kitchen.

"How did the session go?" Kate asked as she filled the teapot and turned on the stove. "If you don't mind me asking."

"No, not at all. It was good, I think. I was freaking out a bit in the waiting room and came really close to bolting. I seriously think if she'd come out to get me a minute later, I would've been gone. But she was easy to talk to once I got going, and by the time we were done I felt a little better."

"Well that sounds positive," Kate said.

Sarah nodded. "Yeah. She said that a lot of what I'm feeling seems normal considering all that's happened. It helped to hear that. Honestly, I felt like I was totally losing it and never going to get better. I feel bad that I've been so out of it. You and Maggie have been great . . . I'm sorry I've been such a mess."

"Sarah, don't talk that way," Kate said. "You're not a mess. You're just grieving and adjusting to some big losses all at once."

"That's just what Monica said."

"Well, there you go! She must be a smart therapist! So, you'll see her again?"

"Yeah. I have another appointment in a week," Sarah said. "And I have homework! I didn't know therapists gave homework!"

Kate laughed. "What kind of homework?"

"It's sort of silly," Sarah said. "Basically, to get up every day, take Lizzy to school, and not go back to bed. And she wants me to get out of the house and do something with a friend every day."

"I was thinking about that myself! You should come back to yoga. I could pick you up for a morning class while the girls are in school, and then we could get some lunch afterwards."

Sarah hesitated. She wasn't sure she wanted to commit to yoga every day. "I don't know. I don't want to put you out."

"It's not putting me out at all. I want to go too. It'll be good for both of us."

"Well, I guess I could try it out." She really wasn't sure. She still felt so tired. Yoga might be too much. She decided to go once and see. If it felt too hard, she could always bail.

"Great!" Kate said. "We'll start tomorrow. I'll pick you up at nine thirty."

Chapter 18

Sarah proudly reported to Monica the next week that she'd followed through with her homework. It hadn't been easy. She still felt sad most of the time and needed afternoon naps every day, but she'd gone to yoga every morning with Kate.

"I'm really glad to hear that," Monica said. "Yoga was a great choice. And what a great effort on your part to go every day."

"Well, to be honest, it really wasn't my choice or my effort. Kate suggested it. I tried to get out of it a couple of times, but she wouldn't let me."

Monica smiled. "She sounds like a good friend."

Sarah nodded. "Yeah, she is. She's helped me so much lately. And as hard as it is to motivate myself to go, I know the yoga is helping. I always feel better afterward."

"That's good. My guess is that each day you'll continue to feel a little better," Monica said. "Do you think you can keep doing it next week?"

Sarah smiled. "I don't think I have a choice. Kate is totally obsessed."

Monica laughed. "Well, I'm glad you have such a dedicated friend!" She squinted a little, as if sizing Sarah up. "I'd like to try something a little different today. Would that be okay with you?"

"Uh, I guess so," Sarah said. Her stomached clenched with anticipation. She didn't really want to do anything more. She was just starting to feel a little better. Why couldn't she just keep doing what she was doing? What was Monica going to ask? What if she didn't want to do it?

Monica frowned slightly. "You're thinking maybe it's too soon?"

"Well, sort of. I guess."

"You'd probably rather just keep doing what you are doing for now."

"Yeah," Sarah said. "How did you know?"

Monica smiled. "Just a guess."

"I mean, I'm still so tired," Sarah said, trying to backpedal. "I just don't want to overdo it."

"Good. I'm glad you're checking in with yourself to see what you're feeling."

Sarah wasn't so sure. Maybe she was just scared. Or depressed. Or both. "I'm still having a hard time knowing what I'm feeling most of the time."

"That's understandable," Monica said. "And I don't want to push you if you don't feel ready."

Sarah was struggling inside. She felt nervous about adding more to her plate. Sure, she'd gotten through last week, but it hadn't been easy. On the other hand, she had to admit that Monica's suggestions had helped so far. And now she was really curious.

"What was it that you were going to suggest?" she asked.

"Actually," Monica said, "I wanted you to try a simple visualization process."

Sarah's eyebrows drew together. She wasn't sure what Monica meant.

"I wanted to ask you to remember a time when you weren't depressed—when you were happy or excited about life."

"Right now, I don't feel like I was ever happy."

"I know," Monica said. "But we both know that you have been. Maybe when Lizzy was born?"

Sarah thought back for a moment. "Yes and no. It was mixed. Robert was very indifferent so it was actually kind of a lonely time for me."

"Okay, so keep thinking," Monica said. "Think about a time when you felt truly happy. Try to visualize where you were, who you were with, what you were doing."

Sarah closed her eyes and sat quietly, letting her mind wander. Finally, she shifted in her seat and opened her eyes. "College," she said. "I was really happy my junior year of college. I had a great boyfriend. I loved my upper-level lit classes. And my writing . . . I loved writing. It seems silly now, but I even had fantasies of being a writer."

Monica shook her head. "It doesn't seem silly. It sounds like something you were passionate about."

Sarah nodded. "It was. I still think about it sometimes. But I really don't have the time with Lizzy and work."

"Well, right now you have time, since you're off work for a while."

"I don't know . . ." It had been so long since she'd written anything. What if she had forgotten how? Lost her touch?

"Would you be willing to try it between now and when we meet again?"

Sarah thought for a moment. She did want to write again. But she felt scared. "I guess I could try . . ."

"That's all I'm asking. Just give it a try. Block out thirty minutes a day to write. Don't worry about the content or whether it's any good or not. Nobody but you will ever have to see it. Just let it be fun."

Sarah thought for a moment. She liked the idea that she'd never have to show it to anyone. If it was awful, she could just throw it away. "Okay, I'll try."

"Good." Monica stood up. "I know everything still feels difficult right now, but think about how you feel today compared to last week. Each week will get a little better. Just keep focusing on Lizzy and your day-to-day activities for now."

"Okay." Sarah extended her hand to Monica. "Thank you."

"You are very welcome." Monica took Sarah's hand in both of hers. "I look forward to seeing you next week."

Sarah ripped the page out of her notebook, crumpled it up in a loose ball, and tossed it onto the floor. She had been trying for an hour to write something at least marginally readable and she felt like screaming. All she wanted to write was "fuck this shit" over and over, and she was pretty sure that wasn't what Monica had in mind. She wasn't ready for this. Monica was wrong. She shouldn't have told her to do this. It was making her feel worse. She'd had so many dreams of writing again, but clearly that ship had sailed. *You're such an idiot, thinking you could write. You obviously can't. Robert was right. It was just a stupid pipe dream. The sooner you recognize that, the better.*

Sarah looked around at the crumpled papers scattered on the floor in front of her chair. She felt hopeless. She wanted to just go crawl into bed. To hell with Monica's rules. Who was she to tell her what to do? She uncrossed her legs and pushed up out of the chair. She dropped the notebook onto the floor and kicked angrily at the pile of crumpled pages—and connected with the leg of the coffee table. Pain shot through her big toe and she dropped to the floor to grab it, tears bursting into her eyes. She felt scared and little and alone.

She wanted to be held, to feel safe, to know that everything would be okay. A child's voice inside her cried out, *I want my mommy. Why did she leave me? Why didn't she love me?* Sarah's tears turned into sobs that racked her entire body until she was so exhausted that she lay down on the floor and fell into a deep sleep.

When she awoke the light in the room had turned dusky. She felt disoriented. How long had she been asleep? She looked around at the balled-up papers on the floor and pushed herself up to look at the clock. Her eyes settled on a framed picture of her, Lizzy, and Robert. Her eyes continued to scan the other framed pictures, evidence of their supposedly happy family. She and Robert had both been good at playing their parts, but it had all been a facade. Behind closed doors and all that. She felt betrayed. She had worked so hard to fulfill her role in their marriage. To be a good wife. But none of that had mattered. He didn't care. He'd never been invested. All this time, he'd had his whole other life that she knew nothing about.

A sense of outrage ballooned in her chest. She slowly pulled herself up to a standing position, walked over to the bookshelves, and methodically picked up picture after picture and threw them across the room. The sound of the breaking glass egged her on and she started moving more quickly and furiously. Screams rose into her throat: "Son of a bitch! Fucking asshole! Liar. Cheater! How could you fucking do this to me? And to Lizzy? You're a worthless, piece of shit father. A good-for-nothing fucking bastard! I hate you! I hate you! I hope you rot in hell!"

After she'd thrown the last picture, Sarah starting throwing books, Robert's golfing trophies, CD cases, anything she could get her hands on. She finally sank to her knees and pounded the carpet with her fists until they started to ache. She dropped down onto her side as the sadness and tears crept back in. She let herself cry for a while, and eventually she began to feel what felt like calm, although it occurred to her that maybe it was just exhaustion. She slowly crawled up off the floor and walked to the kitchen. She needed some food. And she needed to call Kate and check on Lizzy.

She had considered calling to cancel her appointment with Monica. She'd been so drained and tired when she woke up, she hadn't wanted to get out of bed—and she probably wouldn't have if Kate hadn't shown up to take Lizzy to school. She'd all but forced Sarah out of bed and into the shower.

Now that she was here, on Monica's sofa, she felt angry at Kate for pushing her. She crawled into the corner of the couch farthest away from Monica's chair and hugged a big throw pillow to her chest. She didn't want to be here, and she definitely didn't want to talk about how she'd been since their last meeting. Did all therapists start out like that? Was that something they taught them in therapist school? Why couldn't they just talk like normal human beings?

She kept her answers to Monica's questions curt and nearly monosyllabic. Maybe Monica would send her home if she didn't have anything to say. But Monica didn't seem dissuaded; she continued to push on with more questions.

"How has the writing been going?" she asked.

"It hasn't. It just makes me angry."

"I can hear that. What about?"

"Everything!" Sarah forcefully threw the pillow back onto the other side of the sofa. "Robert. The baby. My life. It's all a mess." She pushed herself up and walked to the window. She stood quietly looking out, her sense of outrage permeating the room.

"Nothing has worked out the way you wanted or expected," Monica said.

Sarah continued to stare out the window, refusing to respond to such a stupid comment. Of course she never expected or wanted any of this. It didn't take a rocket scientist to figure that out. Who would ever have wanted any of this?

Monica remained quiet, and Sarah continued staring out the window for several minutes, thoughts rushing through her mind. She was a good person. Why were all these bad things happening to her? Why did Robert cheat on her and leave her? Why did she lose the baby?

When she finally spoke, her voice was slow but steady. "When I was a little kid, my mom would take me to Sunday school. It didn't matter that my parents didn't go to church—she took me anyway, and I listened to the stories and got a naive, childish idea that somehow, if I was good, my father wouldn't get angry. He would leave my mother alone. He would stop his rages and beatings."

"So being good would make everything better."

Sarah turned back to face Monica. "Well, it didn't. But I think I still believed that someday it would make a difference. You know, some Cinderella, happy ending sort of thing. That love and goodness would prevail. But clearly that's not the case. There's nothing good or loving about any of this shit."

"You feel like love has let you down."

Sarah walked back and plopped down heavily on the sofa. "Hasn't it? Look at my life!" She held her hand up to indicate running news headlines. "News flash: Father an abusive drunk. Mother commits suicide. Boyfriend abandons. Husband betrays. Baby dies." She pulled the pillow close to her again and sat quietly for a moment before continuing, her voice more subdued. "Where is the love in any of that?"

Monica waited briefly before responding. "You've had some very painful losses and betrayals, both recently and as a child. And it really hurts."

Sarah curled up into the corner of the sofa and buried her head in the pillow she was hugging. She cried quietly for several minutes before reaching for a Kleenex from the table.

"My friend Maggie recently said something that made me think about my parents and their relationship and how I was impacted by it all. I was really pissed at her. I didn't want to hear it. I've always wanted to think I was above it all. That somehow I'd escaped unscathed and it was all behind me. I wanted it to be behind me. I didn't want to go back and rehash it all." She blew her nose and wiped her face. "I didn't want to remember."

Monica nodded. "I know. Life is hard sometimes. And it's messy. And people don't always act in good or loving ways. But that doesn't mean that goodness and love don't exist."

Sarah reached for another Kleenex. "I wish I could believe that."

"You feel like all is lost," Monica said, leaning in closer to Sarah.

Sarah nodded and wiped her nose. "I do."

"Well, it is true that some of the things we lose we don't ever get back."

Sarah continued to clutch the pillow. "I just feel like I've lost so much."

"I know," Monica said. "And there are also things you have that you haven't lost."

Sarah thought for a moment. "Yeah," she said, letting out a big sigh. "I know that's true. I have Lizzy. And my friends. And my job."

"And you're healthy and strong and insightful and resilient. Even with everything you've been through, you haven't lost those strengths."

"Well, for a while I thought I had." Sarah managed a watery smile. "But I feel like I'm starting to get them back."

Monica nodded. "You are. And there are other things you can get back too." She got up, opened a desk drawer, and pulled out a cloth-covered journal. "Sarah, your mother never got her painting back, but you can *take* back your writing." She handed the journal to Sarah. "Try the writing again. Start with journaling the connections you see with your parents and what you are feeling, even if those feelings are difficult. Write out the anger and sorrow and feelings of betrayal. Don't worry about trying to write a story or trying to write well. Just write about what you are feeling."

Sarah took the journal and looked at Monica. She felt so drained. She wasn't sure she could do this. Or if she wanted to. Thinking about her parents left her feeling sad and overwhelmed. How could writing about it possibly help her get better?

She shook her head. "I don't know if I can do this."

"I think you can."

"Well, you might just be disappointed."

"This isn't about disappointing me or anyone else. It's not about any finished product. It's simply about letting yourself take all those voices in your head and writing them out in your journal."

Sarah's stomach tightened and her pulse quickened. She looked nervously at Monica. How did Monica know about her voices? She felt nauseous and shaky. *She probably thinks you're nuts. You must have said something without realizing it. That's what you get for being such a blabbermouth. Dumb move, Sarah. Now she knows how totally messed up you are.*

"I'm not sure what you mean," she said coolly.

"We all have lots of thoughts running through our minds all the time that we don't say out loud. Much of the time we aren't even aware of them," Monica said. "Writing often helps us get them out into the light of day, so to speak."

"Thoughts, sure," Sarah said. "But you said voices."

"Yes, I guess I did," Monica said. "It seems like that word bothered you."

"I don't know," Sarah said, coaching herself to choose her words carefully. "Hearing voices sounds a bit crazy."

"Crazy?"

"Yeah. I don't know. It just doesn't seem normal."

"Well, in some extreme cases it might not be, but I was talking about the thoughts we all have in our heads and the conversations we have with ourselves."

"Like what?" Sarah still felt cautious.

"Anything from encouraging or supporting ourselves to criticizing and sabotaging ourselves."

"So . . . that's a normal thing?"

"It's a very common thing. Sometimes the thinking is so automatic that we don't even realize we are doing it. But whether we know we're doing it or not, our thinking can really impact how we are feeling."

Sarah frowned, not sure she understood.

"For example, if we have thoughts that are negative or critical, we can end up feeling bad about ourselves."

Sarah's eyes opened wide. "That definitely happens for me."

"I suspected so," Monica said. "You're not alone. That's one of the reasons I suggested the journaling. Many people find it helpful as a way to start to understand more about what they are thinking and feeling."

"I guess that makes sense," Sarah said.

"Try it out and see. Think of it as an experiment. Just remember that it might be hard at first. The feelings that come up are often painful. That's why they've been buried for so long—so you wouldn't have to feel them. You might have to push yourself a little, but many of my clients find that it's worth it in the end."

"So it's worked for other people?"

"Absolutely. Many other people."

Sarah relaxed. "Okay. I'll try again."

"Good. You can tell me how it went when we meet next week."

Sarah stood to leave. "Sounds good." She started toward the door but then turned back to Monica and held up the journal. "Oh, and thanks for this by the way."

Monica smiled. "My pleasure. I'll see you next week."

Chapter 19

Sarah felt lighter as she left Monica's office. More at peace. Her mind was surprisingly quiet. She had several hours before she needed to pick Lizzy up from school, so she got in her car and drove aimlessly for a while—and then an idea struck her. The rain had stopped and the sun was peeking through the patchy clouds. It would be nice to be outside. She turned the car around and headed for Green Lake.

The crispness of the light breeze and the warmth of the sun on her skin energized her as she started her walk. The nice weather had brought more people out than usual. Mothers with strollers, joggers, couples walking hand in hand. She found herself smiling as she thought back to taking walks here with Matt. It had been one of their favorite things to do, just walking and talking.

Her smile turned into a frown as she realized that it wasn't something she and Robert had ever done. In fact, they'd never done much together that was fun. She thought back over their relationship, wondering why she'd been attracted to him. He was clearly handsome and charismatic. And powerful. She'd felt so vulnerable after Matt left, and Robert had made her feel safe right from the beginning. And wanted. When he'd told her he wanted to take her home that first night, she hadn't been able to say no. She'd never told anyone that, not even Maggie. She'd been ashamed. Matt was the only man she'd slept with before Robert, and that had only been after months of dating. And then to turn around and sleep with someone she'd just met—and without protection, no less? She had thought she was okay. She'd counted it out in her head. And she hadn't wanted to do anything to spoil the moment. Thinking about it now made her feel queasy.

What a stupid, slutty, irresponsible thing to do. How could you have been so careless? No wonder Robert was pissed when you told him you were pregnant. What did you expect? You should have taken precautions. This whole mess was your fault.

"Stop it!" Sarah said aloud—and then quickly looked around to see if anyone had heard her. She felt overwhelmed. She couldn't stand the voice anymore. She was tired of it. She just wanted to make it go away. An image of her mother popped into her head. Maybe that was how she had felt. Sarah didn't remember her father ever having anything positive to say to her mother. Or to her, for that matter. He had always been critical. And mean. So abusive, often hitting and choking her mother. She shuddered as she remembered how afraid she'd always felt around him.

Her mother must have felt that too. Maybe that's why she never stood up to him. She'd been too afraid and beaten down. Sarah thought back to her loneliness as a child and how much she had longed for more of her mother—more connection, more affection. She had never been there for Sarah. She'd stayed locked in her room all the time. Sarah had hated her for that. But she hadn't understood depression back then. Tears formed in Sarah's eyes. She'd never fully considered what it had been like for her mother. How the beatings and the verbal abuse must have taken their toll. How helpless and trapped she must have felt.

Anger at her father exploded in her chest. She wanted to stand up to him now in a way she hadn't when she was young. To talk back. To find a way to make him stop. Her stride quickened and she felt a little stronger.

"On your left," a voice called and a bicyclist whizzed by, startling Sarah from her thoughts. She looked at her watch. It was close to noon. Maggie would be getting lunch soon. Maybe she'd be up for a last-minute rendezvous.

To her delight, Maggie picked up on the first ring. "Hey there. I was just about to call you."

"Great minds think alike," Sarah said. "I wanted to see if you had time to grab a quick lunch."

"I'll do you one better. I won a lunch basket from that contest the deli was having. The one, by the way, that you didn't bother to enter because you said we'd never win! Now who told you so!"

Sarah laughed. "That's great. I stand corrected. Good for you!"

"Good for both of us! Why don't I bring it over and we can have a picnic on your deck? Take advantage of this nice day."

"That would be great," Sarah said. "But you won't have enough time for that. I could just meet you at school."

"It's a minimum day today. Which you would know if you weren't lounging around at home."

"I am not lounging around at home," Sarah said, laughing. "I'll have you know that I just walked around Green Lake. Which I dare say is more exercise than you've gotten today."

"Sad but true. I've been trapped inside these cinder block walls. And I'm desperate to escape. Want to just meet at your house? I'll be done here in under an hour."

"Sounds good. I'll see you there."

Sarah was setting the table on the deck when Maggie arrived.

"Hello," Maggie called out from the entryway.

"I'm out here," Sarah called back.

Maggie rushed out onto the deck with a large basket and plopped it down on the table. "Check this out!" She began pulling out a seemingly never-ending stream of items: bread, cheese, lunch meats, salads, and a bottle of Chardonnay.

"Wow! What a feast. Let me grab a corkscrew and a couple wine glasses."

Maggie opened all the containers as Sarah opened and poured the wine. They both loaded up their plates and settled in to eat. Maggie raised her glass to toast.

"To good food, good drink, and BFFs!"

Sarah raised her glass to Maggie's and smiled before taking a sip. The thought of confessing to Maggie about her first time with Robert jumped into her head. She hesitated a moment, trying to talk herself out of it, but then impulsively pushed ahead.

"I was thinking about something today that I've never told anyone."

"You have my attention." Maggie took a big bite of a baguette slathered with Italian salami and Havarti cheese and, with her mouth still full, said, "Do tell."

"I need to start by saying this is hard for me to say. I feel really embarrassed. So no joking, okay?"

Maggie put her food down and looked at Sarah. "Yeah, of course."

"I was thinking about when Robert and I got together. I met him in a coffee shop one morning when I was studying. He asked me out to dinner that night and I ended up going home with him."

"Uh-huh."

"That's it," Sarah said. "I had sex with him the day I met him."

"Okay," Maggie paused. "So, how was it?"

"Maggie! I said no jokes. I feel really ashamed. Like a slut or something."

Maggie visibly struggled to suppress her smile. "I'm sorry. I wasn't joking. I just didn't know what you were getting at."

"Well, you're smiling now. Why aren't you taking this seriously?"

"I'm sorry. I get that this feels big to you, but I've got to tell you, you're not the first good girl to do something like that. And you're sure as hell not the first person to have sex on the first date!"

"So you don't think I'm a terrible person?"

"Hell no," Maggie said as she resumed eating.

"Well, there's more," Sarah said. "That's also when I got pregnant with Lizzy."

Maggie's eyes popped open and she put her food down again. "Well, that's more newsworthy! So is that why he wanted you to get an abortion?"

Sarah nodded. "Yeah. But I was almost three months already when I found out. I'd done a home pregnancy test that was negative, so I just thought my period was messed up or something. And we were getting along well then. We were together all the time. He was upset at first but then completely changed his mind and said we should get married. So we did."

"Wow. That must have created some waves at the Jenkins household!"

"That's an understatement. His parents were really upset, especially his mother. She went off about how I'd trapped him."

"What a bitch!"

"Yeah. It felt pretty yucky to me. But Robert assured them that getting married was what he wanted. And he was able to appease his mother with the promise of a grandchild. In the end they all talked and decided to do the wedding quickly so their friends wouldn't really know."

"Well, people aren't dumb. They could have done the math when the baby was born."

Sarah shook her head again. "They never sent out birth announcements. They never even *talked* about Lizzy until she was older."

"Boy," Maggie said. "They really are something. The powers of denial and deception run deep in that family."

"Yeah. I know that's why Robert is avoiding me. He probably doesn't want to deal with telling them."

"So he hasn't told them you've split up?"

"Not that I'm aware of. But I don't know for sure. He hasn't called me."

"Since when?" Maggie asked as she leaned over her plate to shovel a big spoonful of pasta salad into her mouth.

"Well . . ." Sarah hesitated. She knew Maggie wasn't going to like the answer.

"Well, what?"

"We traded a couple voicemails."

"And when was that?"

"Right after I got out of the hospital." Sarah cringed, anticipating Maggie's negative reaction.

"That's totally lame! He hasn't even called to check up on you? What an asshole! Have you tried the home number?"

Sarah shuddered. "No way! Not after that last fiasco!"

"All the more reason to do it," Maggie said, getting up from the table.

"What are you doing?"

"Getting you the phone," Maggie said before disappearing into the house.

"Forget it, Maggie," Sarah called after her.

"No," Maggie said as she came back out with the phone. "It's high time you stand up to him."

Stand up to him. The words echoed in Sarah's head. She didn't stand up to Robert. Much like her mother never stood up to her father. Maggie was right. She needed to talk to him. Make some kind of plan. For Lizzy, if not for herself.

She took the phone from Maggie. "You're right. He needs to talk to me."

Maggie lifted her wine glass to Sarah. "Damn straight! Be strong!"

"Thanks." Sarah dialed the number, her mind churning. "But what if that woman answers? What should I say?"

"Just ask for Robert. You don't need to say anything to her."

Maggie was right again. She had every right to be calling him. She was still his wife, after all. And Lizzy was their daughter. That was always going to be true. The phone rang four times. Sarah was considering hanging up when a man answered the phone. She was caught off guard. Had she dialed the wrong number?

"Hello?" the man said again.

"Oh, I'm sorry," Sarah said, regaining her composure. "I was trying to reach Robert. Robert Jenkins."

"He can't come to the phone right now," the man said politely. "Can I give him a message?"

"Sure," Sarah said. "I'm sorry, but can I ask who you are?"

"I'm Sam, Robert's partner."

Shit. She was interrupting him during work. Robert hated that.

This was the worst possible time to start a conversation with him. She needed to graciously get off the phone as quickly as possible.

"Hi Sam. I'm really sorry to have bothered you. If you could just ask Robert to call me when he's free, I'd appreciate it."

"I'd be happy to," Sam said good-naturedly, "but you'll have to let me know who you are."

"Oh, I'm sorry. Of course." *So much for a quick, graceful exit!* "This is Sarah. Just ask him to call Sarah."

"I will do that, Sarah."

"Thanks," Sarah said and quickly hung up the phone.

Maggie frowned. "What was that all about?"

"His business partner. They must be working. I got so flustered, I just wanted to get off the phone. It's bad enough that I'm calling on the home phone, but to also be interrupting his work . . . not a good combination."

"Well, the hell with it. Serves him right for not calling you back. Maybe it will get his attention. You need to stop tiptoeing around him and just tell him off."

"I know. Believe me, nothing would feel better. But I also know that I need to find some way to be civil for Lizzy's sake."

"Yeah, I guess you're right. But he really gets my goat sometimes."

Sarah smiled. "Tell me about it!"

When Robert turned the water off and pulled the shower curtain open, Sam's broad smile was beaming up at him.

Robert grabbed a towel from the rack. "That's a shit-eating grin if I ever saw one. What gives?" Sam was an open book, easy to read. Something was clearly going on.

Sam folded his arms and leaned back into the wall. "Guess who I just talked to?"

Robert rubbed his head with the towel. "I haven't a clue. You know I hate these guessing games."

"I know," Sam said feigning a pout, "but it wouldn't hurt you to play along once in a while."

"Fine, your highness. I'll play along. My guess is that it was Tom Ford."

"No, it was not Tom Ford! Which is lucky for you because if it were, your sorry, dripping-wet ass would be standing here alone right now!"

"Okay," Robert said, wrapping the towel around his waist and walking out into the bedroom, "I give up. Who did you just talk to?"

"Your wife."

"Oh, so now you're talking to yourself? And exactly what did you have to say?"

"No, darling. Your female wife. Sarah. She just called here."

Robert pulled a T-shirt over his head. "Really? What did she say?"

"She wanted to know who I was and then asked for you to call her when you were free."

Robert frowned as he stepped into a pair of boxers. "What did you tell her?"

"I said I'd give you the message."

"You know that's not what I meant," Robert said. "What did you say about who you were?"

"I told her my name and said I was your partner."

Robert's face flushed. "You outed me to Sarah? How could you do that?"

"Come on, Robbie. You've been saying for weeks that you needed to tell her."

"I know. But I wanted to tell her myself. I was waiting for the right time."

"Well, fate intervened and the opportunity presented itself." Sam stood up to go back to the living room. "You know, it's for the best. You would have continued to avoid it for weeks. I just saved us both from all that misery!"

Robert wanted to be angry, but Sam was right. He had been avoiding Sarah because he didn't know how to tell her. He had run all the different possible scenarios through his mind, but none of them felt right. It was a relief to have that decision taken out of his hands. He pulled on a pair of sweats and followed Sam.

"What did she say? How did she take it?"

"Very well, actually. Like it was no big deal. Said she just wanted you to call her. Maybe she already suspected."

Robert shook his head. "No, I don't think she suspected. Maybe she was in shock and just checked out. She does that sometimes." He thought for a minute about what to do. "I better call her," he said, as much to himself as to Sam. He picked up the phone and dialed. It rang twice before Sarah picked up.

"Hello," Sarah said.

"Hi Sarah. It's me," Robert said. "Sam said you called?"

"Yes, I did. I'm sorry I bothered you while you're working. It wasn't anything urgent. We can talk later, when you're not busy."

"I'm not working," Robert said, puzzled.

"Oh," Sarah said. "I just thought since your business partner was there—"

"My business partner?"

"Yeah. Sam. He said he was your partner."

Robert paused, putting two and two together. Now he understood why Sarah hadn't reacted to Sam's news, and he was unsure as to how to proceed. Should he let her believe that? It would be easier—but it would just delay the inevitable. He'd have to tell her eventually. She needed to know if he wanted to have any kind of relationship with Lizzy. But was now the right time? On the phone? He thought he should probably tell her in person, but he had to admit it might be easier on the phone . . .

"Robert? Are you still there?"

"Yeah. I'm here. So, what did you want to talk to me about?"

Sarah felt confused. Was it just her or was this a weird conversation? Robert didn't seem himself. Maybe this wasn't a good time.

"I just wanted to touch base. We haven't talked about how we are going to do all this. And Lizzy has been asking about when you will be coming home." She sighed. "She misses you."

"I know. I've been busy, but I'll come up soon. Probably next weekend. I can spend some time with Lizzy and we can meet with the lawyer and start ironing things out."

"That would be good," Sarah said. She felt the urge to say more but held her tongue. Part of her still wanted to plead with him, to make him stay. But a bigger part of her, she finally had to admit to herself, felt relieved. Being alone still felt scary, but being without Robert was freeing.

"I'll look at flights tonight and let you know," he said.

"Thanks. That would be great. I'll just wait to hear from you." Sarah frowned when Robert didn't reply. Something was definitely off. "Well, bye then."

"Sarah, wait. There's something I need to tell you."

Sarah caught her breath. "Okay." A wave of apprehension swept over her. What was Robert going to say?

"Sam isn't my business partner."

"Huh?" He wasn't making any sense.

"I said that Sam isn't my business partner."

"Then why would he say he was your partner?"

"Because he is," Robert said. "He's my partner. We live together."

Sarah's head was spinning. "But there was the woman . . ." She struggled to piece together the disparate pieces of the puzzle Robert was presenting. "When I called you that night, you were with a woman."

"That was Stephanie. She's Sam's sister. And she is my business partner. That's how I met Sam."

"So, he doesn't work with you?"

"No, not at all. He's a film director."

"Film director," Sarah said. "Like movies?"

"Uh, yeah."

Sarah was stunned. Robert was gay? Is that what he was telling her? How could that be possible? Wouldn't she have known? Wouldn't there have been some clues? Or had she just been too blind to see?

Robert broke the silence. "Sarah?"

"You said you were in love with someone else," Sarah said, still feeling dazed.

"I am," Robert said. "I'm in love with Sam." He hesitated, then continued in a rush. "I know this must be a shock. I should have told you a long time ago. I've been hiding for so long. You know my family. I don't know how to even begin to tell them. But I should have told you. You deserved that. I've been a coward, and I don't want to live in fear anymore. I need to be who I am. I don't want to hide. And you need to know the truth. You and Lizzy both need to know."

Sarah sat very still, unable to speak.

"I want you to meet Sam. You and Lizzy. I could fly you down sometime."

Sarah put a hand on the table to steady herself. "Robert, please. Slow down. I can't think."

"I'm sorry. You're right. You need some time to process all of this. Of course. Maybe we can just talk more when I come up."

"Sure," Sarah said vaguely. "We'll do that. Just let me know when you're coming. Then we'll talk more."

"Okay, I'll call—"

Sarah hung up.

"What was that all about?" Maggie said. Once again, Sarah's side of the conversation hadn't given her much, but she could tell by her expression that something had gone down. "You look like you're in shock or something."

Sarah turned slowly to look at Maggie. She stared at her for what seemed an eternity without saying a word.

"Sarah, what's going on? You're seriously freaking me out a little here."

"Robert . . . has . . . a . . . boyfriend." Sarah spoke each word slowly and deliberately.

Had she heard her correctly? "A boyfriend?"

Sarah nodded. "His name is Sam. He and Robert are living together and Robert is in love with him." Sarah continued to stare straight ahead.

"So he's . . . gay?" Maggie asked, trying to make sense of what Sarah was saying. Robert? Gay? She hadn't seen that one coming.

"Seems so. . ."

"Wow. Sarah, I . . . I don't know what to say. What do you think about all this?"

Sarah didn't respond. She seemed a million miles away. The silence made Maggie nervous.

She tried again. "Sarah? Are you okay?"

Sarah turned to look at Maggie. "Robert doesn't even like movies."

Maggie frowned. "What?" She wasn't making any sense. What did liking or not liking movies have to do with any of this? "What are you talking about?"

Sarah shook her head. "Sam. He's a film director. I don't get it. We never went to the movies. Robert didn't like to go."

"Maybe he was going with Sam," Maggie said—and immediately regretted it. She swore at herself for once again not being able to keep her mouth shut. When would she ever learn? Sarah looked at her and Maggie prepared to be yelled at.

Instead, Sarah's eyes opened wide. "I didn't think of that."

Maggie scrambled to backtrack. "It was a stupid thing to say. I don't know why I said it."

"No. I bet you're right. That would explain it, wouldn't it?" Sarah paused, her brow slightly furrowed. She seemed eerily calm. Maggie was afraid to say anything, so she just sat quietly, looking at Sarah.

"You know," Sarah finally said. "I bet a lot of things will make sense once I think about it more." She felt both dazed and aware at the same time. Her mind was moving so quickly that she was having a hard time focusing on any one thought. Her father. Her mother. Robert. Lines of connection between all of them and her. She had a feeling that she was seeing things that made up a cohesive whole, but right now it was all a jumble. Like a jigsaw puzzle with the pieces all scattered about.

"Sure," she heard Maggie say, as if in the distance. "But who was the woman? I thought he was having an affair with a woman."

"Huh?" Sarah said, still lost in thought.

"The woman? In his apartment that night? Who was she?"

Sarah turned to Maggie. "You won't believe this one. She's his business partner. And Sam's sister. That's how Robert met Sam."

"No way! This is too much," Maggie said, shaking her head and sinking back into her chair. "It's scandalous, actually! I'd love to be a fly on the wall when that snooty Cynthia gets wind of this!"

"Yeah, well, she won't hear it from me," Sarah said. "Neither of his parents will. I don't think Robert wants to tell them. Though I'm sure they'll find out somehow."

"Yeah," Maggie said. "And I know how."

Sarah looked at her and frowned, not sure what Maggie was thinking.

"You know what they say: out of the mouths of babes. Lizzy will let it slip."

"Lizzy!" Sarah sat up straight in her chair. "Shit! What time is it? I need to pick her up at two o'clock."

Maggie looked at her watch. "No worries. It's only one forty. Plenty of time."

"Yeah, if I leave now," Sarah said, frantically sizing up the table. "I'll just have to clean all this up later."

"I can do it."

Sarah stood up. "Are you sure?"

Maggie stood to give her a hug good-bye. "Absolutely! Just leave it all and go. I'll take care of it and we can talk later."

"That would actually be great. I wanted to surprise Lizzy with ice cream and a trip to the park. I feel like I've been neglecting her lately."

"No problem. I think that will be good for both of you."

Sarah smiled. "I think so too."

Maggie hesitated. "You know, that's a pretty big bomb that Robert just dropped. Are you okay?"

"Honestly, I think I am. Shocked, but okay." Sarah had so many thoughts running through her mind, she couldn't have articulated any of them to Maggie in that moment even if she'd wanted to. And she didn't—not yet. She needed more time to sort through it all.

"Well, you know where to find me if you want to talk."

"Thanks. And thanks for lunch and thanks for listening." Sarah wrapped her arms around Maggie.

Maggie squeezed her back. "Sure thing. That's what friends are for."

"I think I'm starting to figure that out," Sarah said. She smiled as she turned to leave. She did feel better. She was still reeling from Robert's disclosure, and it would take her a while to process it all. But she also felt something else stirring just under the surface. A strange calmness? Relief, maybe? As if a weight had been lifted. A nascent awareness that she wasn't to blame for Robert not loving her. It wasn't some defect in her or something she'd done wrong. It wasn't about her after all. It was about Robert.

Chapter 20

S arah crawled into bed with her new journal. She thought about what Monica had said: *Just keep the pen moving. Don't worry about the content or whether it's good or bad. Just write.* She smiled. That would be easy tonight. So many thoughts had been running through her mind since her conversation with Robert. She set the timer on her phone for thirty minutes and put her pen to the paper before her.

I actually had fun today. I'm glad I let myself play with Lizzy. We haven't done that for a while. I feel like I have been suffocating in some dark cloud and somehow today a little sun came through . . .

Sarah jumped slightly when her alarm rang. She'd been so absorbed in the writing that she'd lost track of time. She turned it off and finished her last thought, aware that she was feeling better than she had in a long time. She'd actually enjoyed the journaling. She'd tapped into the flow she remembered from years ago, when she was still writing. And she'd had several insights, mostly about her relationship with Robert, that she was excited to talk to Monica about at their next session. Something had definitely shifted. Fleeting images of her old self were endeavoring to creep back in. She realized she no longer felt hopeless.

She carefully closed the journal and rolled over to put it in the drawer of her bedside stand. When she opened the drawer, she saw Matt's unopened letter. She had completely forgotten it was in there. She laid her journal on top of the stand and took the letter out of the drawer. The first thing she noticed was the Tanzania postmark. What had his experience been like there? Had it changed him and how he saw the world? She had so many questions that she'd love to be able to ask him.

She felt nervous. What would the letter say? It felt strange to be opening it now—to be bringing the past into the present. She continued to sit, holding it with both hands, unsure of whether she could go through with it. Maybe not yet. Maybe she wasn't ready. But she *was* curious. And besides, what was the big deal? Did she think she couldn't handle it? What was the worst that could happen? That he was angry—that he had told her to never write him again? To stay away? She'd done that for years. It was time to move forward. Time to just open it.

She turned the envelope over, carefully peeled back the flap, and removed the single sheet of paper inside. She gently opened the page and was caught off guard by a strong upwelling of emotion at the sight of Matt's familiar handwriting. She brushed away a tear and began reading.

Dear Sarah,

I felt very sad after reading your letter. I hope that you don't really believe that I never loved you and was just using you, because that's not at all true. I cherish the time we had together, and you will always hold a special place in my heart. But our lives are in such different places, and we need to honor that. Being true to ourselves is the most loving thing we can do

right now—for ourselves and for each other. Don't ever lose
your faith in love, Sarah. It really is the strongest thing. It's
what makes everything so very worthwhile.

Much love, Matt

Sarah finished the letter and sank back into her pillow, tears flowing freely down her cheeks. She couldn't believe she'd never opened this. For all those years. She'd been so stubborn. Holding on to her anger and not even giving him a chance. What had he thought when she didn't respond? How could she have been so childish and immature? Sarah's mind churned until she was thoroughly drained and finally drifted off to sleep.

She woke the next morning still feeling exhausted but also serene. She lay in bed thinking for several minutes before an idea struck that catapulted her out of bed. She grabbed her laptop, crawled back into bed, and googled "Matt Herringer" and "Boston." Several listings popped up, including LinkedIn and Intelius. Should she try messaging him on LinkedIn? That felt too impersonal. And paying for Intelius seemed a little extreme. Crazy, even. Like, stalker crazy. But she did want to talk to him. To explain. She felt horrible that he'd written such a wonderful and caring letter and she had completely snubbed him. She thought back to seeing him at the restaurant. He hadn't seemed upset or angry with her. Actually, he'd seemed genuinely happy to see her. Maybe it hadn't been a big deal to him.

Sarah knew she shouldn't do anything impulsive. She should just take a breath and think this through. And it would probably be a good idea to wait and talk to Monica first. But she didn't want to wait. Her impulsive urges tugged at her rational thoughts. Each "no" quickly turned into a "yes." She convinced herself that there really wasn't a good reason not to contact him. She reached for her phone on the bedside stand and saw her journal. That's what she should do. That's what Monica would tell her to do. Write.

Sarah picked up the journal and opened to the first empty page as her inner dialogue rushed forward. Why did she want to contact him? What would she want to say to him? She started second-guessing herself. Maybe this was stupid. He might not want to talk to her. But in the restaurant, he'd said he wanted to catch up. She felt conflicted. What should she do? She thought back to Monica again. Monica would definitely tell her to journal. To just get it all out on paper.

Another idea popped into her head. She could write to Matt in her journal, like she was writing him a letter. She grabbed her pen and began:

Dear Matt . . .

By the time she'd finished writing five pages, Sarah felt calm and centered. She was clear that she wanted to reach out to him. It might be awkward, but she owed him an apology. And an explanation. She picked up her phone and called information.

"Boston, Massachusetts," she said in response to the automated voice. "For Matthew Herringer." She wrote down the number and hung up the phone. She sat pensively for a moment, then took a deep breath and dialed.

"Hello?" a man's voice answered.

"Matt?"

"Yes."

"This is a voice from your past," Sarah said—and almost smacked herself on the forehead. *What the fuck! What a lame thing to say. You are such an idiot.*

"Sarah?" Matt asked, interrupting her thoughts.

"Yes! I wasn't sure you'd recognize my voice. I hope it's okay that I'm calling."

"Of course. It's good to hear from you. I was sorry we didn't have more time to catch up when I ran into you at Maxwell's. How are you?"

"I'm okay." Sarah smiled. "Getting better . . ."

Sarah felt almost giddy driving to her next session with Monica. She had so much to tell her. She wasn't sure where to start. Robert's news. The many insights she'd had about their relationship. The connections she'd drawn between their dynamics and her parents'. The letter from Matt. Her new understanding about why she'd reacted the way she did when he left.

She parked the car and took the stairs two at a time. Her excitement bordered on anxiety, and she coached herself to take some deep breaths as she settled into a chair in the waiting room. She picked up a magazine but put it back down after thumbing through a couple of pages. She had too much running through her mind to focus even on the pictures.

When Monica opened the door, Sarah popped up, smiling, and quickly followed her into her office.

"You seem different this week," Monica said when they had settled into their usual seats.

"I feel different. And I have so much to tell you, I don't know where to start."

Monica laughed. "You sound like you're sort of bursting at the seams."

"Exactly!" Sarah said. She launched right into the story about her conversation with Robert, the insights she'd had since then, and the relief she now felt. She talked about realizing that she'd been blaming herself not only for the problems with Robert but also for her parents' problems and their inability to love her.

"Wow," Monica said when Sarah finished. "That's a lot to be processing."

"It has been. But it's helped me feel better. Like a weight has been lifted. Like maybe I'm not so defective after all."

"So, you were feeling defective?"

Sarah nodded. "Like you talked about last time. I had a lot of negative thoughts running through my mind all the time. It really helped to know other people have that too."

"So, you'd been feeling like there was something wrong with you. That you were different from other people."

"I was. But then I realized I was blaming myself for things that really weren't about me. That I wasn't to blame for my father's abusiveness. Or my mother's suicide." The tears came without warning; she reached for a Kleenex.

"That's a big insight," Monica said.

"Yes. And that's not all. It also helped me understand my reaction to Matt when he left."

"That was your college boyfriend?"

Sarah nodded. "Yeah. Remember how I told you that I went a little psycho bitch in a letter to him? I was so hurt and angry."

"I remember. You said you'd gotten a letter back from him but never opened it."

"Right. I put it in a drawer and forgot about it. But then, the same day Robert told me about Sam, I came across it again. The timing couldn't have been more perfect. Reading what he'd written helped me put everything together."

"So, you read it."

"Yes." Sarah reached into her purse and pulled out the letter. "I brought it to read it to you." She carefully unfolded the note. She felt the lump rise up in her throat again as she started to read. She swallowed against it and managed to finish without crying. When she was done, she laid the letter down in her lap and looked up at Monica.

"His words sound very genuine," Monica said. "How did you feel hearing them?"

"Overwhelmed by his caring. And ashamed of how I acted."

"When he broke up with you?"

Sarah nodded, her eyes getting slightly watery. "My feelings were so out of proportion," she said. She took a moment to gather her thoughts. "It was as if all my hurt and anger at my parents came boiling up and I dumped all of that out onto him. I'd convinced myself that he'd never really loved me." She paused and wiped her eyes. "And then to read this . . . To have him respond this way when I was so awful to him . . ."

"It was hard to take in."

Sarah nodded. "The last couple lines really got to me."

"About love making everything worthwhile?"

"Yeah. I was thinking back to last week here, when I was feeling like love had let me down. And then to read this." Sarah lifted up Matt's letter. "It felt overwhelming."

"That love was there after all," Monica said.

Sarah nodded and then smiled broadly.

"What's the smile about?" Monica asked.

"It's silly. And a bit lame. But I was channeling my friend Maggie.

She's always quoting lines from movies. And I thought of the movie *Love Actually*. The idea that love is all around us. We just have to be open to it."

"That doesn't seem lame. It seems like something has shifted for you this past week."

Sarah nodded and weighed whether to tell Monica more, afraid she would judge her for acting impulsively. She pushed away the fear and continued. "I called him."

Monica's eyes opened wide. "Matt?"

Sarah nodded. "I told him about finally reading the letter and apologized for my behavior back then. And I told him about the things I've been going through and how the letter helped me. He said he was glad. And then he said something I won't ever forget. He said that he hadn't loved many people in his life, but he had loved me."

"How did that feel?"

"Good," Sarah said. "But I didn't know what to say back. I got all tongue-tied. I managed to say that it helped me to hear that, but then I changed the subject and asked about him. And he told me about his work and his family. He has a two-year-old boy and he was quite the proud papa as he talked about him."

"How was it to hear all that?"

Sarah shifted in her seat. "It was actually okay. Satisfying, even."

"Satisfying?"

"Yeah." Sarah paused. "In a strange way, reconnecting with him has helped me remember me."

Monica leaned forward in her chair. "Can you say more about that? This seems like an important insight and I really want you to be able to clearly articulate it for yourself."

Sarah thought for a moment. When she spoke, her voice was slow but steady. "It's as if I've been lost or adrift for a while. And now I'm finding my way back by remembering who I was back then. Before Robert. Remembering my zest for life, my dreams of writing, and how encouraging Matt was. He believed in me and that helped me believe in myself."

"That makes sense . . ."

"I guess. I know it feels good."

"I can see that in your face."

Sarah grinned.

"Anything else?" Monica asked.

Sarah's smile widened. She was pretty sure she knew what Monica was thinking. "Like 'what if'? Or 'if only'?"

Monica smiled and raised her eyebrows.

"Nothing gets by you, does it? Yeah. I went there. I actually journaled quite a bit about it. What if things had been different? If I had opened the letter. If I hadn't met Robert. If I hadn't gotten pregnant. I even have to admit that a Cinderella story line was running through my head. The idea that he might be single and still in love with me and rescue me from my messed-up life."

"It's understandable that you'd feel that," Monica said.

"Yeah, I guess." Sarah stared out the window for a moment before continuing. "But maybe it's time to stop waiting to be rescued," she said, more to herself than to Monica, as she turned back from the window. "Maybe it's time for me to create my own happy ending."

Chapter 21

Sarah finished emptying the dishwasher and grabbed the towel to wipe down the counter as she thought back over the past several weeks. Her sessions with Monica were going well; she felt grateful for the many insights she'd gained and changes she'd gone through. She was starting to feel like herself again. She'd been able to meet with Robert and could tell that he was making changes too. He'd actually started his own therapy. She would never have believed it, but it was true. She wasn't quite ready to meet Sam yet, but she knew they would get there.

Lizzy came in dressed in her pajamas, interrupting Sarah's thoughts.

"All ready for bed?" Sarah asked.

"Yep."

"Brush your teeth?"

"Yep."

"Good girl. Okay, go hop into bed and I'll come tuck you in as soon as I'm done here."

"Okay." Lizzy started to leave, but then she turned back to Sarah. "Mommy?"

"Yeah?"

"Why did Daddy leave?"

Sarah froze for half a second, then knelt down in front of Lizzy. "It's kind of a complicated adult thing," she said. "But you miss him, don't you?"

Lizzy nodded, her eyes reddening slightly.

"I know." Sarah swept her up in a hug. "Tell you what. I'll call him tomorrow and find out when he's coming to see you, okay?"

Lizzy nodded again. "Okay."

Sarah tousled Lizzy's hair. "Now, into bed with you. I'll be there in a minute."

Lizzy left and Sarah leaned against the counter, her heart aching. She hated to see Lizzy suffer. She wished there was something she could do to make it easier.

Lizzy was already curled up in bed, hugging a stuffed animal, when Sarah walked in. Sarah saw immediately that she was crying, though she wasn't making a sound, and she lay down behind Lizzy and wrapped her arms around her.

"Sweetie, what's wrong?"

Lizzy rolled over to look at her. "He left because of me, didn't he?"

Sarah shook her head. "No. It wasn't because of you."

Lizzy frowned. "Yeah it was. I did something wrong."

"You didn't do anything wrong. It isn't about you. It's about Mommy and Daddy together being wrong."

"What do you mean?"

"Well, it's hard to explain." How could she explain this in a way Lizzy would understand? Was that even possible? She considered what Lizzy might be needing right now. Sarah knew the important thing was for her to not blame herself, to not think she was the reason Robert left. What would help her get that?

An idea came to her. "Let me tell you a story." She pulled Lizzy in and hugged her close as she began.

"Long ago in a faraway land there was a princess who loved animals. She had two cats who would curl up in her lap and purr, and a dog who would sleep with her at night, and a horse who would take her on long rides through the kingdom. One day she was riding through the kingdom and she heard a blue bird singing. His song was so beautiful that the princess took him home and put him next to her window in a beautiful golden cage. And she was very happy. But then the bird stopped singing, and there wasn't anything the princess could say or do to get him to sing again. Then one night there was a terrible storm. The wind was howling and it blew open the windows and started blowing all over her room. The princess was so scared that she hid under the covers and snuggled up with her dog until she fell asleep. When she woke up the storm had stopped, but her room was a mess. There was stuff everywhere. And then she saw that the golden cage was tipped over and the blue bird was gone. The princess was really sad. She thought he'd left because he didn't love her. But then one morning when she was waking up she heard a bird singing outside her window. She jumped up and ran to the window and guess what?"

"It was her blue bird?" Lizzy said eagerly.

"It was. And when he finished singing he flew away again. But every morning he would come back and sing for her."

"So he still loved her?"

Sarah nodded. "He did. He just needed to be outside flying around. He wasn't meant to live in a cage."

"And Daddy didn't leave because of me?"

"Not at all. He loves you very much and he will always be your daddy."

Lizzy lay quietly for a moment before looking up at Sarah. "Mommy, can we get a dog?"

Sarah smiled. "You've been wanting a dog for a long time, haven't you?"

"Yeah!" Lizzy sat up and bounced up and down. "Can we get one?"

"You know . . . I think that might be a good idea. Why don't we talk about it some more tomorrow?"

"Okay!" Lizzy threw her arms around Sarah, then snuggled under the covers. Sarah crawled out of the bed, leaned over, and kissed Lizzy on the forehead.

"Good night, sweetie."

"Night, Mommy."

Sarah turned out the light and started to close the door.

"Mommy?"

"Yeah?"

"I love you."

"I love you too, honey. Sleep tight." Sarah felt a rush of love and relief as she closed the door. She smiled as she thought about how quickly Lizzy had let go of her fear and moved on to the idea of getting a dog. All she'd needed was a little reassurance.

That's all I need too. A little reassurance. And confidence. Like I said to Monica: it's time to create my own happy ending. I don't have to answer to Robert anymore. We can get a dog. I can take a writing class. And I think I'll try that jazz class.

Plans continued to percolate in Sarah's head, and she grew increasingly excited. She would talk to Robert about selling the house and getting something smaller. She'd always wanted something in the older part of town. Something with character and high-quality craftsmanship. A cozy cottage or a bungalow, maybe. And she would go back to work. It was time. It had been long enough.

Sarah leaned back on her desk and looked out at the sea of faces in her classroom as she discussed the use of symbolism. Some of her students were attentive and engaged. Others seemed bored and indifferent. She didn't take it personally. English was a required subject for all four years of high school, but she knew it wasn't everyone's cup of tea. She'd accepted long ago that her job was about encouraging those kids who enjoyed it or knew it was their passion and maybe inspiring some of the others along the way.

"So, think about the symbolism as you read those chapters tonight, and we'll talk about it more in class tomorrow," she said, wrapping up the day's lesson. She stood up and began to walk around her desk, and the volume in the room went up several notches as her students started packing up to leave. "Oh, and don't forget that I need your short stories by Wednesday if you want to be entered in the state writing contest!" she called out over the noise.

She'd barely finished her sentence when the bell rang and her students rushed to leave. Sarah made her way over to one of her quieter students. "Amanda. Could I talk to you for a second?"

Amanda followed her back to her desk. "Yes?" she asked, looking a little worried.

"I just wanted to check in about the writing contest. I thought you were going to enter."

Amanda was looking down slightly, avoiding eye contact. "I-I don't know," she stammered. "I really don't think I have a chance."

"I wouldn't have encouraged you to enter if I didn't think you had a chance. You're one of the best writers I've had in all of my years of teaching."

Amanda looked up at Sarah, her eyes wide. "Really?"

"Really. You have a distinctive voice; your characterization is rich and your dialogue authentic. So I'd really like you to seriously think about it, okay?"

Amanda's face brightened. "Okay." She was almost out the door when she stopped and leaned back into the room. "Mrs. Jenkins . . ."

Sarah looked up. "Yes?"

"It's good to have you back."

Sarah smiled. "Thanks, Amanda. It's good to be back."

Amanda walked out of the room, and Sarah sat down at her desk. Little did she know. Yes, it was good to be back. And she didn't only mean at school—

"Hallelujah . . ." Maggie sang out, bouncing through the door.

Sarah looked up and smiled. "Hey there."

"You're a sight for sore eyes! It's been dreadful around here without you."

"Yeah, I was feeling terribly guilty leaving you here all by yourself."

"Well, you should!" Maggie said. "You think *you* were suicidal. I was about ready to ask for your shrink's phone number."

Sarah smiled and shook her head.

Maggie dropped the comedy act and became more serious. "Teasing aside, how is it being back?"

"Okay," Sarah said tentatively—and then, more confidently, "Good, actually."

"Well, you look great. More relaxed or something."

Sarah smiled. "Yeah, something like that."

"They posted the summer school list," Maggie said, her tone more animated again. "I see you're abandoning me!"

Sarah scrunched up her face and lifted her shoulders slightly. "Sorry. I want time to hang out with Lizzy and hopefully get moved before school starts up again. And I want to get back to doing some writing, so—I joined a summer writing group."

"That sounds great," Maggie said. "It's about time you did some writing! What have I been telling you forever?"

"I know. I should have listened to you a long time ago."

"You remember that the next time I give you some advice!"

Sarah smiled. "I will. And if I don't, I'm sure you'll remind me!"

"You know it!" Maggie glanced at the clock. "Well, duty calls." She reached out to give Sarah a hug. "It's great to have you back."

"Thanks," Sarah said, returning the hug. "It feels good to be back."

Maggie started for the door.

"Hey, Mags?" Sarah called out to her.

Maggie swung around to face her. "Yeah?"

"Thanks again. For everything."

Maggie cocked her head, raised her eyebrows, and bowed slightly. "Cheer-bully at your service."

Sarah laughed. "Don't think I need the bully part anymore."

Maggie smiled. "You know, I think you're right."

Sarah watched her leave and a wave of gratitude flowed over her. She was very lucky to have Maggie in her life. And Kate. They had been so amazing to her through everything. She vowed to try to be the best friend she could be to both of them.

She looked down at the stack of papers on her desk and continued reading. Grading was always a mixed bag. It could be a tedious task at times, but then the occasional exciting breakthrough or piece of writing by a student would make it all worthwhile. This paper was one of those times. The student had struggled with structure all year, but this time it had clicked.

Grade: A. Great job, Michael.

Sarah began to sign off on the top of the paper—*Mrs. Jenk*—then paused, looking at her signature. *No. It's time for a change.* She scratched it out and re-wrote, "Ms. Reynolds."

Acknowledgements

A cknowledgements, whether in books, awards ceremonies, or in the course of day to day living, have always been important to me. They represent our connection, appreciation, and reliance on one another. Much as it takes a village to raise a child, so too does it take a team to publish a book.

So there are many, far too numerous to name individually, that I would like to thank. First, I want to acknowledge the wonderful She Writes community. I have felt welcomed, supported and encouraged by an amazing group of women writers. To Brooke Warner, Crystal Patriache, and everyone at SheWrites Press and Booksparks: Thank you for your patience, encouragement, and gentle challenge as I made my way along a very steep learning curve.

To the many friends and family members who offered moral support, brainstormed titles, gave feedback, and tolerated all the time I was MIA because I needed to write, thank you. Each and every one of you played a part in the birthing of this book. A special shout out to my first writing partner, Carolina. This all started with those weekly writing dates many years ago at that wonderful but long departed coffee shop in Sausalito.

To David, Kate, and Steven: Thank you for all your help with editing, technical glitches, creative ideas, social media, and most of all moral support when I needed it most. I couldn't have done this without you.

About the Author

© Gina Logan Photography

Cathy Zane is a writer, psychotherapist, and former nurse who draws on her many years of working with women and families to create narratives of growth and empowerment. As a lifelong reader, she believes in the power of story to not only entertain but inspire, connect us to our common humanity, and instill hope. Visit her at www.cathyzane.com.

SELECTED TITLES FROM SHE WRITES PRESS

She Writes Press is an independent publishing company
founded to serve women writers everywhere.
Visit us at www.shewritespress.com.

Center Ring by Nicole Waggoner. $17.95, 978-1-63152-034-1
When a startling confession rattles a group of tightly knit women to its
core, the friends are left analyzing their own roads not taken and the
vastly different choices they've made in life and love.

Fire & Water by Betsy Graziani Fasbinder. $16.95, 978-1-938314-14-8
Kate Murphy has always played by the rules—but when she meets charismatic artist Jake Bloom, she's forced to navigate the treacherous territory of passionate love, friendship, and family devotion.

In a Silent Way by Mary Jo Hetzel. $16.95, 978-1-63152-135-5
When Jeanna Kendall—a young white teacher at a progressive urban
school—becomes involved with a community activist group, she finds
herself grappling with issues of racism, sexism, and oppression of vari-
ous shades in both her professional and personal life.

Shelter Us by Laura Diamond. $16.95, 978-1-63152-970-2
Lawyer-turned-stay-at-home-mom Sarah Shaw is still struggling to find
a steady happiness after the death of her infant daughter when she meets
a young homeless mother and toddler she can't get out of her mind—
and becomes determined to rescue them.

Play for Me by Céline Keating. $16.95, 978-1-63152-972-6
Middle-aged Lily impulsively joins a touring folk-rock band, leaving her
job and marriage behind in an attempt to find a second chance at life,
passion, and art.

A Work of Art by Micayla Lally. $16.95, 978-1631521683
After their break-up—and different ways of dealing with it—Julene and
Samson eventually find their way back to each other, but when she finds
out what he did to keep himself busy while they were apart, she wonders:
Can she trust him again?